As a hybrid of an angel and demon, Nova has never been allowed in either Heaven or Hell. Being adopted by a family of cryptid hunters is all she knows. When the creatures begin hunting her, she is sent a protector. Together, they must figure out why she is being targeted. When the hunter becomes the hunted, they must figure out who is sending them and why. In the midst of their investigation, they become closer than she expected. The pull towards her guardian is more than she could have ever imagined. Can Nova fall in love in a world of nightmares? Or is she destined for a life of horror?

Hybrid Awakening
Copyright © 2023 Christina Abu-Khalaf
ISBN: 978-1-4874-3966-8
Cover art by Martine Jardin

Published by eXtasy Books Inc

Look for us online at:
www.eXtasybooks.com

HYBRID AWAKENING

BY

CHRISTINA ABU-KHALAF

DEDICATION

To my stepmother, Sandra. There are no maidenheads to giggle about in this book, but I hope you can be proud of what I created from Heaven.

CHAPTER ONE

By the age of twenty-three, I thought maybe things would have settled down for me. Nope. There I was fighting a goat man in the middle of the night, in the woods, for stalking a couple of humans. Yes, I said goat man. Mythological creatures were real, and this guy was really creepy. You'd think he would be an embarrassment to the cryptid kind, but he was well over six feet tall and more beast than man. He towered over me and had an insanely muscular build with dark coarse hair that covered almost every inch of his body. His large horns protruded from his goatlike head, with which he'd tried several times to skewer me.

I jumped out of his path when he charged me once more, his clawed fingers outstretched. The goat man managed to catch my black T-shirt with his disgusting nails, shredding the material and catching part of my stomach. I glanced down. "Ouch! You bitch, you tore my favorite shirt!"

I lunged at him and punched him in the snout. He let out a squeal and stumbled backward, gripping his wounded face. I took that moment of weakness and unsheathed my angel blade—which, in appearance, was more like a platinum ice pick than a dagger—and I stabbed him in his chest. The noise he let loose was ear-piercing. I pulled my blade from him and ran a few feet back to get away from the sound. The goat man's body shook unnaturally. After a moment, he imploded, leaving no trace he was ever there.

I wiped the sweat from my forehead with the back of my hand and put my angel blade safely back into its holster at my hip. That was the only thing I owned that was once my

1

mother's, who happened to be an angel. Unfortunately, she'd conceived me with a demon, which was frowned upon in Heaven and Hell. Go figure. I wasn't allowed to stay with her after I was born, so she handed me over to a family of cryptid hunters who were not at all bothered by the fact that I had both angelic and demonic blood running through my veins.

I started weaving through the trees and headed back to my car. I didn't need a flashlight to see in the dark. That made remaining undetected when I was out hunting easier. Aside from having enhanced night vision, and being faster than a human, there wasn't much more I could do. Cryptids tended to stay put during their years of taunting and stalking the human race. I had to give some of them a little credit—not *all* cryptids were horrible, soul sucking creatures. Some were more benevolent and just wanted to be left alone. Like Bigfoot. He hid in the woods, avoiding the limelight, but unfortunately, he'd been caught on camera multiple times.

Now I'd never personally encountered bigfoot, but I happened to know others who had, and most would admit they didn't wreak havoc on the weak unless disturbed. I'd traveled far and wide to hunt all types of creatures that were more troublesome and caused greater grief and fear. Since there were so few of us hunters left, some of us had to pick up the slack. The government assisted. They knew what we did. Everything was very hush-hush, and we received reimbursement for any travel and lodging expenses, as well as a decent paycheck.

We were sent to take care of the problematic creatures of this world before too many people went missing and word spread to the greater population. Sure, there were the normal fuzzy videos and pictures that showed them, but still, there were skeptics.

I stomped up the dirt-covered hill in my boots and reached my car, sliding into the driver's seat. I pulled up my damaged shirt to take a peek at my side where the goat man had gouged me. The wound was already healing, but it would probably take until at least tomorrow to completely close. I released my shirt and started my car.

I had just pulled onto the dark, empty road when my phone buzzed in the cup holder. I answered it, putting the call on speaker.

"What's up?"

"Nova, where are you? You went MIA," my adoptive mother replied.

"I got a heads-up on a cryptid and took care of it."

"Okay, well, you could've taken your sister with you for backup." Good thing I wasn't face to face with my mom — the expression on my face would've spoken volumes.

Tiffany was a great sister, but not so great of a hunter. I could deal with hunting with my parents since they had years of experience, but I felt Tiff was a liability when she was with me. I didn't voice that to my mom. Instead, I said, "I'll tell her next time." Telling her and inviting her were two different things.

"All right. Well, let me know when you make it home."

"I'll text you when I get there."

We hung up, and I drove a while longer to my little house and pulled into the driveway. Making my way to the front door, I heard a low rustling noise. I cocked my head to the side and listened.

"Nova." A deep accented voice. I turned to see Adalrik, a garden gnome, standing between two bushes. I'd picked him up in Germany a few years before on a hunting trip. He'd been shunned by his fellow gnomes for some indiscretion he never wanted to talk about. Although his bushy beard was prominent on his small face, I'd given him children's clothes that I altered to fit him better. He preferred to remain barefoot even though I'd given him several pairs of shoes.

"Hey, Rik, what's going on?" I crouched down to get to his level.

"I was worried about you."

"Worried? Why? You know I'm always in and out at all hours."

"I saw a man come to the door. He was peeking through your windows, and then he disappeared. I tried getting a better look at him. But with my old eyes and the poor lighting, I couldn't make much out." My brows shot up. Not something I was expecting.

"Anything about him that might be helpful?" I asked.

"Like I said, it was dark, but he was big. Lots of muscles."

"Human?" I asked.

"I'm not sure. He appeared human, but he could have been a shapeshifter." Hmmm. Interesting. Was it wishful thinking that perhaps he was just an annoying solicitor?

"Well, I'm fine. You don't need to worry about me." Adalrik nodded, and I patted him gently on the shoulder before I stood to my full height again. "Let me know if he comes back. I'd like to know who the hell's snooping around my house."

I searched my house and made sure no one had managed to weasel their way into my home. It didn't take long for me to realize no one was inside, considering how small my house was. It didn't seem like the man had attempted to enter, so maybe he'd just scoped things out. I wasn't one to feel uneasy because I knew how to defend myself. I was just curious.

I took a quick shower and washed off the sweat and blood from my fight with the goat man and slipped into bed. I tossed and turned for about an hour before I finally was able to drift off to sleep.

Darkness — it surrounded me. But I couldn't see through it like I normally could. I felt unbearable heat, making me sweat as my clothes clung to my body. I reached out my arms, trying to see if there was anything to grab onto. There was nothing. Then a glimmer of light in the distance. I hesitated for a moment but eventually gave in to my curiosity and followed.

My bare feet slapped against the concrete floor. I started out slowly, crossing the distance to the flickering light. Shadows danced around the illumination. I picked up my pace when I saw a figure standing in the distance. My steps quickened as I called out to the person I couldn't quite make out. "Hello?" I yelled. I received no response and I started to run.

The stranger grew larger the closer I approached. Light gleamed off the figure's skin. I realized the stranger was a man. Silhouetted, he stood at least six feet tall. Even in the low glow, I could tell he was well-built and muscular. Without a shirt, the power in his body was evident. I stopped before I ran into him. "Hello?" I said again through ragged breaths. Again, no reply.

His features were obscured in the low light. I stepped forward, trying to get a better view. I squinted through the darkness, which was unnatural for me. The sound of a growl ripped through the air and vibrated through my body. I broke out in goosebumps. Even though the growl seemed like a warning, that didn't deter me. I stepped forward and reached out to touch the stranger. My fingertips grazed his skin, and I jerked my hand away with a gasp.

I jumped out of bed with a hiss, nearly falling on my face as my legs tangled in the bed sheet. My fingers felt as though I'd stuck them into an open flame. Once I untangled myself from the sheets, I ran to the bathroom and stuck my hand under cold water from the faucet. I hissed at the contact of the cool liquid against my throbbing wound. When I inspected my scorched skin, it was red and raw, angry blisters already forming. What was that? The stinging, throbbing pain didn't subside as the cold water flowed over my scalded flesh. I leaned into the countertop, still reeling from whatever the hell that was. Sure, I'd had dreams and premonitions in the past, but nothing like this. This felt like . . . like a bad omen.

CHAPTER TWO

I trekked to the coffee shop around the corner from my house the next morning and hoped some caffeine could shake the fatigue from my body. The dream I'd had the night before hadn't allowed my mind to settle enough for me to get a good night's rest.

The small town we lived in was almost off the grid, which was how I liked it. I wasn't much of a people person but who could blame me? Normal society sucked. I chose to distance myself from the majority of humans. Aside from going to my family's house and hunting, I didn't get out much. Besides, it would be awfully hard to explain to people on the outside where I went and why I disappeared so often.

My phone vibrated in the back pocket of my jeans. I pulled it out and answered.

"Hey, Tiff."

"Hey, Nova. Mom said you never let her know when you got home last night."

"Shit, I was so tired I forgot. Tell her I'm fine." I rubbed my brow. My fingers had completely healed by the time I decided to get out of bed. All that remained of the scalding was mildly pink skin.

"She's also expecting you for dinner tonight," Tiffany said.

"I'll be there," I gritted out. Not that I didn't love seeing my family. Tiff was practically my best friend. Well, pretty much my only friend, really.

"Do I need to call and remind you before?"

"No, I'll remember." I could almost hear the *uh huh, yeah*

sure behind her silence. "On second thought, call me an hour before I'm supposed to be there." Better safe than sorry.

"Will do. And next time, let me know when you're going hunting, will you? I want to come."

"I will." I hung up right as I entered through the door of the coffee shop and then ordered my usual latte from the barista at the counter. Drink in hand, I took a seat at one of the small tables and watched the people milling in and out of the shop. The day was a busy one because of the nice weather. It would probably end up being another hot afternoon, so everyone was getting out before they couldn't stand the heat anymore.

As I watched a customer walk out the door with her coffee and pastries, I caught a glimpse of something unusual across the street. A pale-colored face . . . I stood and hurried closer to the window to get a better view. An elderly woman with gray-tinged skin sauntered by. She must have used a glamour for the benefit of the humans because no one seemed to notice the unusual woman. I glanced around. Everyone in the shop seemed unfazed as they enjoyed their conversations or continued to work on their laptops.

I pulled my rubber band from my wrist and threw my pale blonde hair up in a ponytail. Always had to be prepared. The bell rang on the door as I exited the coffee shop and stalked after her. I followed for about a block or two before she noticed. Her thin, gray hair lifted up around blue-gray skin as she turned back. She caught sight of me coming in her direction and her eyes widened. She most likely recognized me as a hunter. She picked up her pace and I did the same. As I drew closer to her and caught sight of her face, I realized how hag-like she really was. A large, hooked nose, yellowed teeth, and lethal-looking dark nails. Oh shit, it couldn't be . . .

At this point I was sprinting after her. When I reached her, I grabbed the back of her shirt and pulled her into an alley. I slammed her into the brick wall. My forearm pressed against her neck to hold her in place.

"Black Agnes, I presume."

"How can you see past my glamour?" she gasped as she struggled against my hold. I pushed harder to keep her still. Her crepey skin appeared delicate but that didn't stop me. Her black eyes gave me the clue that she had a dark soul. Perhaps no soul at all as they glinted in the light of day. My lips curled over my teeth in disgust.

"How about you tell me why and *how* the hell you're in the States and not in England?" Black Agnes was a myth dating back to the eighteenth century in parts of England. I'd only ever read about her and her penchant for cannibalism, never run across her.

"I'm not telling you." She sliced the air with her sharp nails, narrowly missing my face. I slammed her back again. Her head cracked against the brick, but that didn't seem to faze her. Her nails gouged my forearm at her throat. I wouldn't give her the satisfaction of knowing how much that stung.

"Listen here, you witch. I want to know why you aren't where you're supposed to be."

Using my free hand, I pulled my angel blade from where it was hidden under my loose navy shirt and pressed it into her withered neck. She stiffened at the feel of the metal against her skin. If I pressed hard enough, she knew I could end her in seconds.

"I was summoned." Her raspy voice cracked. She sounded like she'd smoked two packs of cigarettes a day for a hundred years with how gravelly her voice was.

"Summoned by who?" I tilted my head to the side.

"I don't know. I just know I'm supposed to be here to hunt."

"Hunt who?" I pressed my blade harder against her throat.

Her face went from fearful to a wicked sneer.

"You." My brows pinched with confusion. She cackled at the bewilderment that must have been written all over my face.

Who would request such a thing? And why?

"Oh, Aggie, I think you're lying to me." I wiped my face clear of all expression.

"I'm not. But you'll find out soon enough." She continued to squawk with glee. I ignored her goading and decided I had to end this here and now.

"I hear you like to steal children. I don't think that sits well with me." I grazed the tip of my angel blade across her neck, hard enough to draw blood and to make her skin sizzle. She swallowed hard and her smile vanished. She pushed against me, trying to break my hold, but she was weak compared to me. I tightened my grip.

"Oh no, Agnes. You aren't going anywhere." I slowly pushed my blade into her neck. She bucked against me for a moment and ripped with her iron nails into the skin on my forearm before she disintegrated into nothing. I shook out my injured arm, splattering blood onto the concrete floor before I stalked out of the alley and glanced around. Damn, Aggie had gotten me good. I used my shirt and wiped off the excess blood as I headed back to my house to change.

Was Black Agnes the only cryptid around? If she was summoned here to hunt me, I wouldn't doubt there would be more popping up. Maybe the man Rik saw sneaking around my house was one of them. I was going to have to prepare for the worst.

I actually remembered I was having dinner with my parents that night without having to be reminded and I even showed up to their house early. I'd dressed in jeans, but decided to wear a nicer shirt that was loose, per usual, one with a layer of lace over black chiffon. In place of my normal black boots, I wore black strappy sandals. I left the blonde hair that hung down to my waist loose and wavy. I'd even put on some eyeliner and mascara to enhance my violet eyes.

My mom opened the door. "You're early!" She wrapped me in a hug and I buried my face in her dark hair. Where I had lighter features, she had dark. I looked nothing like my adoptive family. They were of Native American descent and I obviously wasn't. Apparently, I resembled my angel mother, whom I didn't remember. I'd been a newborn when she'd left me with the Alexanders.

I untangled myself from her limbs and she took me in with her dark almond-shaped eyes.

"You look beautiful," she said.

"Thanks, Mom. You do too."

She rubbed her hand up and down my arm.

Tiffany strode up behind my mother and broke between us, giving me a hug.

"I didn't have to remind you," she whispered into my ear. I chuckled a little.

"I didn't have anything else going on to distract me," I whispered back. Tiffany had a lighter brown complexion and hair. Naturally high cheekbones a model would kill for and full lips she so expertly painted with lipstick. She was gorgeous and graceful with a dancer's body—I had always envied her beauty. She was a few years younger than I was, but we'd always been pretty close from the moment she was brought home from the hospital.

We headed to the kitchen where my dad was cooking.

"Hey, Nova," he said as we strolled in. He stood at the stove and peered over his shoulder at me. My father gave me a grin, the corners of his eyes crinkling before he turned back to what he was doing. His long black hair was tied back in a low ponytail at the nape of his neck. He wore an apron that said *Domestic Goddess,* one my mother no doubt forced him to wear.

"Nice apron," I teased, and my father chuckled.

I took a seat on the bar stool and swung my legs as I watched him sauté vegetables. My mom slid a beer in front of me and I thanked her.

"So, I wanted to ask you guys something," I said. All eyes turned in my direction. "Have you ever heard of a cryptid coming from another country to terrorize someone?" I purposely left out the fact that the cryptid was sent to terrorize me. I twisted my beer bottle between my hands. The condensation from the bottle left my palms wet.

My dad froze for a moment and seemed to take what I was asking into consideration. Maybe even searched his memory for any other stories similar to what I'd experienced.

"No, I haven't ever heard of a cryptid or mythical coming or going to another country. Why?" My father suddenly seemed very interested in the veggies he was cooking.

"I ran into Black Agnes today."

He nearly dropped his spatula and turned around to completely face me.

"What!" Tiffany practically shouted. "No fucking way!" My mother glared at my sister for her use of foul language in her house. Tiff's mouth snapped shut. "Sorry, Mom."

"Yeah," I continued. "I was drinking my coffee and I saw the hag right across the street, so I followed her. And it was Agnes, for sure. At first, I was wondering why no one was reacting to her. Turned out she'd used a glamour, but I could see through it. I followed her until I was able to corner her in an alley. She didn't give me much information as to why she was there," I spoke my half-truth.

"That's unheard of," my mother said softly. I took a drink of my beer and focused on my dad again. His forehead was crinkled in thought as he stared at the ground.

"I took care of her." I sat back and crossed my arms. My father's gaze lifted to me finally.

"Well, hopefully that's the last of it," he said.

"Also, maybe not related, but Adalrik saw someone skulking around my house last night. He said it was a man. No real description other than he's a big dude. Muscled."

My dad puffed out his chest and took the pan off the burner. "What? I told you there should be cameras installed around the house," he said.

"I bought them, I just haven't installed them, yet." Truth be told, I'd had them for months, I just hadn't done anything with them yet. My bad. Maybe it was my pride, but I figured I could kick most people's ass. I mainly purchased the cameras to make sure no one stole my Amazon packages.

"I'll come over tomorrow to put them up."

"I can do—"

"No, Nova." He cut me off. "I know how you are. You'll wait another six months before you actually do it."

"Okay." I wouldn't win any arguments with him about this.

CHAPTER THREE

During the rest of our dinner, we discussed normal every-day things. I tried not to bring up my recent hunting activities or anything more about Aggie. By the time I was back home, darkness had fallen. As I took the front steps to my door, I noticed the door was ajar.

"Psst!" I heard Adalrik in the bushes. "He's back!"

Oh fuck no. I pulled out my angel blade and spun it expertly in my hand. Taking quiet steps, I slowly opened the door and peered inside. Nothing. I stepped through the threshold but didn't see anyone standing in the dark entry-way or the kitchen. I cocked my head to the side and listened for any type of noise the intruder might unintentionally make. Absolute quiet. I couldn't even hear the crickets chirping, which was unusual for the time of year. The hair on the nape of my neck stood on end, and goosebumps raced across my skin. I started to feel as though my home possessed an electric pulse.

Even though I was on high alert, I continued farther into my home and cautiously stepped into the living room. A large man sat on my couch. His blue eyes glowed as he stared at me, as if he hadn't just been caught breaking and entering. I didn't stop to think before I threw myself at him, my blade coming down in an arc.

Stranger danger was impossibly fast. He managed to end up behind me and grabbed both my arms. His fingers squeezed my wrists, which caused me to drop my angel blade. It clattered to the floor. I twisted expertly and broke free from his hold. Flipping around, I punched him in the gut, causing him to grunt. Good, I hoped it hurt. I took a few steps back to put distance between us, thinking maybe I had slowed him down. But he was only mildly affected by my blow.

He stalked toward me as his blue eyes took me in. I put one foot up on my coffee table and launched myself up and over him, landing on my feet behind him. I kicked the back of his knee and he stumbled slightly. Damn, Rik was right, this dude *was* big. And from behind, the way his body was built . . . my dream flickered through my mind. I shook the thought. I didn't have time to think about the possibility that this was the hulking man from my dream. He towered over my petite frame, and the bulk of muscle was clearly visible to my oh so special eyes.

I kicked out at him again, but he reached behind him and grabbed my leg. He pulled me forward and effectively put me flat on my back. I hit the hardwood floor hard, the wind knocked out of me. The impact sent pain throbbing through my spine. I groaned. He crawled over me and sat on my stomach. His legs pinned my arms by my ears. He definitely wasn't putting his full weight on my midsection because I could still breathe. But when I tried to push up from the floor, he didn't budge.

"Can you stop trying to kick my ass," he said, in a deep growly voice that rumbled. I felt unexpectedly warm.

"I . . . excuse me?" My body relaxed under him because now I was confused. Had he seriously asked me not to kick *his* ass when he broke into *my* home?

"I said, can you stop trying to kick my ass," he repeated.

"You B and E into *my house* and you want me to stop trying to kick your ass?" I said. What?

"Yes. I was sent to watch over you, Nova."

I scoffed at his confession. "Watch over me? Why?"

"Because something is coming for you."

14

He wasn't telling me anything I didn't already know, but how did this stranger know anything about me? My fingers started to tingle from the lack of blood flow. I stared up into the mystery man's face. A calmness stole over me at the soft illumination of his eyes.

"Can you get off of me?"

"If I release you, will you stop coming after me?"

"That depends."

He chuckled, and the sound elicited the need to wiggle beneath him. I didn't understand why but something told me he was telling the truth. Call it gut instinct.

"Depends on what?" I heard the smile in his voice.

"On whether you're a good guy or a bad guy."

"I'm not here to hurt you. So . . . will you behave?"

I shuddered at the smoothness in his voice, and how he was able to produce a tingle that spread across my skin and caused my body to hum.

I nodded, and he removed his knees from my arms and slowly rose. I took a deep breath. This dude was heavy even without his full weight. He stretched out a hand. I took it reluctantly and allowed him to help me to my feet. I stalked over to the light switch and flipped it on.

Holy shit balls. This dude was beyond gorgeous — like only in my wildest dreams kind of sexy. Dark messy hair, bright blue eyes, sharp jawline. He had just the right amount of scruff too. His black T-shirt stretched tautly across his chest and bulging biceps. His jeans fitted perfectly over his long, muscled legs. I bit my bottom lip.

I eyed his body as he strode over to my couch to take a casual seat once again. He leaned forward, his arms resting on his knees. He stared back at me. I couldn't keep from examining him. I watched the veins in his arms bulge, his muscles ripple. Heat rushed to my cheeks as he lifted a brow. He obviously noticed my stare lingering on his body. I cleared my throat.

"Like what you see?" His eyes twinkled with mischief.

Yes. Yes, I did like what I saw. I wasn't going to let him know that though.

I arched a brow. "Do you?" I asked in return.

He chuckled. Before he could say anything more, I moved on.

"Were you here yesterday?" I asked. My hair was a tangled mess from our little scuffle. I pushed it back from my face and then crossed my arms over my chest.

"Yes. I was looking for you." Elias took a seat on the couch.

"Okkaayyyy, well you could have stuck around," I said.

"I was summoned, so I came back tonight." A lot of summoning was going on.

"Summoned by who?" He gave me a sexy grin but didn't answer. "Fine, don't tell me. Can I at least get your name?" I was getting a little irritated.

"Elias."

"So, who sent you . . . Elias?"

"I'm afraid I can't tell you that." That sexy grin came again.

I tried to act like I wasn't having some crazy reaction to this random guy. "All right, I think it's time for you to go." I was fed up. No one seemed to be able to give me answers and that was starting to piss me off. Not that I had dug too deeply into anything. But by that point, if this good-looking jerk had information he wasn't going to share, he could get the hell out.

I headed into the entryway of my petite house. I expected him to follow. When I turned back, Elias still sat on my couch in the same position. No matter how hot this guy was, he needed to leave if he couldn't be upfront with me. "Come on, I don't do well with secrets and bullshit, so out." I threw my arm up toward the front door.

He stood. Wearing a strange expression, he strode to the door as I pulled it open and then stepped outside. He turned back to me and opened his mouth to say something but I slammed the door in his face and locked it. Not that it would've kept him out if he wanted to come back inside. He obviously wasn't part of this world. But I had a feeling if I kept asking him questions, he would've kept avoiding them.

I kicked off my sandals and headed toward my room and pulled off my shirt. I dropped it to the floor and flipped on the light, then screamed when I saw Elias standing in my room. I hadn't even checked before shedding my clothing.

"Did you just slam the door in my face?" He sounded surprised.

"Did you just appear in my room?" I covered my chest with my arms. Elias seemed to notice I was topless, clad only in a black cotton bra. My breasts weren't huge or anything but still. He plastered a smirk across his face and raised that infuriating eyebrow again.

"Get out!" I shrieked.

"I still need to talk to you," he said calmly.

"I tried talking to you. You're an avoidant jerk. If you aren't going to leave, can you at least turn around so I can put a shirt on?"

He did as I asked. I reached into my dresser drawer and pulled on a black tank top.

"Okay," I said. He turned back to me. Never speaking a word, his gaze roamed over the shirt I'd picked out.

I waved my hand as if to tell him to get on with it.

"I was told to keep who sent me a secret." His teeth scraped over his bottom lip. I unintentionally followed the movement with my eyes.

"Fine. Then why are you here?" I asked.

"Like I said before, something is coming."

"And that something is?" I raised an eyebrow as I waited for his response.

"Have you come across anything strange in the last couple

of days?" he asked instead of giving me a straight answer. Nice way to avoid my question. This wasn't my first rodeo, buddy.

"Besides a strange man in my house?" He chuckled. My skin tingled all over again at the sound.

"Yes, besides that."

I contemplated telling him about Black Agnes but why should I give him a straight answer when he'd dodged my questions left and right? Besides, it was only one incident, not anything crazy. Even though the conversation I had with her was worrisome, I was able to hold my own. Screw this aloofness.

"No, not that I can think of," I said with a saccharine smile.

"You're sure?" I could tell he knew I was lying. I clasped my hands innocently in front of me.

"Mmmhmmm." I nodded. He stared at me with his piercing eyes for a moment longer before he sighed.

"Okay. I'll be in touch then. Unless you want me to stay."

Was he flirting?

"I think I can handle myself."

"Oh, I know you can, but I'll be back anyway."

I started to tell him I didn't need him to be my babysitter, but I blinked and he had disappeared. The only evidence of him having been in my room was a feeling of heat that brushed across my exposed skin. Now I was really curious to know what kind of creature Elias was.

CHAPTER FOUR

I had another terrible night's sleep after Elias's little visit. When I'd managed some shut-eye, dreams of strangers in the dark haunted me again. Not the same man, the one I assumed was Elias, but other shadows that lurked in the sweltering heat. I didn't end up burnt this time, but I did wake up drenched in sweat and had to take a cold shower to cool off. I was left still confused as to what it was all about.

"Earth to Nova." Tiffany waved her hand in front of my face. I blinked a couple of times and glanced up at her. We'd made plans to meet for coffee for some girl time, even though it was late afternoon.

"Sorry, I was daydreaming."

"You look like shit," she said as she slid into the chair across from me. I'd gotten to the shop a little before she did and ordered her drink. I watched her slender fingers when they grasped the plastic cup.

"Thanks. You look great too." I gave her a smirk and sipped my latte.

"Have you been sleeping?" she asked.

"Obviously not." I waved a hand in front of my face.

"Maybe you should be drinking decaf this late in the day. Is it because of the whole Black Agnes encounter?" Tiffany's dark brows bunched together.

"I think that's part of it. Dad put up the cameras earlier, but he barely said a word. Have Mom and Dad said anything about it?"

"If they have, it's not when I'm within earshot," she

replied.

"I thought they'd give me more feedback on the issue but it's obviously something I'm going to have to research on my own."

"I don't think anyone's ever seen a cryptid from a different country here in the States. Normally they stay within their home areas."

I tapped my fingers on my cup in thought. If Black Agnes had been summoned to come after me, there were bound to be others. Elias had suddenly showed up out of the blue to keep an eye on me, so he must know something. That was a real crap move on his part to not be upfront about everything. He wanted answers, but I refused to give him any information until he started being straightforward with me. I could've punched the grin right off his handsome face. All of my questions had gone unanswered.

"How did she even make it here?" I asked aloud.

"Good question. Maybe a portal," Tiff said.

I snorted. "That old hag had enough power to make a portal? I thought she just liked to bewitch people and eat children."

Tiffany shrugged. "Just a thought."

I gave her a nod. We sat in silence for a few minutes and mulled everything over in our heads.

We finished our coffee and left together. The evening was balmy, and the sun started to go down as we strolled down the sidewalk.

"I met someone." Tiffany broke the silence.

I jerked my head toward her. "No way!" In all these years, Tiffany had never really talked about boys. Sure, she'd been on dates, but nothing ever stuck. She'd been leaning toward dating women more the last couple of years, but other than ending up in bed together, that had never amounted to anything.

"She's hot and Asian."

I busted out laughing. "That's all you can give me?"

"Her name is Erica, and I ran into her on campus." Tiffany went to the local college, unlike me. She didn't want to be a hunter forever and had lined herself up for real life. I had a side job that I worked from home, and my paychecks were decent. That gig paid the bills and then some. Combined with what the government paid us, I was pretty comfortable.

I listened to Tiff chatter away about Erica as we continued down the street. She suddenly stopped in her tracks and her prattling cut off. Her gaze was focused on the small cemetery at the end of the street. I focused on where she stared and then back to her.

"What is it?"

"I thought . . . I thought I saw something," she stammered.

"Like a cryptid something? Or like Erica naked in the cemetery something?" She didn't laugh the way I'd expected her to.

"Cryptid something. But I don't see it anymore."

"We should check it out," I said.

"I don't have my weapons."

"You should always have something on you." I touched my angel blade through my shirt. "I'll check it out. You stay here." I stalked toward the cemetery without glancing back.

"Nova, I don't think you should go alone."

"Psh. I'll be fine." My boots hit the pavement as I jogged toward the cemetery to scope it out. Tiffany followed me, but she stopped at the entrance. A light breeze picked up the ends of my hair as I slowed and tread in between the headstones. The grass was a little dry because of how hot it had been and crunched beneath my boots. I stopped in the shade of an overgrown oak tree and tried to listen for a moment. I hoped that maybe I'd be able to hear something. All I heard was the sound of the trees swaying in the gentle breeze.

I peered back to where Tiffany stood on the sidewalk with her arms crossed. She seemed hella nervous and her gaze darted everywhere, searching for whatever she claimed to have seen. "I don't see or hear anything," I shouted over to her. At just that moment, I caught a whiff of rotting stench. I covered my nose with my shirt so I wouldn't gag.

Tiffany's eyes widened. Before I was able to see what she stared at, a piece of what I could only assume was a half-decayed human arm fell from the tree above me. The appendage thudded into the grass. Uhhh . . . that was *not* normal.

I slowly lifted my gaze to the tree branches. A spindly figure crouched on one of the limbs. The creature's body was thin and gray, its tendons and bones prominent. Red eyes glared at me from its demonic face. The cryptid's features were heinous — overly sharp cheekbones and a pointed chin. Its jagged teeth were covered with gore from the remainder of the arm. I almost vomited in my mouth at the sight. A ghoul. A cannibalistic ghoul who normally ate the dead. But I was sure that even alive I seemed mighty juicy at that moment.

I reached for my angel blade and wrapped my fingers around the hilt, ready for the creature to drop down from the tree. A moment passed before I heard rustling behind me. I slightly turned my head. In my peripheral vision, I saw several more ghouls, glowing eyes trained on me.

The ghoul in the tree dropped down in front of me. I struck out without hesitation, hitting it in the stomach. He imploded, and then the others descended on me. I spun to face them head on and swung my arm out to block their advances. One crouched and then launched himself at me full force. I brought my blade upward. It glided through pale skin and into the cryptid's gut. Before he even touched the ground, he'd disappeared.

I stepped back and the others charged me. My eyes

widened. If Tiff had been prepared, I wouldn't have been facing all of them alone. She may not have been the best hunter, but two hunters were better than one.

Time seemed to slow down as they rushed me, and a wave of heat appeared in front of me. A form solidified. My lips parted in awe at the large frame that stood before me. The man held a glowing short sword in his hand. He sliced two of the ghouls in half with one swipe. Their blood sprayed across the nearest headstones, the only sign of our fight once they'd vanished.

The last of the ghouls charged and skewered himself on the blade. Ghouls were terrifying, but obviously not smart. The man pulled his sword back and wiped the dark ichor off on his dark jeans before he turned to face me.

"What are you doing here, Elias?" I asked just as Tiffany jogged up to me.

"I told you. I was sent to watch over you," Elias said.

"I totally had it under control." I slid my weapon back in its holster at my hip.

"Yeah, really seemed like it," he said with an annoying smirk on his stupidly handsome face. Tiffany threw her arms around me.

"Are you okay?" She was slightly shaking.

"I'm fine." I patted her back lightly, and she pulled away and regarded Elias before she reached out and shook his hand.

"I'm Tiffany. Thanks for helping my sister when I wasn't prepared."

"I'm Elias. And no problem."

"How do you two know each other?" She glanced back and forth at the two of us. I gave Elias an annoyed look. The last thing I wanted was for my sister to worry about why someone was sent to watch over me.

"He's a hunter friend," I said before Elias could respond.

Tiff frowned. "You never mentioned him before."

"Because he was never worth mentioning." I linked my arm through hers and pulled her away so we could exit the cemetery. She stared back at him as I dragged her along.

I turned back and Elias stood staring after me. He had the nerve to smile and wink at me. I pursed my lips together. *Meet me at my place,* I mouthed to him silently. He gave me a slight nod before disappearing. How did he do that?

"How the hell do you *really* know him, Nova? I know you're lying to me," Tiffany persisted as I lead her down the street to our parents' house.

"I told you. He's a hunter friend."

Tiff knew when I lied because I couldn't maintain eye contact. She pulled her arm from mine and crossed both arms over her chest.

"You don't have any hunter friends other than Matthew. And hunters don't just appear out of thin air."

There were very few of us hunters left. Matt and I had been together for a couple of years, having run into each other at some random cryptid sighting. The attraction had been immediate, and we got along pretty well. But after a while, I felt like I was dating someone I saw as a sibling instead of a lover. My stomach roiled at the thought. I ended our relationship, even though he thought we could work through it, but that just wasn't something I could ever get past. We still talked periodically, and I thought he was still in love with me. I'd avoided most of his calls and texts because of that. I wasn't naive enough to believe that he was the problem . . . I knew it was me. Would always be me.

"Would you believe me if I said I met him in Germany when I picked up Rik?" I asked.

"You would've mentioned him a long time ago. He is not from Germany."

I couldn't help the laugh that bubbled up, but Tiffany was

seriously getting pissed at me. Her nostrils flared at my reac-tion, only making me laugh harder because she was so damn serious.

She huffed. "Come on, Nova. I'm your sister!"

I managed to stifle my laughter after a few moments and admitted, "I really can't tell you. At least not yet, because I can't even explain why he's here."

Tiffany exhaled through her nose, and we ambled to the front door of my parents' house.

"I promise I'll tell you when I can. And please, for the love of God, don't tell Mom and Dad about Elias or the ghouls. Not until we get this figured out."

"Ghouls . . . they aren't from here. I can't remember what I've read about them, but I know those creatures aren't local."

"They're from the Middle East and parts of Europe." I cleared my throat, all seriousness back.

"So Black Agnes isn't the only one."

"Apparently not," I said.

"We need to tell Mom and Dad."

"Not yet. Please, Tiffany. Let me figure out what the fuck is going on before we go there."

She shook her head at me and rolled her eyes. "They can help us." Tiffany was adamant.

I bit my bottom lip. I'd already told them about Agnes, and they hadn't seemed too enthusiastic about that. I wanted to make sure there was a true threat before bringing up another misplaced cryptid.

"Please?" I pleaded.

Tiff's shoulders sagged. "Fine. But you have two weeks to find out what's going on. Then if you don't tell them, I will." She poked me in my boob, and I smacked her hand away.

"Fine. Deal."

"Be careful walking home."

"I'm always careful," I said as I backed away from the door

and gave her my best smile.

"Uh huh, sure."

I stuck my tongue out at her before I turned in the direction of my own house a few blocks away.

CHAPTER FIVE

I strolled up my front steps. The sun had completely set, and no lights were on. I wasn't sure if Elias was inside or not, but I unlocked the door and stepped into the darkness. I didn't see him, so I flipped on the lights, went straight to my room, and kicked off my boots. I disarmed and placed my weapon in my nightstand drawer. Selecting a pair of black leggings, I shimmied out of my jeans before I pulled the leggings on. The moment I finished getting dressed, I felt a lick of heat at my back.

I turned to see Elias standing in my bedroom in all his glorious sexiness. Muscles bulged through his shirt, and my gaze wandered down his body to his slim waist, where his jeans hung low. I bit my lip, and Elias cleared his throat.

"My eyes are up here," he said as he pointed to his face. Nothing wrong with checking out the goods. I may not have been able to really appreciate them the last time he was around, so it was hard not to now.

"I know that." I rolled my eyes as I pushed past him and into the living room. I felt him follow me. A warmth skated up my spine, my skin erupting in goosebumps. Damn, what did this dude have that had my body reacting as though it was his bitch? No one else had ever elicited this type of response. I probably should've been a little worried about that since I'd just met the guy, but with everything else that was going on, I had more important things to be concerned with.

I slumped into a chair and acted like my body hadn't responded to his. Elias stood and crossed his arms across his chest. Those damn biceps of his seemed like they were about to hulk out of his shirt.

"So, the ghouls . . ." he started.

"Tiffany saw them, but she was unarmed. I went to check it out thinking maybe it was something small. I was wrong. I didn't expect there to be more than one."

"You're lucky I stepped in when I did."

"Were you . . . were you watching me?" I scoffed.

"Would it turn you on if I said yes?"

I raised an eyebrow at his response. "You're avoiding my question."

Elias smirked and yet again didn't answer.

"Dammit. Why is it that you can't answer my questions?" I yelled.

"Taking an oath of secrecy is more important than appeasing your curiosity," he said.

"Oath of secrecy," I mocked him. Maybe I was being childish, but I didn't care. I wanted to know the truth — the truth about all of it. Who sent Elias and the creatures? Why was this happening? He laughed outright, unbothered by my derision.

"Look, I'm here to fight alongside you. You don't have to like me, and I don't expect you to. Let's just leave it at that."

I sighed, defeated. "Fine. You win. I'll leave you alone about who sent you to babysit me."

"I wouldn't have to babysit you if you didn't go rushing headfirst into danger."

"It's not like I anticipated there being five ghouls in a cemetery. Since when do they gather in groups?" I threw my hands up.

"You were lucky I was there to help you. Otherwise, who knows what shit you would've gotten into."

"Yeah, nothing like when I ran into Aggie," I muttered.

"Aggie?" Elias cocked his head to the side.

Shit. I swallowed. "I ran into Black Agnes, and I destroyed

her."

"I thought you said nothing strange was going on." Elias's arms dropped to his sides.

"I didn't tell you about her because I was annoyed," I admitted.

"So, that was payback for me not being able to tell you who sent me?"

I tilted my head side-to-side and scrunched up my nose. "Ehhh, yes. Definitely."

"I'm at the mercy of my master. So even if I think protecting you is a waste of my time, we have to learn to trust each other. Besides, I knew about Aggie, as you call her."

"How can I trust someone that I don't even . . . Wait. You knew? Why did you even ask me then?" I asked.

"First, I didn't allow you to become ghoul food. I'm pretty sure that speaks for itself. Second, how do you think I came to be here in the first place? Aggie's dark soul is in Hell. She's spilling all her dark deeds. Even before then, we heard whispers from our sources of someone sending creatures for you. And when my master received word of what's happening, he sent me to assist."

"So, you're from Hell? And that means that your master is there . . ." So, what did that make Elias? A demon? Just great.

He'd proven he was trustworthy so far, but that didn't mean it wasn't all a facade. I knew at that moment having him on my side was good. If he wanted to take me to the enemy, he'd had plenty of opportunities to do so. I sat back in my chair and pulled my legs under me.

Elias didn't respond to my question. Instead he sighed. "So we have Black Agnes and the ghouls, all of whom are outside of their normal territory."

"Right. And when I questioned Agnes, she said she was summoned here to hunt me."

Elias's gaze locked onto mine but they contained no

impression of surprise. If Black Agnes was spilling all her secrets in the underworld, would she ever confess who the culprit was?

"But the thing is, why? What do they have to gain? I'm just a hunter," I said. Albeit an angel-and-demon hunter.

"I don't know what they'd hunt you for. But someone is after something you have. You're the first hybrid in a very long time. We may not have all of the details on what's going on. But we will figure it out."

By the time Elias left, I was ready to strangle the life out of him. I decided to do some research on my own. Google had limited information about folklore cryptids so I headed to the college library since I knew they'd have more resources. Resources that were more than likely to be written by people actually familiar with the creatures in reality rather than in theory.

I slipped into the building virtually unnoticed. I wasn't sure I should have been there since I wasn't actually a student, but no one questioned me. I found the section on folklore and mythology with little difficulty. Located at the far end of the library with no people around was good. I preferred privacy to look up things of this nature.

I searched through the shelves and pulled several books that appeared useful in my search for the truth and took them to a table. I set them down and slid into a wooden chair. The first book I opened seemed like a newer edition. There were cryptids that I hadn't done much research on in the past, so I decided to take advantage of this opportunity and read about them.

I came across an illustration of a Mongolian death worm and shivered. If I had any type of phobia, it'd be a fear of worms. This was the biggest worm I'd ever seen, and I would've hated to fight that thing. Its huge red body could reach up to seven feet, and it could spit corrosive saliva at its victims. Rows of sharp teeth were enough to make me never want to come face to whatever with this thing. The creature had no eyes or nose. Maybe it navigated with heat sensory? The book didn't say.

I continued on and found many cryptids I was already familiar with—bigfoot, mothman, the hodag. All American-based creatures. The list went on. I grew bored and closed the first book and moved on to the second, which seemed a bit more used. The edges of the leather-bound volume were worn, and I was able to tell it had been checked out quite a bit. Maybe there were other folklore enthusiasts here, such as myself. But I didn't really see it as my choice to hunt mythological creatures since I wasn't technically human, even if I could pass for one. My real mother obviously knew I was meant for more than just a normal human life since she'd left me with my adoptive parents who'd taught me how to hunt.

Footsteps echoed through the empty part of the library. I closed the book and stood.

"I have a folklore assignment I need to complete," I heard a familiar voice say.

"I didn't know you were taking folklore," another woman responded.

Tiffany rounded the corner of the bookshelf my table was hiding behind and stopped when she saw me. Next to her was a beautiful woman with dark hair pulled into a ponytail and dark brown eyes. She was lean and she had her arm around my sister's waist—this must be Erica.

"Nova, what are you doing here?" my sister asked.

"Uhh, I was looking for books for your folklore research." I played off of the lie she'd told Erica before I turned to her. "Hi, I'm Nova. Tiffany's sister." I gave her a small, uncomfortable wave. Erica seemed confused for a second as she glanced between Tiffany and me. Probably because we were like night and day in the appearance department.

"I was adopted," I said before she could question our differences. Her confused expression dissipated.

"I'm Erica. It's nice to meet you. Tiffany has told me about you. I just didn't expect you to be . . ." Erica's sentence dropped off.

"So blonde?" I giggled.

"Yeah, that. I'm sorry. That's rude of me."

I waved it off. "No, don't be sorry. That's been a pretty normal response all of our lives."

"Well, still . . ." she said.

"Erica, honestly, Nova is not a super sensitive person. We really have gotten the same response ever since I was born," Tiffany interjected.

I picked up the books from the table and handed them to Tiffany. My gaze went back to Erica. "It was nice meeting you, Erica. Maybe we can all hang out soon." I turned to Tiffany and gave her a wink. Her cheeks turned a little pink. "The newer book isn't much help, but the older one seems to have interesting folklore stories from different countries," I said with a smile and put my hands in my jean pockets.

"I'll check the older one out then," Tiff said.

"I can help if you want. Later, at my house."

"Sure. I'll come by later." She gave me a soft smile.

"I should get going."

"You don't have to go," Tiffany said.

"I have an appointment I need to get to," I lied.

"Oh. So, I'll be at your place around seven?"

"Seven works. I'll grab some takeout."

She nodded, and I gave Erica another small wave before I backed away and turned. I tucked my hair behind my ears and strolled to the library exit. Meeting new people was nice, and I was glad that Tiffany seemed to really like Erica, but I did tend to be standoffish with them at the same time. Aside from my family and Elias, I only had Matt who I was completely comfortable speaking to. Well, maybe not lately. Lately, I hadn't been able to speak to Matt. I was being pretty avoidant about bringing up my feelings. Everything just felt . . . strained.

I arrived back at my house in what seemed like minutes. Probably because my mind was all over the place, I barely remembered my walk home. I entered my house and immediately heard the sound of banging pots and pans. My guard up, I quietly crept toward the kitchen. The noise overpowered the sound of my front door being opened and I managed to sneak in undetected. I peered around the corner and relaxed the second I saw Adalrik busying himself at the stove.

I leaned against the door frame and crossed my arms over my chest.

"I hope you're planning to clean this mess up." He shrieked and dropped the pan in his hand. I cringed at the loud bang.

"You scared the shiza out of me!" He grabbed his chest as he stood on my counter, an assortment of spices laid out around him.

"You scared the shit out of *me*. I thought there was an intruder." He turned back to what he was doing and added ingredients to a pot of something.

"What are you making?" I tried to get a peek at what was in the pot from the doorway.

"Sauerbraten."

"Yum. I didn't know you could cook. Wait . . . Did you get this pot roast from my deep freezer?"

"You weren't going to make it."

"Bullshit, you don't know that."

Adalrik turned and arched a bushy gray brow at me. He knew very well I had no plans to cook the roast. That was fair.

I took a few steps into the kitchen, picked up the dropped

pan from the floor, and peeked into the pot. By the looks of it, Rik had started not too long ago. Maybe we wouldn't need takeout after all.

CHAPTER SIX

Tiffany showed up early and I let her in. Which was perfect because Rik had just finished the slow-cooked sauerbraten, and the smell of the roast made my house feel homier than it ever had.

"Did you cook something?" Tiff wrinkled her nose in disbelief.

"I can't take credit for that. It was Rik."

"Your garden gnome cooks you dinner?"

"This is actually the first time. I didn't even know he could cook. Hell, I don't even know what he eats every day. But he manages," I admitted.

"I cook every day. You're just never home," Rik called from the kitchen where he scooped the food onto plates.

"Okay, well, I guess he's been eating my food for years then." I shrugged. Tiffany and I headed in and helped take the plates to the small dining table. Adalrik jumped down from my counter and hobbled to the table. He climbed the chair before he took a seat on the books stacked for him to be at the proper height.

We talked about nonsense for a while until we were done eating the delicious meal.

"Did you bring the book?" I finally asked.

"I did." Tiffany pulled it out of her bag she'd placed on a chair beside her and set it on the table.

"What are you researching?" Rik asked.

"Cryptids from other countries," I replied.

"You could ask me, an actual cryptid from another

35

country," he said.

"Do you know about any cryptids outside of Germany?"

Rik shifted slightly. "No."

"Okay, well, if there are any from Germany we have questions about, we will ask you." I gave him a slight smile.

As Tiffany opened the leather-bound book, I scooted my chair closer to hers to get a better look.

"Did you find anything when you were at the library earlier?" she asked.

I shook my head. "No, nothing about them country hopping."

We went through the book together, reading descriptions as we viewed the detailed illustrations of the creatures. I had at least heard whispers about most of them, but some of them I'd never heard of. Knowledge was power, and the book even gave details on how best to get rid of them. My angel blade had always been my weapon of choice. Typically, anything angelic or demonic in nature could be used to eliminate them. Even items blessed by a priest were commonly used. Tiffany had been given a sword blessed by a shaman that was passed down for generations in our family. The main reason she didn't carry it often was because there was no way for her to hide it the way I could conceal my weapon.

I felt the heat that was becoming all too familiar before I saw Elias. He stood in my kitchen, weapons drawn. Adalrik shrieked.

"Get your weapons," he said. He didn't even glance our way. His sword was in his hand, and he'd already assumed a fighting stance.

Tiffany and I leapt up without question, our chairs scraping against the tile. Rik jumped from his chair and scurried for cover in one of the lower cabinets since he wasn't much of a fighter. I pulled my blade from beneath my shirt and Tiffany stuck her hand into her bag. I frowned as I watched her. I knew her sword would never fit in that small space. But instead of a sword, she pulled out our mother's smaller dagger set, and held one in each hand.

A freakish shriek came from outside. At first it was only one scream. Then the noise multiplied, coming from all around the house. I peered outside through the blinds. Three pairs of glowing red eyes stared back at me. Elias had taken a position at another window in the living room and was also focused outside.

"There are two over here," he said.

"I have three on this side. There may be more we can't see," I shouted to make myself heard above the cacophony.

"What are they?" Tiffany asked.

"Rakes," Elias and I said in unison. I peered over at him and caught his gaze for a moment.

"I have never seen more than one at a time." I peeped out the window again. The rakes stood on all fours as they watched the house. What baffled me was that they had gathered, which was abnormal for these types of creatures. Most often they were solitary and stayed in the woods.

"I think we're surrounded," Elias said.

"Tiff, I need you to be on your game for this," I told her, and she nodded.

Elias peered again. "I don't see them anymore."

The screeching had stopped too, leaving us in an eerie silence. My grip tightened on the hilt of my weapon as my heartbeat pounded in my ears. I strained my hearing and tried to listen past the annoying thump to locate where they were, but it was no use. Quick footsteps on the roof were the only warning they were coming before a pale body smashed through one of the windows. Glass flew across the living room. Another rake crashed through the kitchen window opposite of where I stood. I threw up my arms to keep the glass from hitting my face. Small shards grazed my bare skin and left small nicks in my flesh. They had all crashed through the windows of my small home.

Elias wasted no time as he slashed and stabbed away at the intruders, and they began to disappear. Their blood was black, and bile rose in my throat at the stench. I held my breath and swung out at the two rakes that had invaded my kitchen. I managed to pierce the first one that came at me directly in the chest the moment he attacked. I didn't stop. By the time I'd freed my blade from the first attacker, the second rake was on me, bony arms swinging at my face. I took a step back at every sloppy attempt to strike at me.

I blocked and ducked until I was against my kitchen wall. When the rake came at me this time, I kicked my foot out. My boot connected with his stomach and he was forced back at least five steps. This was my opening. I lunged, only for it to sidestep me. I pivoted so my back wasn't to it. Instead of aiming low, I struck from above. I jumped forward and aimed my blade downward. My weapon penetrated my opponent's forehead as if it was cutting through butter. Its glowing eyes dimmed before it dissipated.

I ran the short distance to my living room, where Elias was still expertly killing the cryptids that kept coming and glanced around for Tiffany. A rake snuck up behind Elias. I threw my blade and speared the rake between the eyes at the same time Elias slew the one in front of him.

He glanced behind him as the creature fell to the floor. His lips twitched, and he grabbed my angel blade from the disintegrating rake before he quickly handed it back to me just as another rake crashed through the window. Elias could handle this, but I needed to find my sister, and she was nowhere to be seen.

I rushed into my bedroom and found Tiffany tangled with a rake, losing horribly. She was flat on her back, pinned beneath the rake. Its teeth snapped as the cryptid tried to get a taste. Discolored saliva dripped from sharp, decaying teeth. Tiff was barely keeping the creature at arm's length. I stepped in and stabbed the disgusting thing in the back. She was breathing heavily from the exertion as I helped her to her feet.

"You okay?" I asked her.

"Yeah, just grossed out." She wiped the rake's saliva from her cheek with the back of her hand.

"Come on. Elias is by himself handling multiple," I told her.

We jogged our way back to the living room where I'd last seen Elias. When I rounded the corner, a rake launched itself at me and punched me in the face. My nose spurted blood and my eyes watered. With my vision blurred, I stumbled back a step. That creature's shriek of glee would be its last. I wiped away my tears with the back of my hand and stared into the rake's skeletal face. I charged. The monster lurched in surprise and fell onto its back. I jumped on top of it and punched it square in the face. The rake's paper-thin skin tore open, leaving wounds on its nose and cheek. I punched it again, snapping its head to the side. As I hovered over the rake, my blood dripped from my nose and into the creature's open lacerations. Its flesh sizzled and the rake's shrieks ripped through the air. I was certain my eardrums were seconds away from bursting.

I shoved away to put distance between the rake and myself. I bumped into Tiffany's legs. and she helped me to my feet. The rake convulsed uncontrollably and grabbed at its face. No — tore the skin from its face. The exposed muscle bubbled and smoked. The simmering of flesh and muscle only worsened until the rake's head exploded, spattering black ichor across my living room walls and floor. I gagged and covered my injured nose and mouth with my hand. Tiff wasn't so lucky. She raced to the bathroom, and I heard her vomit. I stared wide-eyed at the spot where the decimated rake had been. Only dark sludge was left behind.

My mouth opened, and I tried to figure out what had happened. When Tiffany came out of the bathroom, her normally golden skin was drawn.

The silence was more deafening than the shrieking of the cryptid. The blood from my nose had slowed but I knew my face was covered with it. The metallic flavor was in my mouth. My gaze found where Elias stood, and he stared at me awestruck. He hadn't spoken even though all the cryptids were gone. Broken glass and creature blood covered my living room. I took a deep breath as I held his gaze.

"Did you know that could happen?" I asked in a voice barely above a whisper.

He shook his head and his blue eyes continued to examine me.

"Are you all right?" he asked, his voice raspy.

"Me?"

"Yeah, you're bleeding." As he moved closer, I used the back of my hand to wipe some of the blood from my face and lips. I was pretty sure I ended up smearing it.

"Did your blood make his head explode?" Tiffany asked.

"I . . . I think so."

I washed my face in my bathroom sink with my hand and soap. Elias came in with a washcloth and handed it to me.

"Thanks," I said as I took it from him and ran it under warm water. I scrubbed my face in front of the mirror, watching him in the reflection.

"That was exciting," he said with a sexy smirk.

"Never a dull moment," I murmured. My gaze went back to my face in the mirror. If I were human, I would have been sporting a black eye from that punch.

"Rakes are native to the US," Elias said. I put the washcloth down and turned to glare at him.

"But when have you ever heard of a *pack* of rakes attacking someone out of nowhere?"

"Never."

"Exactly. So, what just happened? How do they know where I am?"

"I don't know."

I pushed away from my sink and sauntered past Elias. I headed to my room and picked up the pieces of glass scattered everywhere. Tiffany had already started to help with clean-up.

"I think I should stay here with you tonight," Elias said from behind me.

"Absolutely not." I shook my head.

"It's not safe here for you anymore. At least not alone."

"I've managed to keep myself alive in this house for years without you here to protect me," I said.

"Why are you being so stubborn?"

"You're an ass. That's why!" Elias's smirk grated on my nerves. I had a feeling he liked my verbal abuse.

"You don't have to like me to let me be here to make sure you stay safe. Besides, you may not like me, but you definitely like to stare at me." His grin widened.

My mouth dropped open. "I . . . what . . ." I blew out a breath, unsure of what to say when he called me out.

He was right though. I did like staring at him, but even still, the thought of him staying in my house rubbed me the wrong way. Maybe it was the way he eluded every question I asked him. How did he even know that the rakes were here? He couldn't just coincidentally show up *twice*.

"Fine, you can sleep on the couch," I said with a sigh. I was too tired to continue arguing with him. The thought of Elias sleeping in my house caused my heart to stutter in my chest. But I refused to acknowledge that.

"I think we should sleep in the same room. Just in case."

He knelt next to me and started picking up glass. My attention shifted to his arm when it grazed mine. The electrical charge from the minor touch shot up my arm and I shuddered. Nope, not happening. I stood quickly and backed away, turning toward the door.

"I'm going to check on Tiffany," I said over my shoulder. I trudged my way to the living room. I couldn't be next to him. Whether it was my traitorous body's reaction or the fact that I was annoyed with him about literally everything. I hoped he didn't follow. I needed space.

I found Tiffany scrubbing the walls, wearing a face mask and rubber gloves. The stench from the rake's blood lingered even though most of my windows were broken, letting in the humid air.

"Thank you for helping me clean up."

"It's the least I can do since you saved my ass," she said.

I picked up a few bigger pieces of glass and threw them into a trash bag filled with other items that couldn't be salvaged.

"That's what sisters do." I shrugged.

"Yeah, but I screwed up and underestimated its strength." Tiff stopped scrubbing and glared at me.

"Tiff, it is what it is. You're here and breathing, that's all that matters." I sighed.

"It's not, though. I suck at this, while you're like a kickass Barbie that sends these creatures back to wherever the hell they came from."

"Shut up. You've killed plenty of cryptids," I said.

"I'm jealous that you're better at it than me."

I'd never thought Tiffany cared enough that she'd be jealous. She'd done so much more with her life than I had.

"I'm not human, Tiffany. You get to go to college and have dates—a normal life. I kill cryptids and have no sense of what normal even is."

Tiffany pulled down her mask and wiped the sweat from her brow with her arm.

"Nova, you are the coolest person I know. Hybrid or not, normal is boring."

My lips twitched as I fought a smile. Tiffany sighed before she started scrubbing again.

"Soon you won't even be dealing with this crap. You'll graduate and become a doctor or something," I told her. There was a beat of silence and I glanced at the clock. I hadn't realized what time it was. "You don't have to finish doing this. It's late."

"No, it's okay," she said.

I sank down next to her and grabbed her arm. She stopped scrubbing. Tiff's dark brown eyes bore into mine.

"Leave it," I said. She dropped the sponge and stood, then pulled off her gloves and mask.

"Elias!" I called out. Elias popped his head out from my room. "Can you escort my sister home?"

"I don't need an escort, Nova," Tiff mumbled.

"You do, and Elias is going to be that escort," I argued.

"And what about you? What if something comes while he's gone?"

"Then I have my weapon and my kickass Barbie skills," I replied with a smirk.

While Elias took Tiffany back to my parents' house, I continued to clean up. I threw glass away, righted the furniture, and covered up the broken windows with large plastic trash bags and duct tape. That would have to do until I could have them replaced. Tiffany had pretty much cleaned up all the rake guts. The smell had finally started to dissipate.

I took a quick shower. Coming out of my bathroom, wrapped in a towel, I ran right into Elias's hard chest. His hands grabbed my shoulders to steady me. The warmth from his touch spread through my body. The sensation ended at the apex of my thighs. I gasped softly. His calloused hands scraped against the smooth skin of my shoulders and I shivered.

When I peeked up at his face, his heated gaze dropped to my mouth. I licked my lips nervously.

"I didn't mean to scare you," he said roughly. Elias's voice broke me from the trance he had me in. My throat went dry.

"I'm just going to get dressed really quick," I managed to get out.

Elias dropped his hands from my shoulders. I hurried to my room and closed the door softly. I dressed in a pair of yoga pants and a semi-baggy T-shirt before I stepped back into the living room. Elias sat on my couch, his legs spread wide.

I took a seat next to him and took care not to let any part of me touch any part of him.

"So, it's more than foreign creatures coming here," I said to break the silence. I pulled my hair up into a messy bun and Elias watched my movements.

"I guess so," he replied.

"And since when do rakes gather together? Like is this something you've ever heard of or seen happen before?"

"No, this is abnormal behavior for them. They're always alone, in wooded areas. They usually don't attack unless provoked or if someone is in their territory."

"So the cryptids are being sent here by someone. How would they know where to go? It's not like they have access to Google maps."

"There has to be someone guiding them," Elias said. He stretched a bit and threw his arm over the back of the couch. His fingers gently grasped a loose strand of my hair, twisting it. "I am curious to know how your blood caused such a reaction to the rake's wounds."

"The only thing I can think of is because I'm part angel and part demon. My blood is angelic and demonic in nature. We know that weapons forged in Heaven and Hell can vanquish cryptids. So why not my blood?"

Elias nodded. His brows formed a furrow, deep in thought.

My gaze found his. His frown softened and he reached over with his free hand and touched my nose. I scrunched it up. "What are you doing?" I asked.

"Does it heal quickly?" he asked softly.

"What? My nose?"

He nodded.

"It does. It's still sore but I'll be fine by tomorrow." I was surprised that he cared.

"You're definitely a kickass Barbie."

"Were you eavesdropping?" I asked.

"I was. I have excellent hearing."

"Good to know. I'll make sure to talk about you when you're back to wherever you go when you're not here," I said, and he chuckled.

CHAPTER SEVEN

Elias refused to let me sleep in my room alone. So I gave him a pillow and blankets and he took up a spot on the floor. I laid in my bed and stared up at the ceiling in the dark. With everything that had happened, sleep wouldn't be possible.

"Elias?" I said, barely above a whisper.

"Nova." His deep voice said my name. My skin prickled.

"Why would someone send you here to watch over me? Who would care?"

"I can't answer that without giving away who sent me."

"Right," I said. "Who in Hell would want me to have a protector?"

There was silence. Not that I expected anything else. I propped myself up on my elbow and stared down at Elias. His blue eyes glowed softly in the dark.

"I don't know if I can sleep," I grumbled.

"Me neither."

"Would it be weird to ask you to play a game with me?" I asked.

"I don't want to play human games with you. Although, we can find other things to occupy our time," he replied flirtatiously. His eyes brightened.

"I doubt it'd be worth my time." I rolled my eyes, unsure if he could even see my reaction.

"I promise it would be."

"Thanks, but no thanks. A game sounds better." I sighed and threw myself back down onto my bed.

Elias chuckled deeply. "Fine. We can play your game."

"Yes!" I tossed my blankets off and hopped out of bed at record speed, running out my bedroom door.

"Uno!" I yelled.

"I have literally twenty cards in my hand," Elias said.

"And I have one. Now drop your next card." He stared at me with a raised brow. He sighed before he put down a red number seven. I slammed down my own red card on top of his and stood.

"I win!" I sang and danced in victory. Elias laughed and threw down the rest of his cards on the coffee table.

"I don't understand these games," he said with a half-smile.

"Because you suck and I'm the queen of Uno." I pointed at him and shimmied my hips, continuing my dance. In the blink of an eye, Elias was in front of me. I fell back onto my couch, which startled me. His eyes glowed brightly as he leaned over me, hovering closely to my face. His breath danced across my lips as he caged me in with his arms. If I leaned in another inch, our lips would touch. I could barely breathe with him so close.

"Don't do that," he growled. Elias's glowing eyes seemed to brighten even more. I swore I saw flames in their depths. His breath stirred the strands of hair that framed my face.

"Do what?" I shivered.

"Don't dance like that."

"Why?"

"Because it makes me want to lose control and you already decided you didn't want to accept my offer," he murmured. His nose brushed against mine.

I swallowed. I knew I shouldn't push the issue and tempt him even more. I told myself I didn't like the guy. I mean he was drop dead sexy, but he was a flirt and an evasive one at that. Which was a no-go in my book.

He pushed off from the couch and stalked toward my bedroom. His form retreated and my gaze wandered to his firm backside. God, I needed to stop checking him out. I shook my head and rose from the couch, following after him.

Elias had lain back in his spot on the floor in the dark. I climbed into my bed and covered myself completely. I forced my mind to stop thinking about everything. I stared at the ceiling and tried to force my mind and body to calm. But with Elias so close to me just moments before, I couldn't help but wonder what if I had just closed that gap between us? Would he have kissed me back? Would he have touched me in return? He seemed to enjoy flirting with me, but would he follow through with his promise? The promise to make it worth my while. I pressed my thighs together and tried to ebb the throbbing that had started. I couldn't think about that. Especially not when there were only a couple of feet between us. I turned to my side and squeezed my eyes shut. I tried to think of anything but the sexy Hell-sent protector. After a while, I somehow managed to drift off to sleep with images of Elias's luscious mouth on my body.

The next morning, Elias was gone. The sun was bright when I pulled the covers from my head. I rubbed my eyes, trying to get them to adjust to the brightness. Grabbing my phone off the nightstand, I saw that it was almost noon already. Holy hell. I'd slept half of the day away. We must have stayed up later than I'd thought.

Several messages were from Tiffany. She was trying to convince me to agree to tell our parents about what was going on. I didn't respond right away. Instead, I threw the covers back and decided to wash the sleep from my body. I showered quickly and dressed in black jeans with a white T-shirt. I strapped my angel blade into its holster. My loose shirt perfectly covered my weapon. While I sat on the edge of my bed, slipping on my boots, my phone rang. I answered without glancing at the caller ID, holding it awkwardly between my shoulder and ear as I tied my laces.

"This is Nova."

"Nova," said a male voice. My phone fell to the carpet. I picked it up quickly and glanced at the call screen. Matthew. I cleared my throat.

"Hey, Matt," I said.

"How are you?"

"I'm good, you know, just living life. Hunting and what-not," I responded nonchalantly.

"I've been getting messages from Tiffany about some strange things going on. How come you haven't asked for my help?"

Fucking Tiffany. I should've clarified that I didn't want *anyone* to know about what was going on, not just our parents. I should've known she would pull this crap. "I've been busy. And honestly, it never crossed my mind," I confessed.

"I'm glad Tiffany's keeping me up to date on it then," Matt said. I could hear the slight disappointment in his voice that he hadn't received a call or text from me with the information.

"I'm sorry, Matt. It's been pretty hectic."

"Well, I guess I'm calling to ask if you need any help."

"I would appreciate that." I cringed inwardly.

"I have some pretty old tomes on the history of cryptids."

"Nice. I think that's what we need, if you could research whether or not there have been any older accounts of creatures catching a ride to other countries or continents. And maybe if they're known to hunt anyone in particular and why." I bit my lip nervously, hoping he wouldn't ask any probing questions. I wasn't sure how much Tiff had shared with Matt. I didn't want to give up the information about me being more than just a hunter. Matt had never questioned why my eyes were unnaturally colored. Or why I was quicker than him.

49

"Sure thing."

"Thank you."

"Nova, I'd like to get together. Like old times," Matt said.

I tried to think of what I should say. I must have been quiet for too long because Matt sighed. "I get it. You don't want to be with me. But it doesn't mean we can't be friends. Hell, we were together for two years. I'm still here for you, you know?"

"I know," I croaked.

"Well, I'll let you go. I'll update you if I find anything."

"Okay, sounds good."

I hung up and exhaled. I felt like a shitty person. Matthew had done nothing wrong. My own feelings had interfered with our relationship. He took our break-up as well as expected. I'd promised to keep in touch so we could be friends. But I couldn't keep that promise and ended up pushing away from him. I knew I was hurting him just by being around him. I guess I should have given him the benefit of the doubt and let him in. Completely platonic, of course. But part of me knew he would always have feelings that would be greater than my own. I didn't want to think about that and filed it away in the back of my mind. This wasn't a priority at the moment.

I pushed off the bed and hauled my ass to my parents' house. I knocked on the door, but it didn't seem like my parents were home. Their cars weren't in the driveway. That was a good thing since I planned on wringing Tiffany's pretty fucking neck.

Tiffany cracked the door open and peeked out before she pulled it open all the way. Her dark hair was up in a high ponytail, and she looked like she'd been working out, dressed in leggings and a pink sports bra. I shoved the door open and rounded on her.

"What the hell, Tiff?"

"Did Matthew call you?" she squeaked, playing with the

ends of her hair. Which was something she did when she was nervous.

"Of course he called me!" I threw my hands up.

"I just think he could help us. If you aren't letting Mom and Dad know, then at least let him help us. The more hunters, the better. Plus, you know he has old books that may clue us in on what's happening."

"You could've at least brought it up to me before you went behind my back and told my *ex-boyfriend* about my personal life."

Tiffany frowned and dropped her hand from her dark strands. "It's not just about you, Nova. This is bigger than the both of us. We need help. We didn't find anything in the books from my school library. Then we were attacked. We could've died. Not once but twice." She wasn't wrong. My anger melted away.

"Well, he's going to look through the tomes and see if there's something in there. He'll let me know."

"Good. I'm glad he's able to help us out in some way," Tiffany said with a smirk.

"Can you at least give me a heads-up before you pull some crap like this again? So I'm prepared?"

She gave me a nod and flipped her dark ponytail over her shoulder. Tiff turned on her heel and strode away from me. I closed the front door and followed her into the home gym. I was never able to stay mad at her for very long.

"What's going on with that Elias guy?" Tiffany threw a glare at me over her shoulder and raised her eyebrows.

"I . . . I don't know. He won't tell me anything other than he's here to help us. Help me."

"Well, he kicked ass last night." She turned to face me.

"Yeah, he did."

"Do you like him?" She tilted her head to the side and squinted. She seemed to be expecting me to lie. My cheeks felt hot. I thought about the sexy dream I'd had about Elias last night.

"Honestly? He's kind of an ass. He acts like he's too good to be watching over me. Last night he refused to leave and slept..." Before I even finished my sentence, Tiff's mouth quirked up in the corner. She gave me a look that said I bet he stayed the night.

"Woah! Not like that. We played Uno and he slept on the floor," I defended myself before she even spoke a word. I held up my hands.

"You played Uno?" Tiffany snorted and started laughing.

I couldn't help but giggle with her. I'd played Uno with my handsome protector from Hell. That was pretty funny. Definitely strange.

"We did. I couldn't sleep after the rush of killing all those rakes. I was still on edge. High on adrenaline and all," I explained.

"That's gotta be one of the weirdest things I've ever heard."

"I'm sure that's not true. I mean, we do hunt creatures," I said. She put her hands on her hips. After our giggles died down, Tiffany was etched in seriousness.

"I need your help," she said.

"With?"

"I want you to teach me how to be a better hunter." Not what I expected.

"How?" I frowned.

"Will you spar with me?" I was a little surprised. She'd never asked me to teach her anything. Our dad normally taught her, but fighting was definitely not her forte.

"Right now?"

"Sure, why not?" Tiffany shrugged and strolled over to the wall where we kept our mats. She pulled out one of the large mats and laid it across the floor.

"I guess. But we're not using weapons. We'll do it hand-to-hand first."

Tiffany's back slammed onto the mat for about the hundredth time in the last hour. We were both breathing heavily, and I was sprawled out next to her. My shirt clung to my sweaty skin. She'd lent me a pair of workout pants before we'd started. There was no way I was going to teach her the moves while wearing jeans.

"I think you're doing better," I panted. I used my shirt to wipe perspiration from my face.

"You're a liar, Nova." Tiff turned her head toward me. Loose strands of hair stuck to her forehead.

"No, seriously. You were able to block more of my advances this last time."

"You're so much quicker than I am. I don't want to be a liability." Damn. I felt like maybe she'd read my mind about some past experiences we'd had.

"Tiff, how many times do I have to tell you, I'm not human. My speed comes from what I am. I've been slowing it down so you can have time to process the moves I'm throwing at you." I hopped up and put my hand out for her to grab onto. She took it and I pulled her to her feet.

When my stomach grumbled, I realized I hadn't eaten all day. With all the extra calories we'd burned, my hunger was almost unbearable. And yes, I felt hunger. I was pretty sure being on Earth had given me some human needs. Needs I wouldn't have in Heaven or Hell, if I had grown up there.

"I need to eat," I said.

"Let's go to the diner in town."

I nodded.

CHAPTER EIGHT

Tiffany dropped me back off at my house after we ate, and I headed inside. Shortly after I kicked off my boots, I heard a knock at my door. Maybe Tiffany forgot something. I peered through the peephole. Matthew stood on the other side. What was he doing here? He said he'd call, not show up at my house. I pressed my head against the cool wood of my front door and took a deep breath. Then I plastered a smile on my face and opened my door.

"Hey, Matt," I said.

"Can I come in?" His brown eyes searched my face. Matt was probably a couple inches shorter than Elias and almost as fit. He looked good with his light brown hair combed and styled. He held a tome under his arm. I pulled the door open farther and motioned for him to step inside.

Matt went straight to my living room and seated himself on the couch. He set the book on the coffee table. The Uno cards from the night before were still laid out. I moved to put the cards back into their box.

"You didn't call." I busied myself so I didn't have to stare at him.

"I thought maybe it would be better to show you. Did . . . did something happen here?"

I froze and snapped my attention back to him. Could he tell that Elias was here? I mean nothing happened but there was that moment that had me thinking there were other thoughts on his mind than just protecting me. But I don't think I could stand the judgment from Matt. Even if there was nothing going on between Elias and me.

"What do you mean?" I queried.

"Um, I happened to notice most of your windows are covered up."

"Oh, yeah. I thought Tiffany told you. We were ambushed by at least ten rakes last night."

"She mentioned the rakes, just not that it happened at your house." Matt frowned.

"They definitely messed my place up." I closed the card box and sat on the couch next to Matt, keeping a decent amount of space between us. He leaned forward and opened the book on top of the stack, carefully turning to a page that listed all the volumes in the set.

"I was researching and didn't find anything that can give you a direct answer. But then I happened to glance at this page and I noticed I don't have all of the volumes. I thought I did."

"Can you locate the missing one?" I asked.

"Well, my grandfather gave me these. Maybe he owns the last one and just forgot to give it to me. I'll have to go snooping around his library and see if he actually has it since he just went out of town."

"Matt, it's fine. I know how he can be about his collectables. Maybe there's a reason he didn't give the other volume to you."

"Nova, this is important. Something big is going on from what I can tell. The cryptids aren't acting normal. That means we're all in danger."

"Did you finish going through these?" I asked him.

"Yeah."

"Do you mind if I keep them for a day or two?"

"Yeah, sure." Matt closed the book and leaned back on the couch. "So, how have you been?"

"I'm good, just busy. You know, dealing with all of this

going on. What about you?"

Oh, how I hated small talk.

"Same." An uncomfortable silence followed. Tension crept into my shoulders and I rubbed my hands on my thighs.

"We don't have to do this, Matt," I said.

"Do what, Nova? Be civil?"

"No, the uncomfortable small talk."

"I genuinely wanted to know how you've been. Is that so hard to believe?" He stood.

"I know. I'm just not good at this, okay?"

"I know you aren't. That was part of our problem as a couple. You never could stand to sit still and relax for a minute."

"Our job as hunters is to *not* sit on our ass. We get shit done." I stood up from the couch. I didn't like how I felt so small next to him, especially when we argued.

"Our life doesn't revolve around hunting cryptids. It's a job, not a life. I like to chill out on some days and just be able to be Matthew. Not Matthew the cryptid hunter."

"Maybe for you it's okay to take a minute to breathe, but I can't, Matt! I'm not hu . . . like you. I don't know what it means to sit still." I'd almost slipped and mentioned not being human. But Matt didn't know about me being a hybrid. My parents had always told me to keep that a well-guarded secret. Even boyfriends weren't privileged to that information.

"If you had been able to loosen up, maybe things would've worked for us." His face started to turn a deep shade of red. He was getting angry with me.

"Wow. You think that was the problem? The problem was that I couldn't stand you touching me anymore. It felt *wrong*. I can't see you as anything other than a friend."

Matt drew back as if I'd slapped him. My gut twisted with the realization that I'd hurt him. Again.

"You know what? Fuck this." Matt stormed out of my house and slammed the door behind him. The walls shook from the impact. A few pieces of the glass left in one of the windows fell and shattered. As a couple, we never used to argue. Maybe I was more . . . agreeable? I squeezed my eyes shut and took a breath.

"Fuck!" I screamed and pulled at my hair. I should've been grateful Matt wanted to help. I had to open my big mouth and start shit. I could've done the normal thing, instead, and been cordial and nice. What the hell was wrong with me?

"That was dramatic."

I jerked my head to see Elias leaning against the doorframe of my kitchen. His arms were crossed over his chest.

"What are you doing here?" I growled out. Elias smirked at me, and that caused my blood to boil. I knew that he'd heard something he shouldn't have.

"Let's call it intuition."

Intuition my ass.

"Actually, if I'm being honest, I was coming to check on you and strolled in on this lovely entertainment," he said.

I slumped back onto the couch, my head in my hands. I felt the heat of Elias next to me. The cushion of the couch dipped under his weight.

"He seems like the forgiving type."

"How would you know?" I asked.

Elias peeled my hands away from my face. He stroked a thumb across my knuckles. "Just a feeling."

I turned my head and stared into his blue eyes. They'd calmed since the last time I'd seen him. There were no flames and they barely glowed. I wanted to smack the smug expression off his face. My gaze wandered to his mouth and back to his eyes. I scooted a couple of inches away from him.

"Are you staying again?"

"If you want me to. We could look through the books together," he suggested.

He grabbed the book off the coffee table and opened it to

the first page with descriptions of the creatures. I clenched my jaw and sighed. "Matt doesn't seem to think there's anything helpful in these. He's going to look for the missing volume."

"We can be the better judge of that. Since he doesn't know."

"Know what?" I asked.

"He doesn't know what you are. Or that they're coming for you."

I took the next book in the pile and settled back. We spent the next couple of hours reading pages and reviewing illustrations. These books were older than the ones from the college library. From what I knew, Matt had access to hundreds of ancient and new age texts about mythology and the creatures we hunted. The pages were thick and discolored along the edges. Elias and I were careful when we turned the pages. There were some side notes in the margins that were handwritten in a different language. One that I couldn't read.

"There's nothing here," I said.

"Not yet at least."

"Look at you, ever the optimist."

Elias chuckled at my smartass comment. I loved how I could be a bitch and he could be amused by that.

"I may or may not have found something of interest." His finger ran over the sloppy writing.

"What?" I sat up straighter and studied the page he referred to.

"This says that there's a portal and tells where to find it."

Holy shit, Tiffany may have been right after all.

"You can read this?" I pointed to the messy penmanship in the margins.

"I can." He gave me a cocky grin.

"Does it tell you where it's located exactly?"

"It does. They're coordinates . . . more or less."

Maybe that was the portal the cryptids were coming through from other locations. There was only one way to find out. I unlocked my phone and asked Elias what the coordinates were. According to Google maps, the location wasn't too far from my house. Maybe if we could get to the entry point of the portal, we could find some clues.

I stood from my couch and pulled on my boots again, then grabbed my keys off the table.

"Wait, you want to go right now? It's almost dark out."

"Are you scared, Elias?" I taunted him.

"Never," he said with a sexy smirk.

It took us a half hour to drive to the mountains where the coordinates indicated. My mood had slightly improved on the drive. But we remained quiet for most of the ride. We parked off the side of the road and I turned off the engine. I knew there were a lot of hiking trails around the area, and I hoped we didn't come across any campers who were staying the night.

I exited the car and closed my door. When I turned around, I bumped into Elias, almost falling back. If it weren't for his strong hands that grabbed onto my upper arms, I would have landed flat on my ass.

"Dude, what the hell? It's called personal space." I stepped back, out of his grip. I didn't realize how warm his hands were until they were gone from my skin. A coldness was left behind that produced a shiver that skated down my body.

"Sorry. You can see in the dark?" Elias asked me. I cleared my throat and tried to ignore the effect Elias had on my body. We marched in unison toward the woods.

"Yeah, for the most part. I mean, I can see well enough to not need a flashlight to kick someone's ass."

"Good to know."

"What about you? Any other superpowers besides teleporting?"

Elias laughed. "Superpowers . . . I like that. Well, as you

know, I have exceptional hearing. And yes, I can teleport, if you want to call it that. I prefer calling it fading."

"Okay, mental note taken." I smiled and continued onto a dirt path.

"I have other advantages. But I can't tell you all my secrets." His lips tipped up at the corner.

"More like you tell me none of them."

"Touché."

"Which, if you think about it, isn't fair. I mean you know more about me than I do about you." I glanced over at him.

"I think you like me more than you let on, Nova." He raised a brow.

"And I think you're delusional." I tripped over a tree root and fell onto my hands and knees. I laughed loudly at my clumsiness and obvious karma for shit talking. Elias started laughing along with me and helped me to my feet.

"I thought you could see in the dark," he said.

"I was—" His finger went to my lips suddenly and he stopped laughing.

"What?" I said against the flesh of his finger.

"Shhh . . ." He pointed to his ear to let me know he heard something.

I listened intently. I was only able to hear a slight hissing noise but that was all. At first, I thought it was snake, but with Elias on such high alert, that was doubtful. The trees covering the trail gently moved in the breeze. Beyond their rustling, I couldn't hear anything. I studied our surroundings. Maybe I could use my visual abilities to make up for the lack of enhanced hearing. I didn't notice anything out of the ordinary. The moon lit our pathway, making it even easier for me to see.

A blur ran past us. I stumbled back from surprise. Another blur passed by. I pulled my blade from its place at my hip and went back-to-back with Elias. We both turned and searched for whatever it was that had been zooming past us.

One of the blurs stopped directly in front of me. A woman with long red hair and pale skin. A smatter of freckles dotted the bridge of her nose and cheeks. Her eyes were completely black with no visible sclera.

"Ona takaya krasivaya," the woman said. She reached out and grabbed a piece of my hair, gently rubbing it between her fingers. For the first time ever, I felt frozen, but not from fear—I was intrigued.

"Obe devushki krasivyye," said another female voice from behind me. She must've been in front of Elias. There was no way I was going to even glance away from this chick.

"Upir," growled Elias, breaking me from my trance. Upirs were the Russian equivalent to vampires. Only they were able to walk in the sun without frying to death. Deadly creatures who didn't have a good reputation.

The woman struck out and grabbed me by the throat. She caught me off guard. I hadn't even raised my weapon. I no longer felt Elias at my back. Before I could stab outward, I was tossed across the forest floor. I tumbled through the dirt. The wind had been knocked out of me, and I struggled to get to my feet. I glanced up to see Elias as he fought the other upir with his sword, but she was fast. I could only make out her blonde hair and white dress as she ran. The speed of Elias's blocks and attacks quickened as he fought. Almost as though he'd learned her moves and predicted them. Maybe even adjusted to her fighting style.

Red stalked toward me. I tried to get the strength to stand before she reached me. She was too quick, though. Before I was able to get my feet under me, she stood over me.

Kicked in the stomach, I tumbled down an embankment. I lost my grip on my angel blade as I fell. Pummeled by sticks and rocks, my exposed skin tore open, and my bones bruised. Eventually a tree trunk to the back stopped my tumble as I coughed and sputtered. I tried to catch my breath, but the pain was nauseating. I struggled to sit up. Pain radiated down my spine and my ribs felt as though they were locked in a vice. Every breath I took was torture. My vision had become blurred as I sought out the upir. My stomach ached and I grabbed onto the tree trunk, pulling myself to my feet. A few of my nails broke in the process. I couldn't stand up straight, hunched over in pain. With a groan, I coughed more, and blood splattered on the ground. The dirt that had been kicked up during my fall had settled and my vision started to clear. The blur came toward me. With no weapon and my injuries, I was helpless.

The redhead stopped in front of me and caught me by the throat again, lifting me from the ground. I tried to dislodge her hand from my throat, but her bruising grasp didn't budge. My airway restricted, I dug my nails into her pale skin, but she didn't flinch. She tilted her head to the side as she ran a long fingernail down the side of my face. Her sharp nail nicked my cheek. The warmth of blood trickled down to my chin, and she swiped her finger through it. She pulled her hand away and moaned as she licked my blood off her finger.

"I'm sure our master won't mind me having a taste. I do love a good chase, but you made it easy for me to find you. He will be pleased with your quick delivery," she said in a thick accent and inhaled deeply. The veins beneath her pale skin darkened and pulsated. The upir's incisors elongated.

"Who . . . is . . . your . . ." I managed to cough out. I gasped for breath, unable to finish my question. Even so, it should have been obvious.

A growl came from behind me. I didn't dare turn my attention away from the upir in front of me to check it out. Her grip loosened, though, and I fell to the ground. I scrambled away from her, taking in long drags of air. The upir backed up a step, her gaze fixated on whatever was behind me. Loud footsteps broke twigs and crunched leaves. Another grunt and an odor permeated the air. And not a good one. The upir's eyes widened a fraction, and she hissed like a cat. That must have been what we heard earlier. What a lame sound. I would have laughed if it didn't hurt so much. I definitely didn't want the attention of whatever creature had stalked the upir.

I turned my head and dared to take a peek at what was coming toward us. Holy mother of God. This being was at least nine feet tall, with a large build and long brown hair that covered almost every inch of its body. An apelike face glared angrily at the upir.

"It's fucking bigfoot," I managed to rasp out. At that moment he charged the upir. The earth trembled beneath his weight. Within three lengthy steps, bigfoot reached her and threw the upir through the air. She landed on her feet and ran at the giant creature. But she suddenly stopped short and grabbed her stomach.

I cocked my head in confusion. I didn't think upirs could get stomach aches. She vomited onto the dirt ground and dropped to the floor in convulsions.

Bigfoot stepped forward. He growled as he stalked toward her. Even though she was obviously incapacitated, he grabbed the upir by her crimson hair and launched her into the air. She exploded before she ever touched the tree she was intended to hit. Gore and blood turned into a fine mist that fell all around us.

He stared in wonder at the misty blood as it fell. I just wanted to scrub my skin raw once it speckled my skin. Bigfoot glanced at me with his dark eyes and grunted. But the sound wasn't aggressive, as if he was making conversation.

"Thank you," I croaked out. My throat was raw. I was sure he couldn't understand a word I said. He grunted again before he strode past me and disappeared back into the overgrowth of bushes and trees. I peeled myself off the ground and panted through the bouts of pain that shot through every inch of my body. Using trees for stability, I started the trek up the hill I'd been kicked down. My injuries had already started to heal but that didn't make them hurt any less. A heat wave appeared beside me and Elias faded in.

"Shit, Nova. Killing that bitch upir took me longer than I expected. I was trying to get to you as fast as I could." He wrapped his muscled arm around my waist and helped me up the hill.

"I'm okay. I think," I said through clenched teeth. I felt intense heat wrap around me in entirety. The world went black and the next thing I knew, Elias and I stood back on the trail.

"You could've faded us in? This whole time?" I was doubled-over and my anger flared. Pissed off that he made me drive a half hour instead of using the convenience of teleporting. If I knew he could take me with him through whatever time and space he went through to teleport, I would've been on board with that.

"You know I can fade. You never asked me to do so."

"You never offered! And I didn't know that you could take people with you! I drove all this way . . ." But I couldn't complete my sentence. I bent over, trying to breathe through the pain of my injuries.

"Do you want me to fade us to the portal?" His arm was still wrapped firmly around my waist and helped me to stay on my feet. I would've loved nothing more than to sit and wait for the pain to subside, but we had shit to do. Delaying wasn't an option.

"Yes!" I shouted. I felt heat wrap around us once more. Elias deposited us right at the point of the coordinates that were in the book. The book materialized in Elias's hand, and he opened it to the bookmarked page.

"My angel blade. I dropped it." I grunted.

"We can come back tomorrow and look when there's better

light."

"I can see in the dark. I need to make sure I get it back. It's the only thing I have of my . . ."

"Your?" Elias stared at me, puzzled.

"Never mind. It's just important," I grumbled.

"Tomorrow. Okay?"

"Fine." I was in too much pain to try to search for my weapon. Scouring the forest floor in my condition didn't sound like a good idea anyway. I scanned the area while he read over the handwritten notes. An entrance to a cave was to the left of where we stood, and the trees thinned.

"I think it may be in there." I pointed in the direction of the cave and stepped out of Elias's arm. I stood a little straighter than a few moments before and limped toward the opening. Elias closed the book and fell into step beside me. I poked my head into the cave and saw a slight glow inside. As I stepped forward, Elias grabbed my arm gently, bringing me to a stop.

I glanced back over my shoulder at him.

"You're injured. Let me go in front of you and check it out," he said.

I had no energy to argue so I nodded. Elias stepped in front of me and I followed closely behind him. The opening was narrow. Elias's broad shoulders nearly touched the walls as we trudged through. Our footsteps echoed lightly. As we continued, the cave widened until we came to a large chamber.

In the center of the chamber stood the portal. I had never seen one before and I stared in awe. I'd only ever read about portals, and they can take different forms. This portal rippled like the surface of water when it's disturbed and reflected the distorted image of Elias and me. A white glow came from the edges illuminating the dark cave.

I reached out to touch it but pulled back my hand at the last second.

"I think we found the portal they're coming through," Elias

said. He peered over his shoulder at me.

"No shit."

CHAPTER NINE

M y injuries felt better by the time we faded back to the car. We figured the upirs and other creatures had come through this particular portal. But it was also possible for there to be multiple portals. We still didn't know who was behind everything. And why it was happening other than them coming for me. Even though I would have liked to try to go through to the other side of the portal, that wasn't a risk I should take. Not knowing what was on the other side, such a move would be dangerous.

There was no way we could close the portal ourselves. Typically, when one is created, only the person who opened it could close it. We had to be vigilant and watch for any new cryptids in the area.

On the way back to my place, my mind still tried to catch up on what it all meant. Had any humans been attacked that I hadn't heard of? Did the upir explode because she ingested my blood? Or was that a coincidence? Most of the cryptids that came through had been cannibalistic. They didn't have a problem killing innocent people. My fear was that if we became severely outnumbered, we wouldn't be able to keep things under control.

When we returned to my house, Elias came inside with me.

"We're going back tomorrow," I said.

"We will." He nodded.

"With all of the brush and trees, I'm going to have to scour the whole area. If that upir bitch hadn't kicked me . . ."

Elias stood still and silent as he stared at me, his expression blank.

"Don't you have other things you can be doing? I mean . . . besides babysitting me?" We stepped into the living area.

"You're my biggest priority," he said.

I whipped my head toward him. "I am?"

"Yes."

I sat down on the couch before I realized how filthy my clothes were. "I'm gonna need a shower."

Elias needed one too. I pushed down thoughts of Elias naked. Elias smirked. Was he able to read minds too? I hoped not.

I swallowed. "Do you want to go first?"

"No, it's your house. I've been covered in worse."

"Have you now?" I teased. I stood and trudged to my bathroom. "I'll be quick," I called out before I closed the bathroom door. I leaned against it for a moment. I was crazy lucky that Bigfoot had showed up, even if in the long run I didn't need him. The situation could've ended much, much worse. I pushed off the door and started the shower. I allowed the water to get hot while I pulled off my blood-and-dirt covered garments.

I set the water temperature high enough to wash off all the gross upir blood and washed my hair thoroughly. When I turned the water off, I realized I hadn't brought a towel into the bathroom with me. Dammit.

I hesitated before I called out, "Elias?" I bit my bottom lip. There was a moment of silence.

"Yes?" he said from the other side of the door.

"I forgot a towel, can you . . . can you grab one from the hall closet for me?"

More silence in response. I worried that maybe he'd left. But then the door slowly opened, and Elias held the towel out in front of him. I covered my body with the shower curtain and reached for it but slipped in the process.

With lightning speed, Elias caught me before I hit the bottom of the tub. He'd gotten a view of all my goodies. My cheeks heated from embarrassment. It hadn't been my intention for Elias to get an eyeful.

"Can you be careful? This is the second time you've fallen tonight." His irritation brought about the heat of embarrassment that swarmed my entire body.

He righted me and covered me with the towel. Then he hurried out of the bathroom and closed the door. Oh my god. I smacked my hand to my forehead and took a deep breath. I stepped onto the blue fuzzy bathmat and dried off. I tried to school my expression before I stepped out of the bathroom. I paused when I gripped the doorknob and turned it. When I pulled open the door and stepped out into the hall, Elias leaned against the wall, his arms crossed over his chest. He was different. I couldn't explain the expression on his face. Maybe he was embarrassed for me? No, he looked angry. I situated my towel tighter around me, my wet hair dripped down my back. I averted my gaze from him.

"I . . ." But before I could get out another word, Elias was on me. His hands were on my waist, his mouth hovered just over mine. I stared up into his eyes, his intentions were clear. I closed my eyes and waited for him to make our lips connect. His forehead touched mine. My eyes fluttered back open, and I stared into his electric blue eyes. Heat rolled off him in waves, lust evident in his gaze. It had been so long since I'd been kissed, I had almost forgotten what it felt like. Elias was close but not close enough. Uncertainty frustrated me. I didn't know what held him back from going that extra inch.

The moment I was about to pull away, he grabbed the back of my neck, pulling my mouth to his. I opened my lips slightly to give him access. My fingertips touched the ends of his hair at the nape of his neck. His soft tongue slid against mine and he growled deeply. I squeezed my thighs together where heat started to pool. Elias's hands tangled in my wet hair, and he pulled gently. I allowed him to taste more of me. Devour more of me. My veins warmed and heat spread from my core to every limb. This kiss ignited my darkest desires. As I reached to touch more of him — more of the muscled torso and warmth of his skin — I moaned softly. When he broke away abruptly, I whimpered. His hands left my waist and hair. He took a couple steps back and bumped into the wall. The fire in his eyes was there again and they glowed brightly. A look of regret flashed across his face. Slight, but I knew it wasn't regret that he had stepped away. It was regret that he'd kissed me.

I sucked my bottom lip into my mouth and bit it softly. I tasted his minty flavor. Elias ran his hand through his dark hair and opened the hall closet. He grabbed a towel, avoiding my gaze as he stalked past me into my bathroom. He closed the door softly. I touched my lips. They still tingled, and the ache between my legs hadn't lessened any. It was going to be a rough couple of weeks.

By the time Elias came out of the bathroom, I was fully dressed in a baggy shirt and shorts. I paced my living room floor but stopped when I saw him. He was shirtless. His perfect abs and chest were on display. A brand was scarred into his chest on his right pec. I thought I'd seen the letter *S* but I couldn't be sure. Elias pulled his shirt over his head as I tried to decipher what it meant. I bit my lip and moved my gaze up to his handsome face. His jaw clenched, and he seemed closed off.

"I'm sorry I kissed you," he said gruffly.

Um, excuse me? My eyebrows slammed down in annoyance. I wasn't going to try to tear his clothes off if he was *sorry* he kissed me.

"I don't want to talk about that." I waved him off. I needed to change the subject in order to forget the embarrassment of what just happened — or didn't happen, actually. My bare feet continued to trace the length of the hardwood floors in my small space.

"And what do you want to talk about?"

I paused and then marched to my couch. I took a seat on the edge of the cushion. Elias kept his distance as he took a seat on the chair across from me.

"Do you think that the person who wrote the notes in the margin of the book is the person who opened the portal? I mean, how long has it been there? Did they open it to let the creatures through? Or was it well before someone discovered it? The upirs must have come through recently since they were still in the forest. The upir tasted my blood and exploded. Oh, and I saw a Bigfoot who threw her through the air by her hair!" I rambled off all the questions that floated around in my brain.

"Whoa, whoa . . . Nova, slow down. I understand this is a lot to process and I definitely have the same questions, but I doubt any of them will be answered tonight."

I let out a sigh and tucked my hair behind my ears.

"But did you say you saw Bigfoot?" Elias asked.

I nodded. "Yeah. He threw that upir chick through the air and she exploded. It wasn't even a minute after she ingested my blood."

"So, your blood spilled into the rake's wounds and the upir drank it," he said.

"Yup." I yawned as I glanced at the clock. It was almost midnight.

"You should get some sleep."

"I've had a lot of trouble sleeping lately. Will you . . . will you watch a movie with me? Just until I'm tired enough to go to bed?" I may have told Elias that I could take care of myself, but I felt better when he was with me. I didn't want to sound

71

needy, but I didn't feel ready to lie down in a dark room and stare at my ceiling.

Elias grunted. I would take that as a yes. I grabbed the remote off the coffee table and turned on the TV. I flipped through the channels until I stopped on one of my favorite movies. *Hocus Pocus*. The three Sanderson sisters were throwing a dead man's toe into a cauldron on the screen.

"You even like to watch movies about the supernatural."

I giggled and lay back on the couch and stuffed the pillow under my head. Elias relaxed into his chair and we both watched the movie in silence. After a while, I struggled to keep my eyes open. Arms underneath my back and legs startled me. But then I heard Elias's voice.

"It's just me. I'm taking you to bed."

I relaxed against him and turned my face into his chest. I breathed in his clean, masculine scent. He placed me on my cool sheets, and he covered me with my comforter. It didn't take me long to completely knock back out.

CHAPTER TEN

The following day, Elias faded us back to the forest so I could search for my angel blade. He wrapped his arm around me and faded us back to the area where the upirs had attacked us on the trail. I found the disturbed dirt where I'd tumbled down easily enough. Elias and I scoured the entire area all the way down to where I'd hit the tree and the upir exploded. Evidence of the redhead was still sprinkled on the dirt and trees. But there was no sign of my blade.

"Dammit." I flopped down on the ground.

"It's gotta be around here somewhere."

"We've been here for two hours, Elias. It's nowhere to be found. It's the only weapon I have to kill evil cryptids." I swallowed the emotions that threatened to come to the surface. My eyes burned and my throat felt tight. But I wouldn't allow the tears to fall.

"We can keep looking, or we can come back tomorrow and try again."

"There's no use. I know this is where I dropped it. If we can't find it now, it's gone."

Elias crouched down in front of me and gently put his fingers beneath my chin. He lifted my head, so I stared into his impossibly blue eyes.

"You may not have your angel blade anymore, but you are not weaponless." What he said caused me to frown. "Come on, I have an idea."

"Do you really think this is going to work?" I whispered to

Elias. We watched a pukwudgie stomp through the trees. I didn't go after cryptids that were harmless, but pukwudgies could be hit or miss. Some were harmless and helpful. Others were more malevolent. So we watched this one for a while. Elias seemed to know just where to teleport us to find one. They were native to the United States but not in the area I resided.

The pukwudgie resembled a goblin. He was around three feet tall with wild gray hair and large pointed ears. His skin had a gray pallor.

"One hundred percent, it'll work," Elias whispered back.

"I don't feel right if he's not doing something wrong."

"I can feel that he's not a good pukwudgie. I wouldn't lie to you."

"And you can just *tell* he's a bad guy?"

Elias nodded but didn't take his attention off the creature. We followed the pukwudgie slowly and tried to keep enough distance that we didn't alert him. The little guy glanced around, and Elias and I ducked behind some shrubs. We watched him enter a makeshift hut constructed of twigs and leaves.

Elias and I waited until the cryptid decided to come back out. He'd had the idea to use my blood on bullets and had loaded them into a gun. Then the most obvious part of all this — shoot the creature. Elias thought that since the upir and rake had exploded from having my blood going directly into their system that the blood-soaked bullet would have the same affect. The only difference was the blood had already dried on the bullets. I wasn't sure it worked the same.

"I hear something," Elias said.

I listened closely, but I didn't have his advanced range. So I just trusted his word. I watched the tiny shack that the pukwudgie had disappeared into. Eventually he came out. He carried a sack over his shoulder that wasn't moving. And now I heard a muffled cry. Holy shit. Elias had been spot-on.

I reached for the gun strapped to my hip. Elias slowly drew his own.

"Wait until he gets closer."

"No duh." I rolled my eyes.

"I know you can go toe-to-toe with many creatures but that's close-range combat."

"I've shot a gun before."

"Okay, and how was your aim?"

I put my hand out and tilted it back and forth. "So-so."

Elias snorted and tried not to laugh. The pukwudgie stopped dead in his tracks and glanced around again. We ducked down farther and lay on our backs. I peered behind me through the brush before I rolled onto my stomach. He'd gotten closer but still not close enough.

Elias rolled to his stomach and scooted closer to me. "When you're ready to pull the trigger, inhale deeply and hold your breath. It'll keep you steadier." He reached over and took the safety off. His fingers brushed against mine. The unexpected touch sent a jolt through my fingertips and up my arm that triggered a tingly sensation inside of me. This was a bad time for my body to have that reaction.

I refocused. All I needed was for the pukwudgie to take a few more steps closer.

"I can't shoot unless he drops the bag. I don't trust myself enough," I said.

"All right."

When he was within range, we both cocked our pistols. Elias intentionally shot and missed. The cryptid dropped the squirming bag. I pulled the trigger and missed. And no, not intentionally. I inhaled, but the pukwudgie ran toward us. I held my breath and took aim. I pulled the trigger and missed the creature again. Fuck this. I pulled the small knife I kept tucked inside my boot for emergencies and slid it across my palm, hissing from the sting. Blood flooded my hand. I gripped the blade, saturating it with my blood.

"What are you doing?" Elias asked.

"Handling this the only way I know how." I stood and pushed through the bushes toward the short pukwudgie. I jammed the knife into his neck without hesitation. The pukwudgie let out a howl that sent a shiver through me. He still stood. I kicked his legs out from under him and dislodged my knife from his throat, then putting a good amount of distance between us. His head whipped back and forth in a frenzy. His howl sent a shudder down my spine . . . and then he exploded. Pieces of him hit the ground a few feet in front of me with a thud. Gross. How had I not figured out this was possible in all the years I'd been hunting? I wiped my knife off on my jeans and tucked it back into my boot.

"I did not see that coming." I heard Elias mutter behind me. I sprinted to the large bag on the ground. Elias followed closely behind me. The sack didn't move. I hoped we weren't too late. I bent down and untied the straps.

When I pulled it opened, the face of a small boy peered up at me. He was no more than five years old, with sandy blond hair and green eyes. His face was red from crying. I could see tear tracks on his dirty freckled face. "You're safe now," I said softly and helped him out of the bag. He burst into tears and wrapped his arms around my waist. My arms went around him gently. I rubbed his back and glanced at Elias. His face was soft and open. "Do you know where you live?" I asked the small child. He sniffled and nodded against my stomach.

Elias crouched to his level and the child peeked at him with a trembling lower lip. "Let's get you home."

We were able to get the boy home. The parents wouldn't know it was Elias and myself that dropped him off. I was sure we would have been people of interest if he just appeared on the doorstep with the both of us.

Elias faded us back to my place. As soon as our feet touched my living room floor, my phone buzzed in my back pocket. I pulled it out and checked my messages. It was from Matt.

"Matt said he found the other book *and* something we need to see," I told Elias.

I replied quickly and asked him to come over to my house. I knew things weren't the best the last time we saw each other, but this was important. We would have to put a pin in our argument.

"Should I stay?" Elias asked in a strained voice.

"What? Of course, you should. You and I are in this to-gether." Elias looked relieved. I tried not to read too much into it.

About an hour later, there was a knock on my door. I let Matt in, and he stepped into my living room. He glared at Elias, whose large frame took up the majority of space, mak-ing him hard to miss. Matt's nostrils flared with irritation.

"I didn't know you already had company," Matt said.

"This is Elias. He's been helping me with the cryptid is-sue," I said. Elias seemed unbothered by Matt's obvious dis-taste for him.

Matt didn't look convinced. "Are you a hunter?" Matt asked.

"Not like you and Nova," Elias replied simply. No further explanation. Matt's brows raised as he turned to me. He pulled out the book from his leather satchel before he settled himself on the couch and I sat right next to him. Elias chose the chair across from us. His forearms rested on his knees. As he rubbed his thumb just below his lower lip, I watched the movement a little too intently. Matt flipped to a page which drew my attention away from Elias's mouth. Elias and I leaned closer to read.

"So, this book was not easy to get my hands on. I found it in my grandfather's library, shoved behind a bunch of books," Matt said. "But I started reading through it and found out that this isn't the first time random cryptids have territory-hopped. This happened about eight hundred years ago when a demon and angel conceived a child. But that hybrid was in Mesopotamia. Whoever is commanding the cryptids to come here, they may know about this historical tidbit. Which is kind of insane. We have never heard of anything like this before."

I nearly choked and Elias's eyes met mine.

"Apparently the hybrid was killed along with the person who tried to kill them. So the question is, why was the hybrid of such importance? And why was the person gunning for the hybrid killed as well?"

"It doesn't say why?" I asked.

Matt shook his head. "A page was ripped out. I can only assume the page we're missing has the rest of the information." Matt sat back against the couch cushion. I inspected the torn page.

"Well, Elias was able to read the writing in the margins of the book you let me borrow and that led us to a portal. So I'm pretty sure that's how they're getting here. Which would mean that the cryptids may have access to other portals."

"And you didn't think to call me?" Matt scoffed. "Or is it that this dude and you are together?" He nodded his head in the direction of Elias. Elias's jaw clenched. He stood in a heartbeat, and Matt's eyes widened.

"What if we are? Does it make you feel insecure?" Elias asked in a low growl.

My head snapped toward Elias. I rose from the couch to put myself between the two of them and prayed there wouldn't be an altercation.

"Look, I appreciate your help, Matt. But I can't have you

come around anymore if it's always going to be an argument with you," I said.

Matt glanced between Elias and me. Matt's jaw clenched. "Fine. I'll keep looking for the missing page."

I gave Matt a quick nod and followed him to the front door.

"And, Nova," he said as he turned back to me, his voice quieter. "I'm sorry I was a jerk. I just . . . I miss you. Miss being part of your life."

My heart cracked a little. But even though I didn't have romantic feelings for him, maybe I could try a little harder to be a decent friend.

"I'm sorry too. And thank you for helping us. I do appreciate it," I said softly. I knew Matt tried to keep his voice lower so Elias couldn't hear, even though he didn't know about the whole super hearing thing. I leaned in with the intention of a quick hug goodbye. But Matt's arms wrapped around me a little tighter and a little longer than necessary. I patted his arm and pulled back once his grip loosened. His brown eyes were sad, and he left without another word. I closed the door behind him and strode back into my living room.

"Sorry. We've been argumentative a lot lately," I told Elias.

"Don't apologize for his insecurity." My eyebrow arched.

Elias faded in next to me in the blink of an eye.

"Holy shit!" I screamed.

Elias started laughing. "He's just mad because I'm here and he feels threatened."

"You think so?" I pushed him but I might as well have pushed a brick wall. He didn't budge.

"I know so." Elias leaned in closely and I took a step back.

"You're so full of yourself."

I headed to my room. But before I entered into the hallway, I turned back. "Feel free to leave," I threw at him before going into my room and shutting my door.

"We need to work on your shooting though." Elias's voice

boomed through the door. I aggressively flipped him off through the wall.

CHAPTER ELEVEN

After going to the shooting range, I felt embarrassed. Even Tiffany, who had tagged along, had better luck shooting the paper torso. Elias assured me I'd get the hang of it. I reminded him that I was so much better at hand-to-hand combat that I didn't need to learn to shoot. I had my blood and other weapons. But Elias insisted that the more I learned, the better off I'd be. If I hadn't lost my angel blade, I wouldn't have been in this predicament.

"Don't beat yourself up, Nova. I have to be better at something than you are," Tiffany teased.

"Shut up," I grumbled and shoved my hands into my jeans.

"We will keep practicing," Elias said.

"Or better yet, find me another angel blade."

"I'm not sure they're just casually laying around. I mean, your mom gave that to my parents for you," Tiff said.

Elias stiffened slightly. "That was a gift from your mother?"

"Yes," I mumbled my response. "The only thing I have of hers."

"And what about your father?"

"My father gave me nothing. I'd be surprised if he even knew I existed."

Elias stopped and turned me toward him. I tilted my head back pretty far to see his face when we were so close together.

"I have no doubt that your father knows about you and cares for you."

I frowned. "What the hell would you know about it? I was dropped off at my adoptive parents' house. Neither one of my biological parents could or would keep me." I stepped back from him and turned on my heel, striding across the parking lot back to the car. I heard Tiff and Elias talk quietly with each other but couldn't make out the words.

I slid into the driver's seat and started the car. Elias hopped into the backseat and Tiffany took shotgun.

"I'm sorry. I shouldn't have mentioned it," Tiffany said.

"It's fine," I grumbled. I didn't even glance at her as I pulled out of the parking lot. My real parents had always been a sore spot. I avoided talking about them as much as I could. When my adoptive parents told me I was the creation of an affair between an angel and a demon, I was surprised. But that made sense. I was never the same as the other kids in school, and I clung to Tiffany when she was born. I had been socially awkward and had violet eyes. That led to being teased and getting into a lot of fights that I inevitably won. I have always been stronger and faster than humans. Now my blood killed cryptids.

When we pulled into my driveway, Tiffany headed back to our parent's house. Elias and I were alone again.

"If I would have known it was from your mother, I would've spent all night searching for your angel blade."

"It's fine," I said. I unlocked my door and pushed it open. Stepping into my small entryway, I dropped my keys onto the console table.

Elias's short sword appeared in his hand. He was instantly on guard.

"Wha—"

An unfamiliar man stepped into the entryway in front of us. He had a tall frame with olive skin and a shaved head. His eyes were dark but still human-like.

"Cryptid," Elias whispered. A little late but still.

"You don't look like a cryptid to me." I sneered as I pulled myself up to my full height. Not that there was much of a difference.

"Oh dear." The stranger tsked as he peered down at his pristine suit and tie. "Let me fix that." His bones started to crack as he hunched over. His suit jacket ripped, and his olive skin turned pale. Dark veins ran beneath his pasty flesh. His face took on an alien form with no nose—just nostrils. His teeth changed from a nice normal smile to wicked and rotted. The creature's long forked tongue slipped out of his mouth. Elias stepped in front of me to shield me. I tried to push him out of the way, but his big body didn't budge. So I squeezed in next to him as much as I could.

I felt small hands on my legs and glanced down for a moment to see that Rik had grabbed onto me. "It'll be all right," I whispered to him.

"It's a shapeshifter," Rik whispered back.

"An aswang." I scrutinized the creature. He had completely transformed. "Why do you guys keep showing up at my house? It's getting really old, really fast."

The aswang didn't speak aloud. Instead, I heard his voice inside my mind. *We've been sent here to retrieve you, hybrid. The one for whom we do their bidding has promised us great power in exchange for your soul.*

"Uh, sorry to break it to you, but I'm not even sure I have a soul," I replied.

Oh, but you do, little one. I can smell it from here. So pure, so full of life. Too bad I am forbidden to eat you. You would've made a delicious meal. His tongue flicked out again.

"You'll have nothing of her," Elias said. He must've been able to hear the aswang's voice too.

I will, sinner. And I'll make sure you watch as our master drains her soul from her lush body, the aswang said. His dark eyes roamed over my body. I wanted to shrink away from his gaze, but I refused to show weakness.

Elias slashed out but the aswang was too fast. With a hard shove, Elias crashed into one of the walls and slid down to the floor. That took some serious strength.

The aswang snarled at me and stalked closer. I pulled out my gun and took the safety off. But that took too long. The creature grabbed me by my legs and pulled them out from under me. I slammed to the floor. Rik tried to beat him off as he climbed over my body. But Adalrik was no match, and he was flung across the room. The creature used his gnarled hand to rip the gun from my grasp and toss it across the room with a thud. The aswang's long tongue slid along my neck, then up my cheek. Drool dripped onto my face.

"Oh my god! Fucking gross!" I screamed. I tried to push him off. With how I was positioned, I was vulnerable.

The cryptid's hand hovered over my chest and his nails dug in deep. I let out a wild scream of pain. I felt my skin being torn. The pressure was too great. I couldn't breathe. My bones cracked and my ribs separated. The pain left me breathless. My back arched off the floor. The creature's long fingers reached into my chest cavity. I bucked and pushed with all my might. I was weakened from the agony. I tried like hell to get him off me and out of my chest. His hand found my heart and squeezed, making the edges of my vision blur, then start to darken. Before I lost it all, Elias charged him. I sucked in a deep breath at the absence of the aswang's hand in my chest. Everything went black.

"I didn't know where else to bring her, Cyrus. You're her father, you know more than anyone what to do."

I heard Elias's deep timber. My eyes were still closed and my chest ached. Definitely from that prick cryptid.

"She isn't supposed to be here. She *doesn't belong* in Hell. What do you think will happen if Lucifer learns of a hybrid taking up a room?"

"I didn't know what else to do. This was the first thing that came to mind. Is she going to be okay?"

"She'll be fine. She's not easily killed, not with her mother's blood in her veins."

My eyes fluttered, and the smell of sulfur burned my nostrils. I stirred slightly and groaned. There was still a pain that throbbed in my chest where my ribs and sternum had been broken apart.

"I think she's waking up," Elias said.

"Will you two stop talking about me like I'm not in the room," I rasped. I opened my eyes and tried to sit up. Elias placed an arm around my shoulders and helped me.

"Nova, you shouldn't get up. You aren't healed completely," Elias said.

"And miss the opportunity to meet my deadbeat dad? Not a chance." My gaze moved past Elias and there stood — someone who I could only assume was my dad. He was tall, with neatly combed dark hair and black eyes. He appeared to be about my age. Obviously he wasn't. He had a slimmer frame than Elias. By the looks of him, I took after my mother.

"Nova . . ." Cyrus said.

I cut him off. "No, you don't get to pretend you care all of a sudden."

"I've always cared. Who do you think sent Elias to watch over you?"

I glared at Elias. "My *dad* sent you to watch over me? And you couldn't tell me?"

"I was sworn to never tell. But I didn't know what else to do when the aswang hurt you so badly."

"So what? You faded us into Hell?" I started to stand, and Elias caught me when I stumbled. I sat back down on the soft bed.

"I had no other choice, Nova."

"Take me back topside. Now!"

My father's expression was blank. As if he hadn't just met his long-lost daughter.

"Daughter."

"What?" I snapped.

"Elias told me you lost the blade your mother left for you."

"Yeah, what about it?"

"I know you would prefer to have something of your mother's, but I do have something you can use in its place." Why would he give me anything? He obviously knew where I had been all along but hadn't bothered to ever send word. Or visit.

"I have a set of blades that were forged in hellfire that should do the job." A black box appeared in his hands. He took a few steps until he stopped right in front of me. I gently took the box from him and opened the lid. I pulled back a piece of red silk to reveal two beautiful onyx blades. Grooves along the curved blade formed words in a strange language.

"I can't take these." I glanced at Cyrus and closed the lid then pushed the box back into his hands.

"You can and you will, Nova," he said gruffly and pushed it back. "It's the least I can do for not being around." I took a beat before I accepted. I did need new blades, and these would do the job.

"Fine. But this doesn't mean I forgive you." I grabbed the box and turned toward Elias. "Can you take me home now?"

Elias nodded. He wrapped his arms around me and we faded into my house. Yet again, it was in shambles. There was an Elias-sized hole in my wall from where he'd been thrown and overturned furniture. No doubt from whatever battle Elias had with the aswang.

"Can I go a week without my house being destroyed?" I said. I pushed out of Elias's arms and examined the mess. "Where's Rik? Is he all right?"

"He's fine. A little banged up but he's okay. I asked if he wanted to come with us, but he declined."

"And the aswang?"

"I killed him."

I nodded and trudged to my room, Elias on my heels the entire way. I placed the box on my dresser and took a seat on the edge of my bed.

"Why didn't you just tell me it was my dad who sent you?"

"I couldn't. If I was to take the position as your protector, I couldn't disobey my master."

I scoffed and pinched the bridge of my nose. "Your master?"

"I have been in debt to your father for centuries, and this is something I have to do to get in his good graces."

"So, the only reason you're here is because your *master* ordered it?" I stared at him. There was a pang in my chest that had nothing to do with the aswang having had his claws in me wrist deep.

"No, Nova. I had the opportunity to decline."

"Well, why didn't you? Why bother? Take another job."

Elias's brows slammed down. "I didn't want to take another job."

"Oh, that's right, just a way to get out from under my dad's thumb."

"Nova . . ."

"Just leave, Elias. This is a little much for me right now."

"I can't leave," he said. "I don't want to leave."

"You know what pisses me off the most? It's that I should've known. I should've known you were helping my father. The signs were all there, but my crush on you made me stupid."

Elias was taken aback. "You have a crush on me?"

If I hadn't been so angry, I probably would've been embarrassed. How could he not know? I'd kissed him.

"Just go." I threw up a hand and pointed toward my bedroom door. Tiny flames danced at my fingertips. My eyes widened and so did Elias's.

"Did you just . . . .is that fire?" Elias asked, stunned.

I smothered the flames with my other hand and dropped them both into my lap.

"I've never done that before," I said just above a whisper.

CHAPTER TWELVE

Elias left shortly after my fingers emitted flames. He said he'd come back, but I didn't even know if I wanted him to. I knew it wasn't his fault that he'd kept my father's involvement quiet. But I was still pissed that he couldn't be honest with me. I couldn't believe, with the hints he dropped, that I hadn't realized his master was my demon daddy. I just thought maybe he didn't care enough.

The fire that came from my fingers had to be some sort of fluke. That had never happened before. I wondered if my father had something to do with it. I decided it was time to tell my parents about what had been going on. I sent a text message to Tiffany. The more people on my side, the better.

She replied almost immediately. Tiff said they'd be over shortly. I paced a bit and nibbled on my thumbnail as I waited for them to arrive. When the doorbell rang, I rushed to answer it.

They came in and took their seats. I stayed standing.

"Tiffany told us you have something to tell us?" my mother said.

"I do. I just don't know where to start."

"Just start from the beginning," Tiffany suggested. I gave her an Okay-Captain-Obvious look.

"There was more than one incident recently where there have been cryptids coming from other territories. I know you guys are aware of the first one. But we've been attacked on several occasions, one of them being today. When I came home with Elias."

"Elias? Who is Elias?" my father interrupted.

"I'll get to that in a bit." I put my hands in a prayer position and rested them against my lips. Then I told my family the whole story. Even about how I met my biological father in Hell.

By the time I finished, my family was talking over each other.

"Stop!" I yelled, and they quieted down. All eyes were on me, waiting for me to continue. "I just need you guys to be aware of what's going on. I'm not asking for your help. Elias has been assisting me. And even Matthew has pitched in, lending me a book, and investigating everything. The only difference is he told me something similar happened about eight centuries ago when another hybrid was born. The book's missing a page so we can't figure out why my soul is suddenly such a hot item."

"Nova, you know we will protect you with our lives," my mother said.

"I know you would, but I have it under control." I peered over at my father. He'd remained tight-lipped about whether he knew anything about the last hybrid's history. "It doesn't sound like you do," he finally spoke.

A knock sounded at the door, and I glanced at my family.

"I may or may not have invited Matt over," Tiffany said with a pained look.

"Dammit, Tiff." I stomped to the front door and let Matt in. He avoided my gaze and plodded straight into my living room and took the last empty seat.

"I think you should tell him, Nova," my dad said. Matt's eyes finally met mine.

"Tell me what?" Matt asked.

"About the whole angel-demon hybrid thing you mentioned . . ."

"Yeah? What about it?" Matt appeared confused.

I took a deep breath before I said the words. "I . . . I am the hybrid," I stuttered.

Matthew stayed silent for a moment and then started laughing hysterically. "You have got to be shitting me."

I pursed my lips together and shook my head.

"It's true, Matthew," my father said. "Nova was given to us by her mother, who is an angel. She wasn't allowed to stay in Heaven or Hell because of what she is."

"So, the two years we dated you never thought to mention to me that you're a hybrid? A nonhuman?" He spat the word *nonhuman* with disgust. I couldn't help the knot that developed in my stomach at seeing his reaction. His words also sent a wave of irritation through me.

"Only my family knows. Well, and Elias. Because he was sent to protect me by my father."

"Of course he knows before me," Matt said.

Here we go again. I rolled my eyes.

A heat wave appeared, and Elias solidified in front of me, his back to everyone else in the room.

"I spoke with your father about the flames coming from your hand. He said that—" I covered his mouth and peeked behind him. Everyone gave me a strange look.

"You didn't tell us that part, Nova," my dad said. He tilted to the side to see me from behind Elias's large frame.

"Sorry, I just think it may have been a one-time thing." I released my hand from Elias's mouth, and he turned to greet my family.

"Well, go on. I want to know what he said about the flames from her fingers." Tiffany sounded excited. She bounced in her seat.

Elias glanced at me for permission. I nodded. There was no point in hiding what happened now.

"Cyrus said this was the reason you were not allowed to reside in Heaven or Hell when you were born. The more time spent in either realm, the more power and abilities you would obtain."

"Uh, that's the reason why? Because I would have powers?"

"Not just a normal amount of powers, Nova. Ridiculous powers. Since you are a hybrid, you could have the powers of both Heaven and Hell combined. You could end up taking over if you wanted."

I stared at Elias for a moment. This was the reason why my father was so mad that Elias brought me to Hell. Even if I had crazy amounts of abilities, it wasn't like I would want either realm. But maybe if I'd grown up with my biological parents, I may have turned out to be a different person.

"So, let me get this straight. I wasn't allowed to stay in either Heaven or Hell because I could likely overpower them?"

"Yes."

"They made me reside on Earth because they were scared?" I asked, my voice pitched higher.

"Yes," Elias said. He seemed a little uncomfortable.

Seriously? They couldn't even give me a chance to see the hybrid I would become.

"They didn't want a war on their hands," Matthew chimed in. "I was researching the last angel and demon hybrid and, he was murdered before he reached twenty-two. There's minimal information, but I'm assuming he was sacrificed by Lucifer's army because whoever was after his soul would be too powerful."

"Thus, being able to use that power against either realm." Tiffany nodded. That was so much information at once, my head began to ache. I rubbed my temples.

"That makes so much sense. But now the question is, who?" my mother said.

"It can't be the same person who wanted the original hybrid because they were also executed," Matt said.

I shrugged. "I have no idea who outside of this room would even know that I'm a hybrid other than my biological parents. And wouldn't they have come for me sooner if it were either one of them?"

"I know it's not your father." Elias peered down at me.

"So that would leave my mother, I guess? I don't know. Why would she want me to be kept safe if she planned this all along?" There had to be someone else who knew this information.

"Maybe someone else knows," Matt said.

"They're sending cryptids instead of coming themselves. Obviously they're afraid," Elias said.

"I'll give them something to be afraid of," I replied with a cocky grin.

After everyone else had gone, Elias and I were the only ones left.

"I'm going to take a shower and wash the smell of sulfur out of my hair," I said.

I made sure to grab a towel. I didn't want any more embarrassing moments in front of Elias. I took my time as I washed my hair and scrubbed my skin of the stench that clung to me. The bathroom mirrors were completely steamed up when I stepped out and dried off. I slipped on my yoga pants and a loose fitted T-shirt. I'd just finished combing out my hair before I stepped into the hall.

I trudged to the living room when I heard Elias talking. I peeked around the corner. He and Rik were playing Uno. I smiled. Who in the world would ever expect to see the two of them playing a mortal game?

"You guys started without me?" I stepped farther into the room.

"We can start over and deal you in," Adalrik offered.

"No, just finish this game and I'll play the next." I sauntered over to the couch and took a seat with my legs tucked under me. Elias sat on the floor at the coffee table. Rik used an upside-down bucket as a chair.

It was times like this, when I wasn't fighting mythological creatures, that I wondered how different my life could've been. If I'd been born human, I would be none the wiser of demons, angels, upir, and everything else that existed. I wouldn't have been the target of some psycho. I wouldn't have any power that simmered just beneath the surface.

Would I have gone to college like Tiffany? Would I be married? Or have a family? I never really thought about those things because it just never was in the cards for me. Maybe a normal job and a house in the suburbs. Maybe a dog. I shook the thoughts from my head. My reality excited me so much more than that. I had learned from my adoptive mother that it was very difficult for angels to procreate. That was because they were typically just manifested by the almighty and not bred. And as far as I knew, the same went for demons.

"Nova, come on. I won this round." Elias gave me a sexy smirk. I slid to the floor next to him and we played for the next couple of hours. We laughed and joked around as though there wasn't someone after me. It was a nice reprieve . . . even if it was only for a night.

CHAPTER THIRTEEN

Over the next couple of days, things were quieter. I couldn't help but think it was the calm before the storm. I hadn't hunted since the incident with the aswang. We researched as much as we could about the previous hybrid, but we hadn't come across anything we didn't already know. Information was few and far between. I couldn't expect the name of the person who wanted my soul to just be in a book. But who knew about me other than the handful of people I was closest to?

Elias had stayed every night, on the floor, and hadn't tried to kiss me again. He was still flirtatious sometimes, but he'd mellowed out a bit. We became more comfortable. He periodically checked in with my father in Hell, to let him know what we had and hadn't found. I wasn't allowed there because . . . well because I might have acquired more abilities. Not that I thought it would necessarily be a bad thing. I mean, it could make up for my lack of being able to shoot.

The only downside to not hunting those couple of days was I hadn't been able to use the blades my father had given me. But I was still upset about the loss of my angel blade.

I bought a new holster for the demon blades. One that I could strap to both sides of my waist.

My phone rang as I worked my side job from home. I saw that it was Tiffany.

"Hey," I answered.

"Hey, so I have a favor to ask of you," she said.

"Okayyyy?"

"Erica and I are going on a date. Like a real date. Tonight. And I suggested making it a double date because I'm a little nervous."

"Haven't you guys been hanging out the last couple of weeks?" I asked.

"Yeah, but not anything romantic or anything."

"And tonight is romantic?" I arched my brow.

"Well, it's dinner at a nice restaurant, and I'd like it if you were there . . . you know, to ease my nerves."

I cringed inwardly. "Tiff, you're a big girl. You have the charm and charisma I lack. You know I don't do well in social situations," I reminded her.

"You do fine with me."

"I've known you since you were born, you turd. It's not the same," I countered.

I really didn't want to go to a dinner where I'd be in an awkward position.

"Please, Nova? I think she might ask me to be her girl-friend," she begged.

"All the more reason you should do it alone." I stuck the pencil in my hand through the bun on top of my head.

"No, you're wrong. I need moral support."

I laughed. "Fine. I'll go. But you owe me."

"Okay, I already asked Elias if he'd be your date—"

"Whoa! Hold on a second." I sat up straighter. "I was gonna go solo. No need to drag Elias into this."

"Too late. You're both going." Tiffany giggled.

"Do we seriously need to have this conversation again about you coming to me first?"

"Gotta go, Nova. I'll see you around six."

"Hey!" The line disconnected. *That little shit.*

I went through my drawers and closet. I hardly had any-thing to wear. Well, I had plenty. But the majority was jeans and T-shirts. I flipped through the clothes in my closet for a second time to see if I owned anything that could resemble dressy casual at least.

"Shit," I whispered to myself. A black piece of material crammed between a pair of jeans caught my eye so I pulled it out. It was dress I wore to a funeral about a year ago. Knee length and form fitting with scalloped edges along the bust. It would have to do since I'd run out of time. I threw off my jeans and T-shirt.

I shimmied the dress over my body and then I dropped back to my knees. Now I had to search for the shoes I'd bought to go with the dress. I felt the heat of Elias when he arrived. I didn't even bother to peer back at him as I continued my search.

"Uh, Nova. What are you doing in there?" his voice rumbled.

"I'm looking for my shoes that go with this dress," I grumbled. I found one of them and threw my other shoes out of the closet in frustration.

"Yes! I found it." I scooted out of the closet and stood. I turned toward Elias. My mouth dropped open at how devilishly handsome he was. He wore a black button-down dress shirt with black slacks. His hair was styled nicely, and his blue eyes stood out against his tanned skin. He eyed me up and down as well.

"You look beautiful," he said.

I blushed at his compliment and cleared my throat, stopping the eye fuck-a-thon.

"I don't really own anything nice since I normally don't go out." I slipped my heels on and ruffled my long hair that cascaded down to my waist in soft platinum waves. I had even decided to wear a little more makeup than usual with a tinted lip balm, blush, and mascara.

"Yeah, I had to go buy this." He waved his hand up and

down his body.

"Huh. Something I've never heard of before."

"What?" He studied me.

"A soldier of Hell going shopping," I said with a grin.

"We can't all go naked in Hell." He unbuttoned the sleeves of his shirt and rolled them up to his elbows. His muscular forearms were out for all to see.

"I think I just had a visual," I said, and Elias smirked. "Don't you dare say anything." I pointed at him.

"I wasn't going to say anything." He put his hands up in innocence.

"Mmmmhmmm. Now let's go. We have to do the human thing and drive."

The restaurant was even nicer than Tiffany had let on, and I felt underdressed.

"You look fine," Tiffany whispered as she grabbed my hand. Unlike me, Tiffany had always been more on the girly side and owned a dress in every color. Tonight, she wore a deep purple dress with ruffles along the short sleeves. The color complimented her complexion perfectly.

Erica and Elias chatted it up behind us. They'd even sat next to each other when we were seated. I was glad Elias was my buffer because I had no idea what Erica and I would've talked about. We ordered our drinks, and I sat in silence as I watched the three of them talk amongst each other. I ordered alcohol so I could relax a bit in the unfamiliar setting.

"So, what do you do, Nova?" Erica asked me from across the table.

I took a sip of my drink before answering but Tiffany cut me off.

"Nova works from home. She does contract jobs for small companies that need a graphic designer." I was grateful for her intervention.

"That's pretty neat. Anything I might have seen?"

I shook my head. "They're normally small companies that are just starting up. What about you?"

"I'm going to the university, computer technology," Erica said.

"Erica's being modest. She's actually a genius. She can probably hack any system she wanted to," Tiffany said.

Erica blushed and gazed at Tiffany sweetly. "I wouldn't, though. Hack the systems. I don't want to get in trouble with the law."

The conversation led to other subjects, and I sipped my beer while I mostly listened. I chimed in here and there. Tiffany and Erica talked to each other as Elias leaned in closely to me. He brushed my hair gently over my shoulder.

"Hey, are you okay?"

"I just don't do well with stuff like this," I whispered. "Fancy stuff."

"We can go if you want."

"No, I told Tiffany that I'd come."

Elias gave me a slight nod. "Well, if you change your mind, I'm sure I can think of something creative."

I gave him a grin and he winked. His lips kicked up into a grin.

The rest of the dinner went by fine, and I even managed to loosen up a bit after a couple of beers. We all strolled out to the parking lot together and said goodnight to Erica and Tiffany, who had come in a separate car. The parking lot was almost empty, only a few cars left.

I went to my driver's side and unlocked the door. But when I reached for the handle, Elias placed his hand against the window and held it shut.

"Come on, Elias, I want to go home. I'm tired." I pouted. His other arm came to the other side of me. He caged me in with my back to his chest. I held my breath, not sure what had gotten into him.

"You shouldn't be driving. I saw how many drinks you had."

"I'm perfectly fine. I can handle my alcohol better than a human." I wasn't lying. I don't typically get drunk, just relaxed. It would've taken way more than a couple of drinks to get this hybrid turnt.

Elias ran one hand along my arm and turned me to face him.

"What are you doing?" I whispered.

He didn't say anything. He leaned in closer, and I felt his breath on my cheek, my neck. His lips brushed against my neck and sent goosebumps across my skin. His tongue flicked out against my sensitive flesh, and I groaned. My nipples hardened and warmth crawled beneath my skin to lower regions. I felt hot, with a warmth that had nothing to do with the humid air outside.

"Elias, you don't want this. "I said. I tried to push him away, but he didn't move. His head snapped up and he examined me. His eyes started to glow softly.

"Why wouldn't I, Nova? You're the first woman in forever that I've felt something . . . it's indescribable. This pull . . . You're fearless and funny. There are days when I want nothing more than to quiet that sassy mouth of ours with my own. You're always beautiful, but tonight you're a goddess. An angel. Angel face. That's what you are." His voice turned huskier, and my stomach did somersaults. Heat crept in under my flesh and begged for him to show me how much he wanted me.

Elias's gaze dropped to my mouth. "I hate how much I want you." He nipped at my ear. His confession was not something I expected, and it was hard for me to keep my body in check. I wanted to grind against his leg that was pressed between my thighs. My dress rode up. His body around mine

100

sent my senses into a frenzy, and the heat that radiated from him comforted me. I wanted to lean into him even more.

Elias tipped his head toward me until his lips gently touched mine. My arms went around his neck. His scent enveloped me. My knees weakened as he bit at my bottom lip. I opened for him and allowed him to slide his silky tongue against mine. So warm and soft. I nearly melted from the fire that built inside of me. Just as I thought there was no way we would make it out of the parking lot, he pulled away abruptly and my eyes snapped open. My hands were covered in flames again.

As soon as I noticed them, the flames vanished. I gasped.

"I'm so sorry. Did I hurt you?" I drew my brows together in concern.

"No, it . . . it surprised me. But it felt like . . ."

"Like what?" I had started to low-key freak out here.

"Like home." His words hit me, but he took a step back, rubbing at his bottom lip.

"I hope that's a good thing?"

Elias smirked. "It's a very good thing. Just unexpected."

Our conversation was brought to a halt as Elias cocked his head to the side. A growl cut through the air a moment later, and we turned to see a dog—no, that couldn't be right. The beast was too damn large to be a domestic dog. Its fur was matted and its head was the size of my entire torso.

Elias's eyes locked onto the weredog . . . werewolf . . . dog man. Whatever you wanted to call it. Drool streamed down its massive jaw to the asphalt.

"Do you have your blades your father gave you?" Elias whispered to me. An identical creature came to the other side of us, snarling. Okay, two big bad wolves. We could handle that.

"The blades are in my car," I said in a low voice. All traces of arousal had vanished. The wolves had ruined the moment.

"Slowly . . . and I mean slowly . . . open the door and get them out. I think I can hold them off until you're armed." A third came up behind Elias.

"Uh, Elias." I didn't need to say more. He peeked out of the corner of his eye. His short sword appeared in one hand and a pistol loaded with my blood-covered bullets in the other. I wished I could do that.

"Now!" Shots rang out as I rushed to get my weapons from the car. No way was I going to do this slowly. I heard a whine from one of the dogs and saw that Elias had charged. I gripped both blades and jumped into action.

A werewolf at Elias's back was ready to pounce, but I jumped on top of the huge beast. I slammed one of my blades into its ribcage. The cryptid let out a howl of pain and tried to buck me off of him, but my thighs were tightly clamped around its midsection. My second blade shoved into its other side. The werewolf fell to the ground. Blood coated my hands, and its legs kicked feverishly. I rolled off and quickly stood, pulling the blades free. The engraved writing glowed red.

I wasted no time as I stepped in to help Elias fight off the other two beasts. The one he hit with a blood-coated bullet shook feverishly. Elias must've been right about the effectiveness of the bullets. I put my arms up to keep from getting my face splattered. Thankfully, I didn't feel the wetness of werewolf guts. When I dropped my arms, Elias had his short sword halfway down the werewolf's throat. I guess he didn't need my help after all. The bodies of the dogs disappeared. I breathed heavily as I stood in front of Elias.

"Um, Nova?" Elias said.

"Yeah?"

"Your dress is up to your waist." He pointed at me with his sword. I pulled the bottom of my dress down to cover my bare ass.

"Nova?"

"What? I'm pretty sure you got a great view of my ass in a thong!" I yelled.

"I did, but..." He peered past me. I glanced over my shoulder to see three more werewolves stalking toward us. They gnashed and growled at us. I backed up to stand beside Elias.

"On three?" I peered up at Elias, whose eyes were trained on our attackers. He gave a slight nod.

"One, two . . ."

"Three!" we said in unison and charged. Elias took the one on the right and I took on the other two on the left. Throwing a blade, I hit one between the eyes as I advanced on the other. My demon blade sunk into the werewolf's neck, making the creature cry out in pain. Both creatures dropped and vanished, leaving no evidence they were ever there.

At the same time, Elias finished off his opponent. I put my hands on my knees and bent over. I tried to catch my breath.

"We should get out of here. I'm sure people will be coming out to see what all the noise was about."

"I created a noise barrier around the fight."

"You what?"

"I kept the noise inside a bubble."

"You managed to do that while fighting a pack of werewolves?" I stood up straight.

Elias just smirked and we turned to go back to the car.

"So many secrets, Elias."

"I have to keep you on your toes."

CHAPTER FOURTEEN

"Can you create the flames just by thought?"

"I haven't really tried to do it on purpose. I think it's when I'm angry or stressed."

"And turned on," he added.

I flushed at the thought but bit my lip to keep from replying.

"Try to manifest them right now."

We'd just arrived back at my house. I was still in my dress I'd worn to dinner with Tiffany and Erica. I kicked off my heels, took a seat on the couch, and rubbed the arch of my foot. Fighting in those shoes was not practical. "I don't know if I can."

"Well, try," he pushed.

I leaned my head against the back of the couch and covered my eyes with my forearm. I felt Elias seat himself on the couch next to me. He pulled my arm from my face and stared down at me.

"What?"

"Nova, can you at least try?"

"Ugh, fine." I pushed his arm away and stood. Putting my hands out in front of me, I focused on my fingers. Elias stared at me in silence. When nothing happened after a few moments, I dropped my arms.

"Come on, Nova. Try harder," Elias gritted out. He was starting to piss me off.

"I *am* trying!" I put my hands out in front of me again. A small spark was emitted from my fingers.

"Try, dammit!" Elias yelled at me. Which annoyed me

more. I gritted my teeth.

"*I am!*" My hands sparked and fire erupted, trailing up my arms. But as quickly as the fire had come, it disappeared.

Elias chuckled.

"You jerk! You did that on purpose."

He gave me a grin. "Your eyes are glowing. I haven't seen them like this before." He stood and stepped into my space, tucking my hair behind my ear.

"They are?" I rushed over to the mirror hung on one of the walls. And sure as shit, my eyes glowed, flames in their depths, much like Elias's sometimes had.

"Are you happy now?" I turned back to where Elias lounged on my couch.

"Very. You will need to hone that skill. It will take a lot of practice to be able to control it."

"Do you think I gained any other skills while I was in Hell?"

"I'm not sure. You weren't there too long."

I wondered if I had stayed longer, would more abilities have popped up.

"I'm going to change." I headed toward my bedroom and peeled off my dress the moment I closed the door. I was grateful the dinner was over with and I could put my yoga pants on with a T-shirt. When I returned to the living room, Elias was in the same spot I had left him in. I took a seat next to him, and his eyes studied my new attire.

"Don't like my outfit?" I asked while I tied my hair up in a messy bun.

"I like you like this." Uhhh, what?

"What do you mean?"

"It's like seeing a sloth in its natural habitat."

"Shut up!" I yelled. I hit him with a pillow in the face. He laughed all the while I beat him, blocking most of the blows. I started laughing with him, and he gently grabbed my wrist when I swung to hit him again. Our laughter died down, and his eyes roamed over my face. I dropped my pillow and stared at Elias. I leaned in and placed a soft kiss on his lips. Elias released my wrist and took my face between his hands.

"Do you even know what a sloth is?" I whispered. Elias and I chuckled. He silenced me with his mouth.

Our soft kisses turned more frantic. My hands ran over his muscular arms to his chest. I started to unbutton his dress shirt. He hadn't changed from dinner as I had. We broke our kiss only for me to pull my shirt over my head, baring me to him. Elias's hot mouth enveloped the peak of one of my small breasts. My back arched and a moan escaped my throat. His rough hand roamed to my other breast and lightly pinched and pulled my nipple. My fingers tangled in his hair, and I tugged lightly.

He broke his hold on my breasts, pulling me so I lay full length on my couch. His body covered mine, and his rigid cock hard against my thigh. My body ignited and tingled at his gentle touch and the soft kisses he placed along the length of me. I wanted more. More of Elias and his touch.

I pushed my hands beneath his unbuttoned shirt and pulled it down his arms. Caressed his skin as his bare chest warmed my body further. I noticed the raised brand again and brushed my fingers across it. Elias grabbed my hand and pulled it away. His mouth kissed each pad of my fingertips.

"I didn't think you would try to get into my daughter's pants, Elias. After all, you are serving me."

Elias jerked back, and his hands left my body. I sat up quickly and covered my chest with a decorative pillow. Grabbed my shirt and quickly pulled it over my head. Cyrus stood in my living room. My face felt hot from embarrassment. My father just stared at the two of us with his black eyes. My lips must've been pink and swollen from our kissing. What would have happened if we hadn't been interrupted was obvious.

Elias pulled his shirt back on and buttoned it. He ran his hand through his hair, probably to fix the mess I'd made of it. But he just ended up messing it up more.

"I . . ."

"This was one of my rules and you've broken it." My father's face turned into a snarl, transforming him into the epitome of a demon. A face you'd only see in your nightmares. The hair on the back of my neck stood on end. My father's rage was palpable, and the temperature became stifling, making it harder to breathe.

"I kissed him. I pushed him into kissing me. This wasn't his fault." I rose to my feet.

"Do you think I'm stupid, daughter?" he growled.

"He serves you, and Elias isn't one to disobey orders."

My father glared at Elias. "Is what Nova says true?"

Elias glanced at me. I gave him the slightest of nods.

"Yes. She kissed me." Which technically wasn't a lie. But demons were deceitful, so who cared.

"You and Elias are not to have a romantic relationship."

"Oh, no, that's not gonna work for me," I said. "I'm twenty-three years old and just met my demon father for the first time. You show up at *my house* and think you can tell me what or *who* to do?" I threw at him.

"He is but a soldier and servant. If you want a mate, I can provide one of higher stature."

Did my dad really just tell me he'd set me up? I laughed. But not a joyful laugh. One that was filled with disbelief that Cyrus thought he could just order me around and tell me what to do.

"Leave."

He cocked his head to the side as if he hadn't heard me right. "Elias, you will come with me."

"I won't leave Nova unprotected," Elias said.

"She can handle herself for the night. I'll put up a ward that will last long enough to protect her through the night. Only the two of us will be able to enter and exit."

Elias seemed inclined to argue but I could tell that wouldn't go well for him. He tensed, but then he gave my father a nod. My father faded out and Elias remained for a moment.

"I'll be back as soon as I can." he said.

"Be careful," I said softly and then he was gone.

As I lay in bed, I couldn't keep my thoughts from straying to Elias and how much I hoped he was okay. Cyrus was pretty pissed off that we were kissing. If he hadn't faded in, I don't think I would've stopped Elias from fucking me until the sun rose. I'd started to like the bastard. And for more than just his heart-stopping good looks. He could be a jackass, but he did have a sense of humor. Even if no one else could see it. And even though he tried to act like a hard ass sometimes, I knew he was really a softy.

My phone vibrated, breaking me from my thoughts. I grabbed it from my nightstand. It was Tiffany. Erica had asked her to officially be her girlfriend. I smiled. I sent her a series of heart emojis in response. Maybe next time I met her, I wouldn't need drinks in order to have a normal conversation.

I heard footsteps as they came down the hall and I froze. I reached for my demon blades on the nightstand. The writing on the onyx blades glowed red from my touch. When the door creaked open, I saw the short silhouette of Adalrik. I relaxed and put them back in the box.

"I thought someone was in the house," I told him.

"I wanted to check on you."

"Why?"

"I heard your father and everything earlier."

I rolled my eyes and laid back down on the bed. "He's on some sort of power trip," I said.

"I can tell he's an important demon down there."

"How?"

"Just a feeling. His power spilled into the whole house when he was here. Put me on high alert."

"I didn't notice," I said dryly.

Adalrik stepped farther into my room. "I think you have just as much, if not more power inside of you."

"How do you figure?" I turned to stare at Rik's silhouette.

"It's inside of you. Hidden. You just haven't come into it yet."

I was pretty sure that's what everyone was afraid of. And the only reason I had fire abilities was my short trip to Hell.

"I don't think it'll come to the surface unless I somehow end up in Heaven or Hell for a longer period of time. But I did think of something. Since I've spent my life on Earth, I think I have acquired human habits and needs."

"What do you mean?" he asked.

"I think being here for so long has given me the need to eat and sleep among other things. I can't help but wonder if I was in Heaven or Hell, would I lack those human needs."

"Perhaps. But being here has made you who you are. If it were different, you wouldn't be the Nova I know and love. I'm glad you're here."

"You're too sweet, Rik. If we hadn't met, you'd still be stuck in Germany with your clan," I pointed out.

Rik shuffled closer and gently gripped my hand at my side. "I probably would have been killed, but you saved me. If you hadn't, I would no longer be here."

"I'm glad you're here too, Adalrik."

"Goodnight, Nova," he said softly.

"Goodnight, Adalrik." He turned and closed the door softly.

Chapter Fifteen

I woke up to a loud crash from my living room, sitting up with a jolt. My hands were covered in flames. They snuffed out quickly. Grabbing my blades, I crept slowly into my hallway. My back against the wall, I reached the corner where I peeked out into my living room.

My gaze landed on the large object that lay limply on the floor. It was Elias. I dropped my weapons with a clatter and rushed toward his still body. I slid on my knees when I dropped to the floor next to him.

"Oh my god, Elias." I took his head in my hands and his eyes opened in slits. The blue barely shone in the dark room. My hands felt slick. He was covered in blood, and my hands began to shake. They roamed over his body, trying to find the source.

"Rik!" I shouted out as I kept my attention on Elias's wounded body.

"Christ, Nova what is all the ruckus about?" He stumbled into the room and rubbed his eyes.

"Turn on the light! Now!"

His eyes widened and he hobbled over to the light switch. He flipped the switch and I swallowed a scream when I saw Elias's battered body. His shirt was gone, and he looked as though he'd been whipped and beaten half to death.

"Can you ... can you help me get him to the couch?" I asked Adalrik.

"I can try." He rushed over to help me get Elias off the floor.

I picked up Elias's upper half and Adalrik barely managed to lift one of his legs. A grunt left me from the effort of moving him as I dragged Elias to the couch. His head in my lap, I tried to keep him on his side and check for other injuries. Tears blurred my vision. I cleared my throat and tried to keep a level head. If I would've known this was going to happen, I wouldn't have let Cyrus take him. I would have fought if I had to.

"Okay, I need washcloths and warm water."

Adalrik hurried to get the supplies.

Did I need antibiotic ointment? Did beings of Hell get infections? I didn't think so. I tried to think of an illness or injury that required me to see a doctor. But nothing sparked in my memory.

Elias groaned. I pushed his hair from his forehead, noticing a laceration at his hairline.

"Hey, Elias," I said softly. I stroked his hair, avoiding his injury. His eyes slowly opened. A tear slipped free down my cheek. I wiped it away hastily. I didn't want Elias to know I'd been crying.

"Nova."

"What happened?" My voice cracked.

"I was punished," he managed to say.

"Punished? By Cyrus?" He nodded slightly, but I knew without asking that it was him.

"Because of our kiss?" My nostrils flared with rage.

"Yes."

"He punished you, even though I kissed you," I seethed.

"I think he still holds me responsible for being weak."

Adalrik came in with a bowl of warm water and washcloths.

"I'm going to clean your wounds and the blood off of you, okay?"

"You don't have to do that, Nova," he rasped. "I'll heal in

the next few days." There was no way I wouldn't clean him up.

"I want to. Now, roll onto your stomach." I scooted to the edge of my couch and placed Elias's head on a pillow. With a wet washcloth, I gently cleaned the blood that dried on his torn back. He hissed and jerked back when his open flesh was touched. Making out flesh from muscle was difficult with how deep the lacerations ran.

"Sorry." I sniffled.

I rinsed the washcloth in the warm water and wrung it out. The water turned pink from the blood.

"Will . . . will you scar?"

"If I'm here, most likely."

"So why did you come? If you're in Hell, won't you heal faster?" I continued to gently clean his shredded back.

He hissed again. "I came to protect you. And yes, I'd heal faster."

"You idiot. Why would you come for me? You have to go back and heal."

Elias visibly swallowed and shook his head. "I won't."

"You stubborn jerk." I threw the bloodied towel into the bowl. His blood stuck beneath my fingernails, but it didn't bother me.

Elias let out a weak chuckle. "Even when I'm injured, you name call."

"There's no reason for you to suffer just to protect me. You should've stayed until you were healed. You couldn't even fade out while you were being punished?"

"I was chained to a whipping post with manacles that canceled my abilities. As soon as I was freed, I used the last of my strength to come here. So even if I wanted to go back to Hell, I couldn't. Not right now."

"I can't believe my father would do something like this."

"He's a demon, Nova. It's in his nature," Elias said.

"And does that mean it's in your nature . . . or mine?"

"I don't hand out punishments for the higher ups. And as for you, you're more human than you think."

"What do you mean?"

Elias shifted slightly so his gaze met mine. "Do you think if you hadn't been raised on Earth, that you'd be cleaning my wounds?"

"I . . . I don't know." My brows pulled into a frown. I guess it would have depended on if I was raised among the angels or the demons. I mean, demons and beings from Hell were known for being ruthless. But then again, Elias wasn't what I would call evil. I'm sure he wasn't all sugar and spice when it came to business. Elias gripped my hand and squeezed.

"Thank you."

"You don't need to thank me." I squeezed back. "But Cyrus will not be happy to be on my shit list."

"Oh, calling him by his name is going to piss him off." Elias chuckled.

"Good."

Elias spent the night on the couch. I didn't want to leave him, so I slept awkwardly on the chair across from him. I bandaged him and cleaned the blood that stained his skin the best I could manage. I felt awful that he was punished because of me. When I saw Cyrus again, he was going to know just how unhappy he had made me.

I still wanted Elias to go back to Hell to heal, but he couldn't. Even if he could, I didn't think he would. It would take time for his wounds to close completely. And time was one thing we didn't have enough of. I drifted in and out of sleep the rest of the night. At one point, I had a vivid dream.

Bright light assaulted my eyes. The smell of flowers was heavy in the air. I was in a large field of yellow flowers that gently swayed in the breeze. The sun warmed my skin. I glanced down to find I wore a pale blue cotton sundress. Not my normal attire. My skin was iridescent. I put my arms out in front of me, watching the shimmer. "Nova." I heard a melodic voice say my name. I caught sight of a woman who stood in front of me. Her long blonde hair fell in soft waves down to her breasts, and her violet eyes stood out against her pale skin. Her heart-shaped face, so much like my own.

"Are you . . ." She nodded before I finished my sentence.

"I am your mother."

"Why am I here?"

"Because I have something for you . . . for Elias," she said. Her voice calmed my nerves. It was so odd, not to know my mother my whole life, but there was a certain calmness that her presence created inside of me. She showed me a small vial with a purple liquid inside. She took my hand in hers and placed the vial in my palm.

"What is it? And how do you know about Elias?" I frowned.

"My dear daughter, I've been watching you your whole life. The vial contains properties that will heal your mate." Her fingers gently tucked my hair behind my ear.

"Wait, what?"

"Elias needs this to help you. It will speed his healing and you will be able to continue on your path."

"No, don't skip over the part where you just called Elias my mate." My mother gave me a soft smile but said nothing more. Her form started to fade away slowly.

"Wait! Don't leave me! Tell me who is doing this so we can stop them!"

"Daughter, I cannot interfere with such things. But I will assist you in any way I can. Trust Elias. He will protect you at all costs." Her words echoed around me even though the space was empty where she just stood.

I woke with a gasp and a kink in my neck from my unnatural position in my lounge chair. I sat up and rubbed my neck. A small thud sounded on the floor below. I sat forward and searched for the source of the noise. I saw what appeared to be the vial from my dream. How did she do that?

I picked it up and my hands shook. I held it up in the morning light that streamed through one of my unbroken windows. The liquid shimmered, and I wrapped my fingers around the small ampule. I stood and stepped toward Elias's sleeping form. Adalrik still slept on the floor, snoring up a storm.

"Elias," I whispered softly.

"Hmm?"

"I have something for your wounds." He stirred and hissed when he turned.

"Don't move." I opened the lid of the vial. "Open your mouth and drink this."

"What is it?" he asked.

"I'm not sure."

"You don't know what you're giving me but you want me to drink it anyway?"

"Yes."

"Okay, but if I die, I'm going to haunt you."

I giggled. "Okay, deal. If you die, you can haunt me for eternity. But if you don't, you owe me a latte."

Elias took the vial from my hand and glanced at me before he drank down the contents.

"It's sweet. Like nectar." He licked his lips. My eyes locked onto the movement. How could I get aroused at a time like this?

"Not what I'd expect." After a moment, his expression turned pained, and the veins beneath his skin started to bulge along his neck and forearms. Elias let out an inhuman roar that shook the walls of my house. I tripped over my own feet as I backed up, my back hitting the wall. His body arched off the couch, and the bellow that came from him was one of pain. I couldn't help but think I screwed up. That I had let my mother trick me into killing Elias. Maybe it wasn't my mother. Maybe it was someone who'd pretended to be her. Someone with nefarious plans. His body levitated off the couch. The wound on his face started to knit back together. I covered my mouth with my hand but couldn't tear my eyes away from the scene. His eyes were the brightest they'd ever been. Like they could give Superman a run for his money.

The bandages that I had placed around his torso burned to ashes and fell to the couch below. I watched his open wounds on his back mend together as a white light emanated from each lash in his flesh. The light gradually brightened until I had to cover my eyes. All the while, Elias continued to let out noises of pain, sending my body into tremors. I couldn't stand seeing him in pain. This may not be what would kill him, but he wouldn't be happy with me now that he'd gone through agony to be healed.

The light started to dissipate, and I was able to drop my arm to take in the scene. The wounds on his back had completely healed. Elias's body slowly lowered back onto the couch, but his breathing was heavy. I waited a few moments before I drew closer.

"Elias?"

"Where did you get that vial?" His voice was husky, teeth bared. That was the last evidence of the pain he had experienced.

"From my . . . from my mother." I swallowed. His face was contorted in anger, and I should have told him beforehand where I had acquired it. But I'd thought we trusted each other.

"Your adoptive mother?"

I shook my head.

"You didn't think to tell me before I drank it that this was something from Heaven?"

"I just knew I wanted you to be healed."

Elias sat up and rubbed his hand across his unshaven jaw. I reached toward him but he jerked back. I dropped my arm. My stomach twisted with nervousness. What had I done? I should've told him exactly where I'd acquired the tonic before he downed it.

"Do you realize that by ingesting something the exact opposite of what I am—the opposite of where I reside in the realms—that it can change me?"

I flinched at his raised voice.

"What's all the noise about?" Adalrik said groggily. Oh, now he wakes up, but the whole house shaking like an earthquake didn't rouse him? I ignored Rik.

"I . . . I didn't realize. She didn't tell me it would change you, just that it'd heal you."

"That's right . . . because you didn't *think*, Nova. Like always. You could have killed me!"

I shrank back. I wasn't scared of Elias, but I didn't want to be the object of his anger. "I'm sorry, Elias. I just—"

"You just what? Wanted me to feel better so we can get on with this bullshit with the cryptids? Was it even for me? Or was it for your convenience?" His nostrils flared.

My jaw dropped. "Are you kidding me? Of course, I wanted you to be healed. Your skin was torn apart and it's my fault!" I yelled back. Tears pricked the back of my eyes. How dare he think I'd done it for my own selfish needs. "I didn't want to see you in pain. I didn't want you to be reminded every day that the reason you bear scars is because of my bastard father!" Tears fell from my eyes and streaked down my face.

"What else did she tell you, Nova?" Elias said in a voice that was lower but no less angry. The brightness in his eyes had returned. There was no way I was going to tell him anything about the whole mate thing. He'd think I was crazy.

I shook my head. "Nothing," I croaked. Elias stood and his muscles bulged as he clenched his fists tightly together. The scarred *S* on his chest was stark against his tanned skin.

"I'll be back later."

117

"Wait . . ." I stepped closer.

But he was gone. At some point, Adalrik had left the room without me noticing. It was probably a good thing since I couldn't stand when people saw me cry. I angrily wiped the tears from my cheeks, staring at the empty spot on the couch where Elias had slept. His blood stained the cushions. So much had changed in the last twelve hours. From fighting together, to kissing, to my father beating him. If there was one thing I knew, it was that I couldn't stay home and dwell on it. I decided to text Tiff and see if she was up to either sparring or going to the shooting range. I threw my phone on the couch and headed to shower.

CHAPTER SIXTEEN

Tiffany and I ended up back at the shooting range. With my ear plugs in, standing inside in my booth, I tried to calm my mind as I released the safety. With my arms raised out in front of me and took aim. I took a few deep breaths and slightly squeezed the trigger but not enough pressure to actually shoot. With slowed breathing, I pulled the trigger. This time, hitting the silhouette on the paper.

I repeated the process again and again, until I started getting chest and head shots.

Tiffany bounced up and down. She hugged me when I was done and stepped out of my booth. I pulled out my ear plugs. "You're doing amazing!"

"Thanks," I said without enthusiasm.

"Hey." She grabbed my shoulders. "What's wrong? You haven't been yourself today."

"I just had an argument with Elias, that's all."

"Like a lovers quarrel?" Her lips tilted up into a grin.

"What? No. Just an argument, Tiff." I shook my head.

"About what?"

"It's a long story, one I don't really want to talk about."

"Okayyy. Well, you know I'm here for you if you need to vent. How about we go get you a latte?"

I gave her a weak smile. "Sure."

Once we packed up our belongings, I swung my bag over my shoulder and we headed to the coffee shop. When we arrived, Tiffany kept me distracted with her updates on Erica and how she asked her out. I tried to keep my mind from

119

wandering but it was no use. Elias had been so angry with me. I hadn't thought of the possible repercussions of giving him the tonic my mother had given me. I'd trusted her to be honest. For me, that had been stupid to take her word for it, that the mother I'd never met helped me. Helped Elias. I didn't even know her. What if Elias had died? What if he hadn't healed and instead the contents of the vial had done more harm than good?

During the time in my dream, was I really in Heaven? Or was that another realm? I had so many questions I wanted to ask her, but it wasn't like I could call her.

"Nova?"

"Hmm?" I took a sip of my latte.

"Your eyes . . . they're glowing."

I blinked a couple of times and peeked at Tiffany. "How about now?"

"Not as intense but still."

I grabbed my bag but left my latte and stood from the table.

"Wait, I'll come with you."

"I should head home. I have some work to do on a website," I said. Not a lie, I did have a project I needed to work on.

"Oh, okay. Well Mom and Dad wanted me to ask you to dinner tonight."

"I guess it depends on how much work I get done. I'll text you." Tiffany frowned but I turned to leave anyway. The bell on the door to the coffee shop jingled as it slammed shut behind me.

I marched in the direction of my house. When I reached the end of the block, I felt as though I was being followed. I glimpsed over my shoulder, but there was no one there. The hairs on the back of my neck stood on end and my body became hyperaware. I knew someone or something was watching me. This wasn't the way Elias made me feel with his heat — this was a sensation of dread and coldness. A chill skated down my spine, but I kept myself from shivering. I was on high alert and shifted my bag, unzipping it for quick access to my weapons.

I decided to get off the main street and turned to an open field that was less populated. Just in case whatever was following me decided to attack. Not something we would want the general public to witness. Especially since the government hated to do damage control on stuff like that. I strolled at a normal pace and kept checking behind me. I still didn't see anything. But just because I didn't see anything, didn't mean something wasn't there.

I pulled my blades from my bag and held them in one hand. A foul smell burned my nostrils and I wanted to gag. When I peered back again, I saw a pair of antlers atop a decaying deer head. A skeletal body spotted with random patches of filthy brown hair. The height of this creature was close to that of Bigfoot. But this wasn't Bigfoot.

It was a wendigo.

Wendigos were known to possess humans and invoke cannibalism in its host. I had a feeling that if he succeeded in getting his hands on me, he wouldn't be possessing me. He'd be taking my soul.

Empty eye sockets stared at me for a few moments. Then it advanced on me. Long boney legs shortened the distance between us quickly.

I dropped my bag and gripped a blade in each empty hand. When the wendigo was close enough, I swung out a little too hard. I missed the creature and I fell onto my back. Bad move. I shouldn't have put all my weight into my attack. I scooted back across the ground and rolled backward, my legs over my head and landed in a crouch.

When I popped back up, the wendigo swiped his long fingers. The force was so great, I fell to the side. My arm burned, and I felt wetness spread. When I glanced down, long gashes ran down my upper arm. Blood started to cascade in rivulets. I tried to grip my blade, but with the pain in my arm, it was impossible to hold on tightly. The wendigo stood over me and grabbed me by my shirt. I was lifted into the air. I kicked out and managed to hit his stomach. But he hardly flinched. With my uninjured side, I swung out my blade, slicing the wendigo's arm—or what was left of it. With no real flesh to come into contact with, that did nothing. Unfazed, it used its other hand to grip my neck. If the wendigo wanted to, it could've snapped my neck in an instant.

I was so screwed. Its grip on my neck tightened. I dropped my demon blades. My hands went to the skeletal fingers wrapped around my throat. I tried to loosen the hold. I tried to drag in air, but I could tell I was going to lose this battle. I kicked out again and tried my damnedest to release myself from the wendigo's grip. I wasn't sure I could even die this way, but I was running out of air. My vision started to blur. If I passed out, it would be game over and who knew what would happen.

A giant boney hand pressed flat against my stomach, but the creature hadn't disemboweled me as I'd expected. Its hand laid across my belly, and I felt something being pulled from me. My vision swam from the searing pain. I tried to scream out in agony, but nothing came out. With every pull, I felt weaker. I didn't have much fight left. I tried to peer down at what the wendigo was doing. But I couldn't move my neck. My throat was in a death grip. Another pull and my vision faded, going black around the edges. My body went limp. My arms dropped to my sides and my legs stilled. My eyes fluttered closed. Then there was nothing.

CHAPTER SEVENTEEN

I blinked a couple of times and tried to focus on my surroundings. The brightness of the room was disorienting. I rubbed my eyes, trying to get them to adjust. When I opened my eyes again, I was in a bed I didn't recognize. The sheets were silky, and everything was a bright white in color. I was dressed in a white nightgown. I had no recollection of changing clothing. I sat up with a start.

Did the wendigo kill me?

"Where am I?" I whispered to myself.

"You're in Heaven." My head snapped toward the ethereal voice. My mother sat in a chair by the bed.

"Did I die? I thought my soul was supposed to be taken to whoever is trying to usurp God and Lucifer."

My mother gave me a bright smile and gripped my hand. "No, Elias killed the wendigo before it took your soul. He came very close to draining your life force though. But the wendigo's plan involved taking your soul for itself."

"Then why am I here?" My brows pulled into a frown.

"You need to heal. When you're ready, you can go back into your body."

"I think I feel fine. I'd like to go back now." I threw back the sheets and tried to stand.

"Shhhh, at least give yourself a little time. The wendigo succeeded in taking part of your soul. It was released once he was killed," she said soothingly. "I didn't expect to see you so soon."

"What does Elias think? Does he think I'm dead?"

"No, he has your body back at your home in your bed. He's very worried."

"Last time I saw him we fought." I focused on my hands in my lap.

"No one is perfect. And just because you two are meant for each other doesn't mean you won't quarrel."

I lifted my eyes to my mother's violet gaze, so identical to my own. "I don't know if he'll forgive me. He thinks I gave him the vial for my own selfish purposes."

"Did you?" she asked and tilted her head to the side. Not an accusation, just pure curiosity.

"What? No! It killed me to see him in pain. I didn't want him to suffer because of me. It's my fault that he was beaten to a bloody pulp by Cyrus." My mother's face became hard to read.

"Cyrus does have a mean streak. My thoughts are that he thought he was doing what's best for his only child."

"How could he think hurting my protector is for my well-being?" I was getting a little annoyed.

"Cyrus doesn't know that Elias is your mate."

"Then how do you?"

"Soulmates are created in Heaven." My mother stood from her chair and clasped her hands in front of her.

"But Elias isn't from Heaven, he's one of Hell's soldiers." I frowned. Now I was confused.

"He wasn't always a soldier of Hell. It isn't my story to tell but maybe you should ask him. When the time is right." We were silent for a moment while I thought that over.

"Did you ever love him?" I asked.

My mother strode across the room gracefully. Her lavender gown flowed behind her, the only color in the room.

"Cyrus? Yes. I think at one time I did." She poured hot water into a cup and steeped a teabag. "I met your father during one of the Holy Wars."

"As in on Earth? Like the Crusades?"

"No, this was an otherworldly war. I'm sure Lucifer would call it something else." She held the cup of tea in both hands. She came back over to the bed and tried to hand me the cup of tea. I hesitated. "Drink. It will help."

"I'm more of a latte type of girl." She pushed the cup toward me. I took it and she sat on the edge of the bed.

"This will help you feel whole again."

I peered into the steaming cup and blew on the tea. It smelled like rosemary and something else I couldn't quite identify. I took a sip. It was slightly bitter but not bad.

"Cyrus and I battled against each other for some time. But the pull I had toward him became unbearable. We would meet in secret. He wanted to ask for permission to take me back to Hell with him, but I refused. I would never leave Heaven, and if he tried to force me, then it wasn't meant to be. He accepted my refusal for centuries until I became pregnant with you. We both weren't expecting a child. It's a rarity for our kind to procreate."

"Was he ever loving toward you?"

My mother smiled shyly. "Oh yes. He was very attentive." My mother's cheeks turned pink. Gross. "When I became pregnant, he no longer would accept my refusal of not being with him in Hell. I wasn't going to obey his wishes just because I was going to have his child. He wanted to hide you from everyone so we could keep you with us. And of course, I wanted nothing more than to keep my daughter with me. Hiding you on Earth was my own idea and was for your own protection. I feared you would be killed if anyone knew what you were. I wanted you to have a life even if it meant I wasn't going to be there. When I gave birth to you, I made the decision to give you to a family who wouldn't be afraid of the supernatural and the possible powers you may have. If you obtained any. The Alexanders willingly took you in without question and made sure you'd be able to blend in with humans and even gain human characteristics."

"I hated every minute of trying to be normal," I muttered as I took another sip of my tea.

"I'm sorry you felt out of place." She sounded sincere. "When your father found out I'd given you to a family of hunters, well, let's just say all the love he may have felt for me diminished. I haven't seen him since. It pained me to give you away, but I didn't have a choice."

"I'm sorry he was so cruel." I tapped my finger against my cup. I'd almost emptied it, and I felt stronger than I did when I woke up. I hadn't even noticed until now. A knock sounded at the door, and it cracked open.

"Seraphina, it's time," said a woman. I assumed another angel. Her long cobalt dress clung to her slender body and ended at her ankles, accenting her dark skin beautifully. My mother took the cup from me and set it on a nearby table.

"Come, Erela will take us. It's time for you to go back. Wouldn't want to keep you here too long and get in trouble."

I took her outstretched hand and rose from the bed. I followed behind my mother and the other woman down a long hallway. My bare feet pattered across the warm stone flooring. We came to a stop when we reached a room with a large dome. I examined the inside of the dome. I could see intricate painted details that would've taken years for a human to complete.

Someone cleared their throat which pulled me from my inspection. I took quick steps to catch up to my mother. We stopped at the edge of a large balcony. Only this balcony had no railing. When I stared out past the edge, there was a vast expanse of greenery that floated above the clouds. But directly over the edge, when I glanced down, I couldn't see anything past a blanket of clouds below. I'd never been afraid of heights, but it was a little unnerving.

"Do I have to jump?" I asked.

"Yes, but it's more like a slow descent," the woman, Erela, said. I nodded and before I stepped off the ledge, my mother stopped me.

"I think you dropped this." My angel blade materialized in her hand. I nearly burst into tears right then. I threw my arms around my mother. She hugged me in return and stroked my hair.

"Where did you find it? I searched everywhere."

"I have my ways," was all the explanation I received.

"Thank you." I sighed.

"If you ever need me, I'm here." I pulled back, accepting the angel blade. There was a feeling of rightness once the weapon was back in my hand. Cyrus's blades got the job done, but this blade felt like home. I turned and took tentative steps back to the edge of the balcony. Clouds covered the majority of sky below. Unable to tell how far down the drop was, my toes hung over the edge, and I glanced back at my mother and Erela. They both nodded in reassurance. I leaned forward and spread my arms wide before jumping.

Clouds blurred past me as I free-fell. As soon as I exited the cloud coverage, I slowed. The endless sky disappeared quicker than I would've expected. A pull in my gut blossomed. My soul felt as if it was tethered to my body and guided me home. As I was pulled closer to the call my body gave me, my neighborhood came into view. Homed in on my tiny white house with its terracotta roof from above, and I went right through the top. Elias sat on the edge of my bed. He held my hand. Slipping back into my body, I jolted when settling back in and woke with a gasp, sitting up quickly. Elias nearly fell off the bed from surprise.

"Nova." He gripped my face between his large hands. The callouses scraped gently across my cheeks.

"Elias," I rasped. My throat felt dry. Elias was sporting

some serious dark circles beneath his eyes. The hair on his face was longer than usual.

"I was so damn worried. I thought you were gone for good." He placed his forehead against mine.

"I'm okay."

"I'm so sorry, Nova. I was so mad at you, but I shouldn't have let that get in the way of protecting you. I felt something was wrong, but I ignored it because I was still so pissed off. I figured you could handle whatever it was. I fucked up and I'm sorry I waited. And then I had a vision of a woman who looks just like you. She told me you needed me."

"My mother."

He nodded. "She told me that you needed me and that second I faded in. You were limp, and the wendigo was taking your soul. I could literally see the life being drained from you. I cut his head from his body and faded us in back here. I was so afraid he'd succeeded, but your mother told me otherwise. That you needed to heal." His voice was pained, and his dark brows furrowed. I wanted to reach out and touch his face, his lips . . . but I restrained myself.

"How long have I been gone?" I placed my hands over his.

"Two days."

"Two days? She said I would stay for a little while," I said.

"Time works differently in the realms."

"What do you mean you felt something was wrong?"

"Ever since I met you the first time, I've had this strange connection. I know when something is wrong. A gut feeling. I didn't mention it before . . . I wasn't really sure why."

"Maybe Cyrus?" I suggested.

"Doubtful." His hands slid down to my neck and he brushed my hair back. I felt the warmth of him and his face inched closer to mine. His lips mere inches away. Warmth bloomed in my belly, but my thoughts went to the battered body I found on my living room floor a couple of days ago.

I'd rather not risk the wrath of Cyrus. I didn't want him to hurt Elias again.

"I don't want Cyrus to punish you again," I whispered, and he pulled back.

Elias gave a soft grunt and released me completely. I felt instant regret for having to block his advances. I craved his kiss just as much I'm sure he did mine. I was going to deal with Cyrus in my own way, but for now I wanted to protect Elias.

CHAPTER EIGHTEEN

Being absent from my normal life left me with crazy amounts of missed calls and texts from my family. I honestly didn't even want to tell them what had happened. All it would do was cause them to worry. I didn't need that right now. They needed to keep a calm mind and help me the best they could with the information I needed. There were even texts from Matt.

I dialed Tiffany's number, and it only rang twice.

"Oh my god, Nova! Where the hell have you been? Did you forget about dinner the other night? I didn't think you'd totally ghost me!"

"Whoa, hold on. I lost my phone, and I was super busy with the website job I was doing."

Elias sat on my couch, watching me pace as I talked on my phone.

"So busy that you couldn't answer the door?"

"You came by?" I glanced at Elias for some help. He shrugged because honestly, neither of us were good enough at fibbing to make up a lie.

"Of course I came by. And so did Mom and Dad. I know you're lying to me so spill it. Dad even checked your camera feed."

I licked my lips and tried to get the words right in my head before I spoke them. Especially since Tiff tended to be a blabbermouth.

"Dad has access to the cameras outside my house? Never mind. Okay, but if I tell you, you have to keep your mouth shut to Mom and Dad. And that includes Matt and anyone else you like to blab to."

"Fine. I promise as your sister to keep the information you tell me to myself." My gut feeling told me I was going to regret telling her. Even so, I filled Tiffany in on what had happened but left out some parts. Especially about being in Heaven with my real mom. When I'd finished, there was silence on the other end. I peeked at my phone screen to make sure the call hadn't dropped. Tiffany finally spoke.

"So, you were attacked by a wendigo and YOU were hurt. And you needed time to heal."

"Yes. I didn't want Mom and Dad to worry so I laid low for a couple of days." I could tell Tiffany wasn't buying the whole story, but she didn't say anything. She accepted my confession for what it was.

Tiffany and I hung up a few minutes later. We planned to meet up at some point the next day. I turned to Elias, who still watched me with an expressionless face.

"So, what's the plan?"

"We could go hunting. See if we can find a creature that we can get some answers out of."

"Nova!" Rik shouted.

I jumped at the sound of his voice. A searing pain ripped through my back and I doubled over. When the intensity settled, I froze for a moment. I slowly turned to Elias—he had a face full of feathers. Feathers that were very large and very much attached to me. They were white that bled to black tips. Reaching back, I touched the very top of the wings that protruded from my back. The soft feathers slipped through my fingers. I could feel my hand as it caressed the giant wings.

Rik stopped dead in his tracks, his mouth hung open.

"Oh my god. Oh my god. Help me put them back!" I started to freak out a little bit. Elias brushed the feathers out of his face. His fingers sent a shiver up my wing and through my body.

"I was wondering if you'd gained anything from your time in Heaven," Elias said in a calm voice. A little too calm.

"And now you're going to help me figure out how to put them away. I wasn't sure if I would gain anything because my body wasn't physically there." I tried to take deep breaths so I wouldn't panic. Elias stood and grabbed my shoulders gently.

"Don't freak out. Take a breath, Nova."

I took in a shaky breath through my nose and blew out of my mouth.

"Good. Do it a few more times until you feel calmer."

I did as Elias said until I managed to get a grip on myself.

"Now, picture them being pulled into your body."

I gave him a nod and closed my eyes. I tried to picture my wings folding and disappearing into my back. When I opened my eyes again, they were still out. I gazed into Elias's eyes. I'd felt even more nervous that they didn't go back where they came from. "I can't."

He gave me a soft smile and his hands grounded me. "You can, Nova. Not everything happens the first time you try."

I felt a gust of wind on my face. I was taken by surprise when a pair of onyx wings extended from Elias's back. My mouth fell open. The high shine from the light in the room drew me in and I reached out my fingers. I brushed them against the arch peeking out above his shoulder. His eyes closed as my fingertips ran through the soft feathers. I could see his body shiver from the touch. Good to know we both had the same reaction.

"Does it tickle?" I asked.

He opened his eyes, and they glowed softly. "No, it feels . . . nice." My stomach clenched at the sound of Elias's raspy voice.

"You two need to get a room already." Adalrik's accented

voice pulled me out of the moment.

I drew my hand back and cleared my throat. "Do you mind, Rik? I'm trying to learn to put these things away, and obviously you are lacking in the wing department." I didn't take my eyes off Elias as I spoke, and my wings almost touched the floor as they folded.

"I'll be in the kitchen if I'm needed," Rik said. As he left the room, I could hear him mutter under his breath in German.

"How come you didn't tell me you have wings?"

"Well, these are a new development. You see, that special drink your mother gave you did manage to change me in some ways. Which is what I was afraid of."

"They're beautiful," I said.

Elias shifted slightly, still with his hands on my shoulders. "Okay, let's focus on getting yours put away."

I only managed to nod in response. I was barely able to tear my gaze away from Elias's. I could've drowned in them, and my body hummed for him. I closed my eyes and felt much calmer than I originally had. I imagined my wings becoming one with my body. My wings pulled in close to my back and the pressure became unreal. My ribs felt like they'd expanded past the point they should, and I feared they'd break. My face scrunched up from the pain but as quickly as it came, it was gone. I opened my eyes and Elias stared at me. His hands slid down my arms and grabbed onto my hands.

"You did it."

"I did?" I turned my head. I no longer had the wings that took up a good portion of my living room. Elias's were still out but he quickly folded them in, and they disappeared. He was adept at dealing with his newly acquired wings.

"The pain will get better the more often you do it," Elias said.

"Are you mad that you have wings now? Because of me?"

"At first, I was. But now, I think it's kind of badass." Elias smirked. I felt as though our relationship had shifted. I felt closer to him. Maybe it was the fact that we were soul-mates . . . or maybe it was because I'd come so close to death.

If I was being honest with myself, I didn't know how long I'd be able to keep Elias at arm's length.

Going hunting was the last thing I felt like doing. But Elias and I needed to get information somehow. There were more creatures in wooded areas than any other place. Armed to the teeth, we faded into the forest where we fought the upirs. We stayed clear of the trail but were pretty close to the portal. We'd set up a post to see if anyone or anything decided to come through.

I grew tired of crouching and decided to stretch my legs.

"You all right?" Elias asked from his seat on the ground. He leaned back against a large rock and picked his nails with a small blade. His legs were out in front of him, his ankles crossed.

Dressed in his usual jeans and taut T-shirt. I eyed his muscular body as he glanced back down at his hands. Did my father really think he would be able to get his soldier to protect me and I wouldn't go goo-goo gaga over him? I mean he wasn't just cute—he was drop-dead gorgeous. His dark messy hair, sharp jawline covered in scruff, his perfectly straight nose . . . and those eyes. I bit my bottom lip.

"Nova?" Elias peered up at me.

"Huh? I'm sorry, what did you say?"

He gave me a smile. "I asked if you are all right? You're fidgeting."

"Oh, I'm fine. I just needed to stretch my legs. They were cramping."

"You can take a seat on the ground, you know."

"Right. I'm just gonna stay here . . . standing." I was so awkward. If Elias knew how much of a hard time I was having keeping space between us, he didn't let on.

I heard the sound of a flute in the distance and frowned. Elias perked up and put his blade in his boot. He brushed the dirt from his jeans as he stood.

His brows knitted together, and we listened for a while longer.

"I don't think normal forest animals play the flute," I said.

"Yeah. But fauns do."

Fauns had the upper body of a man and lower body of a goat. They also had the horns and ears of goats. Fauns typically played the flute to lure women and take them prisoner.

"I have an idea."

Elias studied me with curiosity. I gave him my best smile. "No, absolutely not." He knew right away that I would use myself as bait.

"Oh, Elias. Since when I have ever listened to anyone?"

"If you do this, I am to have eyes on you at all times."

"Dude, it's a faun. What superpowers could he possibly have that would overpower me?"

"Superpowers," Elias whispered and shook his head. He placed his hands on his hips.

"We need to follow the sound before he stops playing. Or worse, before he lures a human in." Since I wasn't human, the flute didn't affect me. But if any women were out hiking today, they would undoubtedly be hypnotized to follow the sound. I'd just had to make sure we found him first.

Fauns were typically jovial creatures and not all of them were wicked. Better safe than sorry.

We hiked up a small hill and followed the sound of the flute until we finally spotted the faun. He was in the center of a clearing surrounded by trees. Elias was easily able to stay out of sight in the heavy brush.

I glanced at Elias before I took down my hair. I ran my fingers through it quickly and turned to meet the faun head on.

Elias caught my hand. "Do you think this is a good idea?"

"What? Of course, what's he gonna do? Play me to death on the flute?" Elias's lips tilted up and I smirked in return. "I'll be fine. Besides, I have a big, strong Hell soldier watching me just in case." I patted him on the shoulder.

I acted entranced as I entered the clearing and the faun stopped playing.

"Oh, what a beauty I have called in," the faun said in a gruff voice. He was quite a bit shorter than I was. His brown hair was shaggy around where his horns poked out. He stepped closer to me. I watched him calmly as his hooves beat against the dirt ground.

He took my hand and kissed it. "My dear, what is your name?" He gazed up from my hand.

"Stephanie," I said softly. I didn't know if he'd recognize my true name.

"Well, Stephanie. I have quite a treat for you." He pulled me gently to a blanket that was laid out under a nearby tree. I followed him and willingly seated myself. A variety of treats and food were arranged before me. What did he plan on doing? Seduce women with food? He offered me a plate of pastries and fruit. I took it but didn't eat anything from it. I watched as he indulged and poured himself a goblet of what seemed to be red wine. Braids were woven throughout his beard and his eyes were as green as the grass in spring.

"Here you go." He handed me the glass and I took it from him.

"Thank you."

"You're very welcome. Now, you heard my playing? How did you like it? Did it ensnare you?" He grinned and I gave him a nod. I tried my hardest to maintain a blank expression.

The faun scooted closer to me, and my body tensed. His cool fingers brushed against my neck as he entwined them in my hair, twisting a piece. His eyes hungrily took in my appearance until they reached my eyes. The faun paused and released my hair.

"I don't know who you're trying to fool, child."

I stayed quiet for a moment, and he spoke again.

"No human would have eyes the color of yours. So what do you want, *Stephanie*?"

Dammit. I sighed.

"I'm looking for answers. Answers regarding the portal and who is letting the creatures through."

The faun scooted away from me. "I have no answers for you."

"Come on, you have to know something."

"Nothing I can give you to you freely." He took a sip from his goblet.

"So, you do know?" I arched a brow.

"Only of the portal, but nothing of the individual who opened it. That's all I can say."

"You know more than you're letting on, faun. You came through here, obviously. You don't belong here." I stood, knocking over my wine. The liquid spread across the blanket and soaked into the fabric.

As Elias stepped out from his hiding spot, his footsteps crunched. I turned my head slightly, catching his towering figure in my peripheral. "We could definitely give him reason to talk." Elias manifested his sword out of thin air.

"Oh please, I've lived a long time. I am not afraid of you or death." The faun rolled his eyes, resembling a defiant teenager.

"What will it take for you to give us some information?" I asked. I turned to face him again. His eyes lit up. I knew I'd made a mistake—he could ask me for just about anything and I would have to comply.

"I've been needing a new flute for a century or two." He thoughtfully stroked his braided beard.

137

"That's all?" I asked. "I buy you a new flute and you tell me about the portal and who's after me?"

"Top of the line. Yamaha Professional. Should only cost you about seven thousand in American currency."

I nearly choked. "Seven thousand dollars? That's insane. No. No way."

The faun shrugged. "Suit yourself, darling."

Elias joined us then, his hand landing on the small of my back. "I think Cyrus may be able to help with the funds for this," he whispered against my ear.

"There's no way I would ask him for money. Or help for that matter. Not after what he did to you."

"What I mean is, Cyrus gave me funds for being here on Earth. I have enough to cover the cost since I haven't needed to touch a dime. Well, other than when I had to buy an outfit when we went out with Tiffany and Erica."

"Oh . . . I don't want to take your money." Even if the thought was very sweet.

"I want to help you, Nova. We need this information. We're in this together."

"I don't want to take your money, Elias." I glanced back at the faun, who casually popped grapes into his mouth. He pretended he couldn't hear us as we argued.

"We have a deal," Elias said loudly to the faun.

"Wonderful." The faun clapped his hands together with glee.

"We'll be back as soon as we have your flute."

"Wha—" I barely managed to spit out before Elias turned and pulled me by the arm. He dragged me back into the heavily forested area. I pulled my arm from his grasp.

"Elias, I said I don't want you to do this!"

He turned and clasped my face in between his hands. "And I told you, I want to help. So let me help, Nova. This may be the lead we need."

I exhaled. There was no way I would win this argument. Either I just agreed and we'd get the ridiculously priced flute for Mister Creepy Faun. Or I disagreed and we'd still get the ridiculously priced flute for Mister Creepy Faun.

"Fine," I gritted out. Elias released my face and turned to continue striding through the forest. I followed him.

CHAPTER NINETEEN

It took Elias and I two hours to get to the only music shop that confirmed that they had the flute in stock. No shop within a fifty-mile radius carried the exact brand of flute the creature had requested. The traffic made our excursion longer than it should have been, which only added to my irritation. By the time we had the instrument in hand, I was tired and hangry. Not a good combination to deal with the faun at this point. So we stopped at a diner for some dinner on the way back to the forest.

We sat in a booth by a window, and I ordered a cheese-burger with fries and a milkshake. Elias didn't order anything.

"Come on, don't you want to try some of this delicious human food?" I waved my fry in the air toward him.

Elias grinned and leaned forward. "You forget, I don't need to eat. I haven't spent enough time here to warrant eating."

"Fine, more for me." I shoved a disgusting number of fries into my mouth and took a huge gulp of my milkshake. Elias watched, but all he did was chuckle, while I gave him a smirk in return. If I had done that in front of Matt, he would have been embarrassed. But maybe because Elias wasn't used to human normalities, he didn't know better. Or maybe he did, and he just didn't care. I liked the latter idea better.

"Do you think the faun will be there when we get back?" I asked after I swallowed my food.

"He'd better be. Otherwise, we'll be going faun hunting."

"I'm down for that. But if he goes back through the portal, we'll have no idea where he's gone."

"We'll just have to wait and see when we get back."

"How about we play a game?"

"We don't have an Uno deck here." He arched a brow.

"No, more of a question asking game. Like I ask you a question and vice versa. But on a more personal level." I dipped my fry into my shake and took an over-exaggerated bite.

"Okay, and why would we do that?" he asked.

"To get to know each other better. You go first—ask me a question."

"Was Matthew your first boyfriend?" he asked me. Dang, went straight for the super personal stuff.

"Boyfriend, yes. Sexual experience, no," I answered honestly.

"Were your other sexual experiences with humans?"

"Oh no, it's my turn," I said. "How long have you been a soldier?"

"Five centuries, give or take."

My mouth dropped open.

"Answer my last question."

I wondered if there was a reason Elias was so interested in my sex life. Since I'd come back from Heaven, the intensity I'd felt between us had been amplified. I knew I'd never felt anything so electric with anyone. I wondered if he felt that too.

"Yes, all humans. It's not like I encountered much of anything else. How'd you become a soldier in Hell?"

Elias sucked his bottom lip in between his teeth. Maybe he'd give me an idea of what my mother was talking about. That Elias hadn't always been a soldier and he did have a soul.

"I was given the option by Lucifer to either be a prisoner and feel unbearable pain for eternity or become a soldier. I chose to not deal with pain day in and day out."

"I don't blame you. I would've made the same choice." I took a big bite of my burger. Ketchup squirted out and onto my chin. Elias grabbed a napkin and reached across the table to wipe it off. I stared at him for a moment as I swallowed.

"You're not very good with human interaction. How did you manage to have human partners?" he asked as he pulled his hand away.

"So, you've noticed? Sex was never complicated. It's more of the nervousness of conversation. All I've ever known is hunting. I'm not sure I have much to talk about with humans. Nothing in common, that's for sure."

"You seem very capable of conversation to me."

"Well, because you aren't human now, are you?" Wait . . . It just dawned on me. "You said that you could have been a prisoner of Lucifer's. Does that mean you were once human?"

Elias leaned back against the cushion of the booth. "I was," he replied.

"How come you didn't tell me this?"

"Per your rules, it's my turn to ask a question."

Touché, Elias. Touché.

"Fine," I grumbled.

"Have you been with anyone recently?" The question caught me off guard. This was getting next level personal.

"No, Matt was the last person." I glanced down at my plate of half-eaten burger and fries. Heat crept in my cheeks, and I wasn't even sure why. I was never ashamed of my sexuality. "Who were you in your human life?"

"My name is the same. I look the same but with more muscle mass, since I train and fight."

"No, what I mean is, why were you sent to Hell? Were you some sort of mass murderer?"

Elias seemed to tense a bit at my question. I wondered if I'd overstepped a boundary.

"I'm sorry, you don't have to answer that."

Elias was quiet for a minute more before he responded. "I killed the men who attacked my wife."

My stomach dropped.

"I'd left home to tend to the cattle and farms of my employers and didn't return until the afternoon. By then, they'd beaten her bloody, raped her, and stolen all our savings. When she told me who they were, I took my vengeance. And then was hanged for my crimes by the towns people."

My blood ran cold and I felt sick to my stomach. There was no way I could have finished my burger. What a horrible scene to come home to. His poor wife. Poor Elias.

"I'm so sorry, Elias. That's such a horrible thing for the both of you to go through." The heat in my cheeks had drained.

"It was a long time ago. I'm being punished for my sins."

"That doesn't seem fair." I frowned.

"I believe my sin was wrath. Also, murder," Elias replied.

"You were protecting your wife. You probably saved another family from going through the same trauma."

"I don't want to talk about it anymore. Are you done eating?"

I nodded and threw cash on the table before I stood. Elias headed toward the front door before I'd even gotten out of the booth. Now I was sorry I ever thought a question game was a good idea. I didn't think it would end on such a sour note.

The ride back to the forest was quiet. and I couldn't bring myself to bother Elias with any more stupid questions. I just wanted to know more about my protector, friend, whatever he was. *Mate.* I decided to give him time to process the memories I'd dredged up. The sun was setting, and I hoped the faun was still in the same spot and hopefully not luring women into his trap.

We pulled into the empty parking lot. Slamming the door,

I double-checked all my weapons were still secured to me before I took a step toward the trail. Elias wrapped an arm around me and faded us into the clearing we'd been at earlier. I stumbled slightly, not ready for the transition from one place to the next. When I scanned the area, I spotted the faun. He leaned against a tree and smoked a cigarette. The end brightened as he took a long drag.

"About damn time you two showed up. I was getting ready to give up on you." He flicked his cigarette, and it landed in front of me. I stepped on the butt, extinguishing it completely. The last thing we needed was a forest fire.

"You sent us on a hunt for the most expensive flute known to man and thought it would be simple?" I asked.

"No, not at all. Did you get it?"

I glanced at Elias, and he materialized the flute case in his hand. The faun stood on his hooved feet and clomped toward us. With hardly any light to illuminate the clearing, I wasn't sure if he could see clearly. But he didn't seem to have any trouble spotting the case.

He took his *gift* gently from Elias's grip and opened the case, eyeing the brand-new flute before he confirmed it was the one he'd requested.

"Wonderful. Now what did you want to know about the portal?" He snapped the case closed and latched it.

"Everything you know," Elias said.

"The portal has been open for years. However, not many have come through until recently. I've heard whispers of there being a price on someone's head. I don't buy into all those promises of power. I keep to myself and listen to the gossip of others."

"Have you heard anything else?" I asked.

"Only a whisper of a name."

"I thought you only knew of the portal. Who's sending the cryptids?"

"That was before you came through with what I requested. As for their master's name, I've heard Azvameth a few times. Why he's sending these inexperienced creatures is beyond me." He grinned.

"Shit," Elias said. My gaze went to him.

"So, you've heard of him?" asked the faun.

Elias nodded but said nothing more.

"If he asks, tell him I've never met you or he'll slaughter me."

"I give you my word. Thank you," I replied. We turned to fade back to the car but just as Elias gripped my arm gently, I stopped and peered back at the faun. "One more thing. If I catch you luring humans here again, I will end you."

The faun gave me a pouty face. "As you wish, darling."

Elias pulled me closer and put his arm around my waist. We reappeared next to my car.

"Who is Azvameth?"

"Your uncle."

That was not what I expected. "Where do we find him?"

"No one has seen him in the last few years. He doesn't reside in Hell. Or at least he hasn't recently. Azvameth just disappeared one day. No one asked questions and no one cared enough to go looking for that prick," Elias explained.

"Cyrus must have told him about my mother and me."

"That's the only explanation as to how he knows you exist. That you're a hybrid, and he's probably old enough to have lived during the last hybrid's life."

I swallowed.

He may be old enough that he was alive from the time of the first hybrid.

CHAPTER TWENTY

By the time we reached my house, Elias still had barely spoken to me since the diner version of twenty questions, aside from a few comments about Azvameth. Apparently, Azvameth used to be Lucifer's favored. For some reason or another, Azvameth had lost his privileges and had been MIA for the last few years.

I peeked over at Elias. He seemed so sad. Should I apologize again? I didn't want to continue to make him think of his wife and the unfair punishment he'd suffered for hundreds of years. I decided to think everything that Elias had confessed over while I changed out of my clothes. I put on cotton shorts and an oversized shirt. I threw my hair up into a messy bun. When I checked my reflection in the mirror, stray blonde hairs stuck out of my hair tie messily.

When I came out of my room, Elias stood stoically in my living room and faced away from me. His jaw was clenched tightly. I admired the mere perfection. I craved his full lips. I would love to feel them move across the soft skin of my stomach to the apex of my thighs. To feel the scratchiness of his stubble against my legs. I clenched my thighs together at the thought.

"I'm not mad at you, Nova," he said gruffly, breaking me from my dirty thoughts.

"I didn't mean to bring up bad memories." I took a seat on the edge of my couch. My shoulders slumped. I felt horrible, even if he said he wasn't angry.

"My wife was my reason for living at that time. When I

found her, I was enraged. I decided to act since I knew no one else would. Go figure. I was punished for taking their lives when nothing would have happened if they hadn't taken hers."

I picked at my cuticles, unable to witness the pain on Elias's face. My stomach was in knots, and I felt for him. I really did. To seek revenge for the love of your life and be reprimanded in such a way that you lose your life and your soul. He turned and took a few steps toward me before taking a seat next to me on my sofa. His hand covered mine to stop me from picking before I drew blood.

I peeked up at him through lowered lashes. His blue eyes were soft as he searched my face. Maybe he was looking for any type of sign of what I felt. I felt rage for him — sadness, and pain. I took it all on because I knew that this had ultimately killed him in more ways than one.

"I still don't think it's fair," I whispered.

"Maybe not. But I can't change what happened now." He was right but if I ever had the opportunity to fix this for him, I would. I promised that to myself. But I didn't speak it aloud.

He removed his hand from mine and reached up, stroking my cheek with his thumb. His calloused skin evoked goosebumps that raced across my body. I melted into his touch. Closing my eyes, I breathed out softly as I tried to control my urges.

When I opened my eyes again, Elias stared at me and the fire in his irises was hard to ignore. His lips kicked up into a grin. A slight dimple in his left cheek appeared that I'd never noticed before.

"Your eyes are glowing," he said.

I lowered my lashes to cover up the fire in them. "No, don't do that." Elias's hand brushed back stray hairs that'd fallen forward.

"What?"

"Hide from me." Elias was closer, and the heat of him sent a shiver through me. He leaned in and placed a soft kiss on my lips. I pulled back after a moment and pressed my forehead to his.

"Cyrus . . . I don't want him to—"

Elias silenced me with a finger against my lips. "I don't care anymore. I lived through the worst of it. I haven't felt this way about anyone in five hundred years."

I stared at him for a moment and tried to decide if this was worth the risk to Elias. There was no doubt that I wanted him and that he wanted me.

"I would gladly accept any punishment from your father if it meant I could have you. Be with you." Elias's hand brushed against my jaw and down my neck, intensifying my shivers. His words hit me hard. This time I was the one who pressed my lips to his. A few softly placed kisses as I slid my tongue along his mouth. He opened. My tongue slid against his. Soft and velvety. A deep growl came from his chest. I placed my hand against it, felt the vibrations. Never breaking our kiss, I threw my leg over both of his. He leaned back into the couch cushions.

His hands gripped the bare skin of my thighs, and heat spread beneath my skin. My fingers explored his chest, shoulders, stomach. Down to the buttons on his jeans, where I flicked the button open and unzipped them. I reached my hand between us, and the deep groan from Elias vibrated through me. I clenched my thighs tightly around him. He was big, much bigger than I would've thought.

I continued to run my hand beneath Elias's briefs exploring his silky cock as he slid his hands up to my rear. He gripped me hard. A moan escaped me, and Elias trailed his long fingers under the edge of my shirt. And then farther. His palms scratched against my smooth back, and it caused me to arch. I pressed my breasts into his chest and my nipples hardened.

"I can't let this happen out here," Elias said as he pulled his mouth from mine.

My brows furrowed in confusion. "What I mean is, not on the couch in your living room. Especially when Rik likes to pop up unexpectedly." True. In one swift movement, Elias stood and held me against him. I wrapped my legs around his waist.

He faded us into my bedroom where I landed on my back on the soft sheets. Elias's hard body covered mine. I giggled. He used his mouth to slowly seduce and explore my body. He started at my neck and then moved lower. I pulled my shirt over my head. Nude from the waist up, he took an eyeful of my breasts. He brought his mouth to my nipple. The heat compelling me to arch my back.

"I want you," I said huskily. I lightly pulled at the strands of Elias's dark hair and his bright eyes flicked up to my face. His mouth left my breast.

"You have me."

"But I want you want you."

He chuckled deeply. "You'll have me inside of you soon enough. There's no way in hell I'm going to rush this."

I groaned in frustration. Elias's fingers hooked into my shorts and underwear, pulling them down my legs.

"If I'm going to be completely naked in front of you, you better start taking your clothes off too," I said as he tossed the last of my clothing behind him.

Without a word, Elias peeled off his shirt and tossed it to the side. I admired the fit form of his chest and abs. The deep V that ran beneath his jeans tempting me even more to see the well-endowed appendage that I had felt moments before. Elias removed his jeans and then slowly lowered his briefs. His cock sprang free. I smirked with delight as I checked out the perfection of him. His large cock was a bonus, and I had a feeling I'd be experiencing the best sex of my life.

Elias hooked his arms under my knees and pulled me toward him to the edge of the mattress. He lowered himself to the floor, and his hot breath on my flesh sent a quiver through me. Elias flicked his tongue against my clit and I gasped. I threw my head back. The ache between my thighs intensified. If he didn't get down to business soon, I might lose my mind.

"You taste like heaven," he said against my sensitive flesh. His mouth engulfed my entire center. The sounds that came from me echoed throughout my room. His tongue lapped at my clit until I was so close to coming, my legs shook uncontrollably. Then he stopped. He slowly pushed a finger into my slit. And then another. I nearly came apart at the welcome intrusion, I was so worked up and wet. He pumped his hand at a steady, maddening rhythm. My hips started to rock and I shamelessly grinded against his hand. I whimpered when he withdrew his fingers from me.

"Elias," I said with a gasp. He licked my slickness from his fingers and a satisfied growl rumbled through him.

Elias hovered over my body. His eyes burned with fire. Brighter than they'd ever been.

"I want the first time I make you come to be on my cock," he growled. I could feel his thick erection as it pushed against my slick entrance. No way would I argue with him.

His crown pushed into me slightly, and my hips bucked. I tried to impale myself on him, but he held my hips in place. He chuckled. "Not yet, Nova. I won't be rushed."

"I really want to punch you right now," I said between clenched teeth. Elias laughed and withdrew himself from me before he pushed into me a little farther. He did this multiple times, never completely seating himself inside of me. A moan escaped me, and Elias finally pushed into me fully. My eyes rolled back from the feel of his smooth cock. He stayed still for a moment and kissed me. Then he started his slow and torturous thrusts. My nails gripped his buttocks as I tried to push him to go faster but my prodding didn't work.

"Is there something you're trying to tell me, Nova?"

"More," I whimpered.

"More what?" He nipped at my neck and pulled the hair tie from my hair. He gripped my hair roughly and tingles erupted across my scalp.

"I want more of you." I moaned.

"I don't want to hurt you," he whispered against my throat.

"You won't. Please . . . fuck me," I begged him.

"I thought that's what I was doing." He chuckled.

"I want it faster . . . harder."

Elias kissed my mouth and picked up his pace, pounding into me. He gave me what I'd asked for. His fingers found my clit and rubbed steady circles over the bundle of nerves. It took less than a minute for me to come apart around him. Elias didn't show any signs of slowing down. I wrapped my legs around his waist and rolled us, ending with me on top. Taking control, I rode him roughly. He gripped my hips and helped to lift and lower me onto his shaft. Another orgasm tore through me, leaving me weak. But Elias continued to pummel into me from below. He roared as he spilled into me. Our bodies were slick with sweat, and I rested my head on his chest. We both breathed heavily.

"That was amazing." I sighed. Elias's fingers brushed down my spine and he kissed the top of my head. I fell to the side and his still engorged erection withdrew from me. We both lay in silence as I idly drew circles around his nipple and then up to his scar on his pec. He let me and didn't even flinch.

"What does it mean?" I asked. Elias peered down at me and I peeked up at him. His eyes had dimmed but there was still a soft glow.

"Sinner. It's Lucifer's brand of ownership," he replied. I pressed a kiss to his damaged flesh.

"You're anything but a sinner," I whispered.

I woke the next morning to a pounding at my door. When I slipped out of bed, Elias was already up, pulling on his jeans. He had stayed all night. Normally he'd be gone before I woke up. I found my baggy shirt and shorts in a pile on the floor and slipped them on quickly. Elias went to the door shirtless. I trailed after him, probably crazy disheveled from the incredible sex the night before. He pulled the front door open without glancing through the peep hole. Tiffany and my mother stood in front of me. Their mouths dropped open.

"What are you guys doing here so early?" I asked. I peeked out from behind Elias.

"Nova, we haven't seen you in days and we've been worried. We came here to . . ." Tiffany stopped mid-sentence. Thoughts clicked together in her head. My appearance . . . Elias shirtless . . . and I probably screamed the walk of shame.

"Ohhh, I see why you weren't answering last night." Tiff pointed a finger at me.

"Nova, we're here for more than just checking in. Your father is missing," my mother said, changing the subject.

"What? Since when?" I ushered them inside. Elias went back to the bedroom. I closed the door behind my mother and sister.

"Since last night. He never came home after saying he was going to the store," My mother looked like she was ready to cry. I sat next to her and clasped her hand in mine.

"We'll find him. I promise." I tried to comfort her. My stomach was in knots at the thought of my father not coming home. That was definitely out of character for him.

"Do you think this could have something to do with the whole cryptid situation you're dealing with?" she asked me. Honestly, I didn't know. I couldn't see why he would just up and disappear.

"I don't think so, but I can't be sure. Unless someone knows he's my father and that I care about him. They could be using him to get to me." My mother broke down then and I wrapped an arm around her shoulders.

Elias strolled out of the bedroom and pulled his shirt down over his trim waist. "We could get eyes and ears sent out from Cyrus."

I didn't necessarily want to use Cyrus's minions to help search for my adoptive father. The less I had to do with him the better. If he found out about Elias and me, he'd undoubtedly send him to the Hell fire pits. But did I have any other choice? Not really.

"I guess."

"Cyrus? He's your biological father, right?" Tiffany asked. I gave her a nod.

My mother's shoulders shook as she cried, and I rubbed my hand up and down her arm. She eventually calmed down and took a deep breath. "Please, Nova. Please help me find him."

"I will, Mom. Don't worry. We'll get word to Cyrus."

Elias gave me a quick nod and faded out.

"Does he do that often?" Tiffany stared at the empty space Elias had stood in moments before.

"Not at first. But he does now. Did you guys locate Dad's car?" My mother shook her head against me. "Maybe we should check the parking lot of the store. See if it's still there."

"Good idea. I'll go now," Tiffany said. She headed to the door quickly and left. There were only a couple of stores in town that he could have gone to. This whole situation was becoming a nightmare. I worried that maybe someone may have gotten word that he was my family. If that was the case, then this had just become even more serious.

CHAPTER TWENTY-ONE

Tiffany found my father's car in one of the grocery store parking lots. This wasn't the news I'd hoped for. Even if he'd fled for some reason, that would have been better news than this. There was no sign of a struggle or foul play of any kind. No blood or anything out of place inside or outside of his car.

Tiffany took our mother home. My heart broke for her, and I knew the worrying could make her physically sick. I wanted her to hold off on the worrying until we had more evidence.

I sat on my couch and gnawed at my bottom lip when Rik hobbled into the room.

"Hi, Nova. Any luck with the creatures?" he asked.

"Actually, yes. We came across a faun in the woods that was able to give me the name of my uncle."

Rik shuffled his way over to me and put his small hand on my knee. "What could your uncle want with your soul?"

"I'm not sure. I just hope I can find him before I can't fight back anymore and he takes it."

"You will. You're a strong one, girl. Have you told your mother? Your sister?" His thick accent was rough around the words, but that didn't make it any less sweet that he had so much faith in me.

I gave his hand a gentle squeeze. "They already know quite a bit of what's going on. But right now, I don't want to burden my mother any more than she already is with my dad missing."

"I'm sure your family would appreciate your honesty even

though it's already a hard time for your mother and sister. You take too much on yourself. You need to let us be there to help."

My face softened.

Elias faded in at that moment.

"Good news?" I asked. Rik dropped his hand from my leg.

"Your father agreed to assist with finding Victor. He didn't look happy when I asked. When I told him you'd requested his help, he gave in more quickly. Still, it took some convincing."

I breathed a sigh of relief. The more eyes on the streets, the better.

"I wish there was a way I could help you, Nova. I'm sorry I'm useless to you when you need as much help as you can get," Rik said.

"Adalrik, you are not useless. You keep me company and you let me know when strange men come to my door when I'm not home," I teased and glanced over at Elias. His lips kicked up in a slight grin.

"So much good that did. Now you have cameras to tell you who's been around."

I kept forgetting about the damn cameras. I didn't even have access to the feed. I'd never asked my dad for it. Then it hit me.

"Stores have cameras in parking lots, don't they?" I glanced back and forth between Rik and Elias. They glanced at each other and I remembered they'd probably never stepped foot inside a grocery store.

"Never mind. I'm going over there right now to ask if they have the footage from last night."

"I'll go with you," Elias said.

I dressed in more appropriate clothes and brushed my teeth and hair quickly. We headed over to the grocery store immediately, leaving Rik behind, of course. I explained the situation to the teenager behind the customer service counter and he called his manager to the front.

"How can I help you two?" he asked. The man was stout and balding. His badge read *Glenn*. I took a deep breath and hoped he could help us.

"My father's car is in the parking lot, and he disappeared last night. I want to see the surveillance footage from the parking lot last night?" My words came out as a question instead of a statement.

Elias placed a hand on my lower back which gave me a comforting feeling. My shoulders relaxed. I hadn't realized how tense I was.

"Sure, let me pull up the footage real quick. Come into my office." I thought it would be harder to convince him.

Elias and I followed him into a small, cramped office with an oversized desk. We squeezed between the wall and desk to take a seat in the two available chairs. Elias's body took up the majority of the room and the space seemed even smaller than it already was. Glenn slid his glasses onto his nose and pulled up the security footage.

"You said from last night, dear?" He glanced at me from over the rim of his glasses.

I cleared my throat. "Yea . . . yes. Last night."

"Sometime between eight and ten pm," Elias chimed in.

Glenn turned the monitor to give us a better view. He rewound the footage to start at eight and fast forwarded it until I spotted my father's car.

"Right there." I sat up straighter and leaned in. Glenn paused the image so I could take a closer look.

"That's his car for sure."

Glenn pressed play and we watched the screen as nothing happened. He just sat in the car. After about five minutes, a dark vehicle pulled up next to him and my father exited his car. He strolled around to the passenger side of the stranger's car and got in.

The car drove off. The license plate of the second car wasn't visible from the angle we were viewing.

"He just left with someone." I frowned, confused.

"Maybe another woman?" Elias suggested.

My stomach sank at the thought. I mean, it wasn't unheard of for men to step out on their wives. My mother was already heartbroken and worried. That thought would just destroy her.

"It's a possibility but doubtful." I sighed. "Glenn, can we get another angle on the black car?"

"Sorry, we only have the ones you see here on the screen."

"Well, thank you for your time." I started to stand.

"Good luck finding your dad." Glenn sounded sincere. I gave him a slight nod and an awkward smile. Elias and I squeezed back toward the office door.

As soon as we stepped into the night air, Elias bumped his shoulder into mine gently.

"We'll figure it out," he said.

When we arrived at my house, I realized the second we started up the sidewalk that, my front door was ajar. Dammit. I know I closed and locked the door. If another cryptid had come into my house, I was going to lose my mind.

"Wait here," Elias said.

"There's no way I'm waiting here." I pulled my angel blade from my sheath.

We crept slowly into the house and listened. There was only silence.

"Rik?!" I called out and Elias glared at me. "I want to make sure he's okay."

There was no response. I called out for him again and Elias joined in.

"Nova." I barely heard the sound. But it didn't sound right.

The voice sounded strained.

"Rik? Where are you?" There was no response. I started tearing through my house to find my friend. It wasn't until I entered my room that I heard a gurgling sound. My heart dropped. I rushed to the other side of my bed, where the noise was coming from.

Adalrik's mangled body was strewn across my floor. I dropped to my knees beside him. His face was so swollen I barely recognized him. If it weren't for his small stature and bearded face, I didn't know that I would have. I reached out and brushed my fingers down his bloodied cheek.

"Rik, what happened? Oh god." I sobbed. Elias stood behind me.

"Hu . . ." The gurgling took over once more.

"Who, Rik? Who did this to you?" Tears fell down my face as I realized there was no way to save my friend. Not when he was this battered and hardly able to take a breath.

He rasped a few more times until silence took over. My friend's chest no longer rose and fell. There was no sign of life . . . no breath, no accented remarks . . .

"Rik?" I cried and my shoulders shook with my sobbing. I gently grabbed his small body and pulled him into my lap, cradling him. "Please don't leave me."

Elias put a warm hand on my shoulder. I felt him lower himself to his knees, and he held me as I held one of my only friends in this world. I leaned my head into Elias and screamed until my throat was raw.

"I'm going to find him. Whoever did this to Rik, I'm going to find him."

"We will find him together," Elias whispered close to my ear and kissed my head.

Elias let me cry and hold Adalrik until I could hardly see through my swollen eyelids anymore. It was so silent in the house, and I could only hear the sound of Elias's heartbeat where my ear was pressed against his chest.

"What would you like to do with Rik?" His voice was soft and the vibration of his words pulled me from my thoughts. The thoughts of revenge I had so deeply rooted in my mind in such a short amount of time. The thoughts of it twisted through my body, through my bones. Into my gut. Promises of what I planned to do to the person who killed one of my best friends.

"I want him here. In my garden." I sniffled. Elias stood and helped me to my feet. I still held Rik's small, crumpled form in my arms. I was covered in his blood. "Do you have a shovel?"

I gave him a nod and told him where to find it. He disappeared for a few minutes and came back with the shovel in hand.

"I'm ready whenever you are. Take your time, Nova."

Even though my heart ached for Rik, I was touched by Elias's kindness. The notion never left my mind that this man was not a sinner. I'd never expected him to do this for me, but I was grateful. The experience of our pleasure last night may have brought us closer than I'd realized. It wasn't just sex. If my mother was right, Elias was my mate. The one I was supposed to be with. My stomach tightened at the thought. I didn't know when I'd ever be ready to tell him that secret, or if I ever could. He'd had five hundred years to dwell on the loss of his wife. I'm not sure I could measure up to her memory. And I wasn't sure how he felt about me—if this relationship was anything more than sex for him.

"I'm ready," I managed to croak out through my raw throat. I followed Elias out into my backyard. The flowers I'd planted last spring were dead from lack of nurturing. But I'd decided that was where I wanted him. Elias dug a small but deep hole, and I wrapped Rik in an extra white sheet I had for my bed. When Elias was done, I took a hesitant step forward.

I knelt next to the makeshift grave and peered down at Rik's wrapped body in my arms. The blood that hadn't dried had seeped through the sheet. I hugged him a little tighter for a moment before gently placing him into the hole.

"I promise I'll keep the garden in better shape for you," I said to Rik. Tears began to spill down my face again and I stood. Elias handed me the shovel and I tossed the loose dirt over Rik's body. Once I'd completely filled the hole, I dropped the shovel.

Elias pulled me into his arms. "I'm so sorry, Nova. We will find who did this."

"I need to find out how to log into my video feed."

CHAPTER TWENTY-TWO

I texted Tiffany and asked her if our dad happened to leave his phone behind. I'd planned to tell her about checking out the grocery store cameras when I saw her. That felt like something I should tell her in person. Our father hadn't been kidnapped — he'd chosen to leave. For what? Who knew. But this all seemed like suspicious timing. He'd left without a word and now Adalrik was dead.

I'd known this man my entire life and had never felt as though he'd betray me. But now, I wasn't so sure. He'd taught me everything I knew about cryptid hunting and raised me as his own. There was a twisting pain in my chest knowing that this could all be connected. Maybe my adoptive father wasn't who I thought he was. My father leaving, Adalrik's death, my uncle that wanted my soul . . . it was a lot all at once. Now I needed to figure out how to get into my home video feed.

I kept a brave face for Elias because he'd dealt with enough of my crying over the last few hours. With a quick shower, I roughly scrubbed the dirt and blood from my skin and ended it with cool water to soothe my swollen eyelids. I dried off, wrapped the towel around my body and hoped that Tiffany had responded. When I checked my phone, I saw her reply.

Tiff: *No sign of his phone. Why?*
Me: *I need to get into my camera that he put up around my house.*

The dots of Tiffany responding appeared.

161

Tiff: *He may have it on his laptop?*
Me: *I'm coming over.*

I dressed in a hurry in jeans and my typical loose T-shirt.

"Hey, can you fade us into my parents' house?" I asked Elias as I came out of my bedroom.

"Sure. What's going on?"

"Tiffany thinks there might be access to the videos on my dad's laptop. I want to see what this guy looks like who killed Rik."

Elias placed his hands in my wet strands of hair, then leaned down and placed a soft kiss on my lips. The gesture relaxed my tense muscles a bit as we faded out and then stood in my parents' living room. I hadn't even felt the heat I normally did.

Tiffany wandered in, a bowl of ice cream in her hands, and nearly dropped it when she saw us standing there.

"Holy shit," she said as she grabbed her chest. "I didn't think you'd appear within minutes."

"Sorry, it was the quickest way." Elias let his hands drop from my hair and took a step back.

"Dad's laptop is on the table in the kitchen." Tiffany headed toward the kitchen. Elias and I followed, and she set her bowl down on the counter. I strode straight to the table, flopped into the chair, and opened the laptop and naturally the first screen asked for a password.

"Do you know Dad's password?"

"No, he was always super secretive. I always thought maybe it was because he didn't want Mom or me to see his browser history."

I turned to her and arched a brow. "What? Gross." I tried a few different possible passwords until I ended up locked out. Dammit. I closed the laptop and glanced at Elias. He stood quietly in the corner of the room with his arms crossed over his chest.

"Lock yourself out?" Tiffany put a spoonful of ice cream in her mouth.

"What do you think?" I asked sarcastically.

"You know, Erica is really good with computers. Remember we talked about it at dinner the other night?"

"Do you think she can help with password stuff?"

"Probably." She pulled her phone from her back pocket and sent off a text. It took less than a minute for her phone to ding with a response.

"She said she's pretty sure she can hack into it. No problem."

"Can she come now?"

"What's the hurry, Nova? You never cared about the cameras before."

I swallowed against the burn in the back of my throat. I didn't even want to say the words because it made it so much more real.

"Nova, what's going on?" Tiff asked again. This time more urgently.

"Adalrik . . . Rik . . . is dead. Someone came into the house while Elias and I were gone and attacked him." My eyes started to water but I refused to allow the tears to fall.

Tiffany's brown eyes glistened instantly, and a tear tracked down her face. "Oh my god, Nova." She sat on a nearby stool and her face paled.

"I have to find out who came into the house."

Tiffany's head snapped toward me. "Do you think we'll be able to see who was responsible for this? Poor Rik." She sniffled.

"I'm not sure, but I really hope I have a clear shot of the killer's face on that feed."

"I'll see if Erica can come over right now."

"Thank you," I said softly. I tried to hold it together and Elias must've known. He stepped closer to me and reached out to grip my hand, squeezing gently. While we waited, I filled Tiffany in on the visit to the store and the videos Glenn had showed us.

"I can't believe that," Tiffany said.

"I don't know what Dad's doing. I really hope it isn't something that's going to hurt Mom even more."

A short while later, Erica arrived. I vacated the seat I was in so she could have full access to the laptop. I stood next to Elias as close as I could without touching his body. The heat that radiated from him was a comfort, and I wished I could crawl into his arms. I just wanted to sleep the rest of this horrible day away.

Erica pulled out a thumb drive from her backpack and plugged it into our dad's computer. She typed away for a few minutes. Tiffany and I shared a hopeful glance. "I've got it unlocked."

"Oh my god! Thank you, Erica!" Tiffany jumped up and down. She planted a kiss on her girlfriend's cheek.

"Okay, okay. You're welcome." She grinned. Elias cleared his throat. "We need to get into the camera feed at Nova's house. She doesn't have access to it, but Vincent does. He set it up for her."

Erica's dark brows furrowed. "How do you not have access?"

"Long story." I tried to wave off the excuses that came to the tip of my tongue.

"She basically figured she didn't need it until tall, dark, and handsome over there started showing up at her front door." Tiffany threw her thumb in Elias's direction. Elias smirked and his blue gaze took me in.

"That's not creepy or anything," Erica said.

I snorted and slapped my hand over my mouth. Elias and

Tiffany started laughing.

"How do you know your father has the camera software on his laptop?" Erica clicked a few more things on the computer screen.

"I saw him when he downloaded it after setting up the cameras at Nova's house," Tiff said.

"Well, luckily for you guys, looks like the credentials for the software was saved." Erica spun the laptop to face us.

As we viewed the footage, we came to the part where Elias and I left to go to the grocery store. Sometime later, a figure with a dark hoodie came to the door. Judging by this person's build, I would have guessed a male. But the hood over his head covered the majority of his face. I couldn't make out any definitive features. Dammit, Dad, why didn't you get the right angles?

"Is there any way to make the picture clearer?" I asked from behind Erica. Even if I couldn't see his face, maybe there was something else I could recognize.

"I can, but this guy has a hood covering his face. I don't think cleaning up the image will do any good." The hope I'd had that we would be able to see who killed Adalrik drained from me. I watched as the stranger on the screen picked the lock on my front door.

Elias and I shared a glance. This would mean the intruder was human. Picking locks wasn't something a cryptid would choose to do. Elias stood straighter, more alert. My gaze locked onto his. I already knew he'd heard something I couldn't.

What is it? I mouthed to him. I hoped Erica was distracted enough that she wouldn't notice.

"We need to get Erica out of here," Elias said aloud. So much for being discreet. Erica peeked up from the computer screen and glanced around at us. Pure confusion etched in her features.

"What?"

"Uhhh, we should go, babe. You know, just go to dinner or something," Tiffany said, trying to redirect her attention. She pulled Erica up by her arm, standing just as the door leading to the backyard burst open and sent chips of wood flying into the room.

My arm went up to protect my face and head. I stepped closer to Elias, and pulled my demon blades from my holster. Without warning, my wings shot out from my back. I really needed to practice how to control my abilities.

A rake stood on all fours in the doorway and glared at us.

"Do you assholes always have to destroy stuff? Can't you knock on the front door?" I growled. In response, the rake let out a shriek.

"I think that was a no," growled Elias.

"What the fuck is that?" I heard Erica shriek. But I was focused on this cryptid that stood halfway in my parent's house.

"Tiffany, get Erica out of here." Erica and Tiffany ran from the room just as the rake charged me. I spun my blades in my hands before I struck out to hit it in the chest. That was too easy. I watched as the dead rake fell to the kitchen floor and disappeared.

Elias came to my side and lightly touched my feathers, making me shiver.

"There's more out there."

"Then maybe we should take this outside, so we don't mess up my parent's house."

We headed out the door. I tucked my wings close to my body so I could fit through the doorway. I wasn't used to my wings being out. I hoped they would benefit me more than hinder my fighting capabilities.

In the yard stood several other creatures. Another rake, several ghouls, and a large scorpion man. Now, the ghouls and rake, I wasn't so worried about. The scorpion man, however, towered over Elias and me. His torso was that of a human with two large pincers, and a stinger the size of my entire body. In his human hands, he held a sword of his own.

"Uh, Elias, how do we kill the scorpion dude?" I whispered.

"Don't worry about it, I'll take him, and you take the others, angel face." We charged the creatures, and Elias's blade came out before we reached them. I cut down the last rake first. I sliced my blade through his abdomen, disemboweling him. The stench of his blood hit me. I didn't have time to be sick to my stomach. The ghouls surrounded me.

One of them jumped into the air and landed in a crouch directly in front of me. I slammed my dagger into its neck and kicked the ghoul back with my foot. I pulled my blade out in the same motion. He landed several feet away.

A second ghoul jumped on my back and crushed my sensitive wings. I screamed out of annoyance more than pain. I tried to knock him off by flexing my wings. The third creature was in front of me with a satisfied smirk on his face as he stalked forward. His grotesque rotted teeth gleamed with saliva. I refused to be these guy's dinner. Or worse, have them take me to the one who wanted my soul. My hands erupted into flames of their own accord. I tried to push the inferno towards the sneering cryptid but nothing happened. So, instead, I threw one of my blades at him, aiming for his head. The steel embedded into his forehead. It let out a blood curdling scream and stumbled back before fading away.

My hands still blazed. I dropped my remaining weapon on the grass and grabbed onto the arms of the ghoul that was still on my back. His skin sizzled and he let go of me immediately. I spun and dropped low to the ground, picking up my demon blade. I kicked out my leg, taking the ghoul to the ground. Before I had the opportunity to give it a killing blow, Tiffany brought her sword down, decapitating it. Its head rolled across the grass. My flames evaporated from my hands. I took a few deep breaths and grabbed my blood-soaked demon blade I had thrown from the ground.

"Sorry, it took me so long. I had to get Erica away from here."

"No worries.". I spotted Elias over her shoulder. He was still in a battle with the scorpion man. It seemed like they are both pretty good at holding each other off. I lifted my chin toward them, and Tiffany turned, her jaw dropped.

"What the hell?"

"Let's go." We ran over to help Elias. Tiffany kept up with me. The moment we were within range, the scorpion's pincer tried to take a chunk out of Tiffany. She narrowly blocked it with her sword. She jumped back a few feet to get out of the creature's reach.

"We want the hybrid. Give us the girl and we will stop coming," the scorpion man said.

"Not a chance in hell," Elias said through clenched teeth and lunged. He barely missed one of his legs.

"Then you will all die."

"Been there, done that, asshole," Elias retorted.

The cryptid tried to clasp Tiffany with his pincer again. But this time, Tiff brought her sword down, removing the appendage. Blood spilled out of the wound, and he let out a roar that shook the ground. Elias took his opportunity. All he needed was a distraction. His onyx wings broke free from his back. He leapt into the air; his wings beating a few times before he landed on the shoulders of the scorpion. Elias's sword quickly glided across the creature's thick neck. Blood spurted out several feet. The scorpion man stumbled and gripped his gushing throat.

Elias jumped to the ground before the creature fell. The creature gasped for air. But with the deep laceration, he choked on his own blood. It took a moment for him to still.

When he did, he evaporated. Elias came to stand in front of me. His hand brushed against my cheek gently.

"Are you all right?" he asked me. He wasn't even out of breath and pulled his wings in tightly.

"I am. Are you?" He nodded before and placed a kiss on my lips.

"That was insane!" We whipped around toward Erica's voice. Her face was pale and her eyes wide.

"I told you to stay where I put you," Tiffany grumbled.

"There's no way I was missing out on this. Is this why you're taking folklore? Because they're real?"

"Erica." Tiffany stepped toward her. "I'm not taking folklore; it was research for personal use. But you can't tell anyone what you saw. Not about the creatures or us." Tiffany pointed to herself then to Elias and me.

"I promise, I won't. And even if I did, who would believe me? My girlfriend just kicked some weird demon's ass! This is so cool." I giggled and rolled my eyes. My attention went back to Elias who also had a smirk on his face.

"Technically, not a demon," Tiffany giggled.

Chapter Twenty-Three

"Have you been able to get ahold of Matthew? See if he found anything?" I asked.

"You know, since the last time we saw him, he hasn't been responding to my texts," Tiffany said. I sighed as I crossed my arms. It was probably my fault. I should've never let Tiff bring him into this. He was still too hurt by our breakup even though it was a while back. I wouldn't blame him for stepping away from this problem because of the tension between us. I could have been nicer, more caring. I knew it was my fault.

I pulled my phone out and dialed his number. It rang and rang and then went to voicemail. I hung up and sent him a text.

Me: *Hey, Matt. Can you call me when you have a sec?*

I waited for a few moments to see if the dots appear, letting me know that he was responding. But nothing. I put my phone in my back pocket. I would have to let him take his time answering me. I didn't deserve his immediate attention anyway.

Erica was in the corner of my parent's living room with Elias. Her eyes were bright, and she questioned Elias about what she had just witnessed. I strode over to them.

"So, how do you guys have wings? Does Tiff have them too?" I heard her ask.

"No, Tiffany doesn't have wings," I replied and met Elias's gaze. "Elias and I aren't technically human. Tiffany is considered a human, just like you."

"How did you come into this life? I mean I'm still shaking from watching you guys. You must be pumped full of adrenaline."

"Normally, hunters are born into their rolls. I was given to the Alexanders because my mother and father couldn't care for me in their realms." I didn't go into too much into detail. Although, it wasn't like she would be surprised at this point.

"And I'm not a hunter by nature. I'm a soldier," Elias chimed in. Erica frowned slightly.

"A soldier? For whom?"

"Okayyyy, enough badgering my sister and her boyfriend," Tiffany said. She placed a hand on Erica's shoulder. We hadn't corrected Tiffany's boyfriend comment and I felt my cheeks warm.

"This is stuff that I only see in movies or video games. I'm not trying to bombard them, but this is insane."

"One day, I'll tell you everything. But right now, we should get you home, where it's safer."

"How do you know I'm safer at home? What if those things come after me?" Erica asked.

"It's unlikely, since they want Nova," Elias said.

"What do they want from Nova?" Tiffany pulled her away and I let them both know we would be leaving.

"I'm going to make sure Erica gets home okay."

"But I want to know more!" Erica whined.

"There's plenty of time for those answers . . . another time." Tiffany disappeared down the hall with Erica. I heard the front door as it opened and closed.

"That chick asks a lot of questions." Elias leaned against the wall and crossed his arms over his chest. His muscles flexed. I tried not to gape openly at him. Not that I thought he would mind.

"Can you blame her? She just saw a bunch of cryptids that

are only rumored to exist."

"True." He unraveled his body and stalked toward me. He wrapped an arm around my waist and pulled me into him. He gave me a quick kiss on the lips and when he started to pull away. I pulled him back down to my mouth. My stomach dipped and Elias's deep growl sent a shiver through me.

My phone buzzed. It pulled me from the haze of oncoming lust and Elias broke our kiss. He stroked my cheek with his thumb. I let out a sigh of frustration and reached into my back pocket and pulled out my phone.

"Sorry," I mumbled. But he didn't seem the least bit bothered. I unlocked the screen and sure enough, there was a text from Matt.

Matt: *Can we meet up?*

I glided my thumbs across the touchscreen and replied.

Me: *Sure. Where and when?*

Matt: *Can we meet at my place? The sooner the better. I have something I want to go over with you, and it'd be better if you came alone.*

Me: *I'll be over soon.*

I put my phone back in my pocket.

"Matt wants me to go to his place to discuss something. Maybe he finally has answers for us."

"Great, let's go." Elias took a step forward, but I put my hand against his hard chest. He glanced down at my hand and frowned.

"He doesn't want anyone else coming. I know you make him uncomfortable," I said. "Can you go back to my house, and I'll come back and tell you all about it."

"Are you sure it's a good idea you're going by yourself?" His hands rubbed up and down my bare upper arms. I was glad Elias worried about me and I knew that was his job. But did he honestly think that Matthew would hurt me? I mean, I had known him for a good amount of time. I never felt like he'd harm me.

"I'll be fine. I can take care of myself, you know?"

"There have been few times where my intervention was needed if I remember correctly." Elias's smirk appeared and I wanted to kiss those sensual lips of his. But this wasn't the time and there would be plenty of all that and then some later. Maybe Elias and I could reenact what happened between us last night.

"Okay, but you have to wait outside and make sure Matt doesn't know you're there." I ran my hand over his chest.

"Deal. But if anything seems strange, you yell for me." He took my hand from his chest and kissed my knuckles. "Be safe, angel face."

I strolled up the stone walkway to Matthew's place. He lived with his grandfather since he often needed help around the house and had become more forgetful. But I didn't see his grandfather's car in the driveway. So, it must just be Matthew that was home. Low lights illuminated the windows. The home was an older brick-faced house that had been in Matt's family for generations. And one day, it would be passed down to him. Elias faded us to Matt's house and waited across the street for me. I peeked over my shoulder at Elias. His eyes glowed softly in the fading light. The sun was setting fast.

I turned back and took a deep breath before I raised my hand to knock on the door. I didn't want us to argue tonight. I knew I was a bitch to him, but I was going to do my best to play nice. My knuckles rapped against the wooden door, and I heard footsteps approach from inside.

Matt opened the door and stepped back to allow me to come in. I noticed he looked tense. His hair wasn't styled like it normally was. His brown hair is fell across his forehead, and he pushed it back. He was dressed in a black T-shirt and jeans with boots he normally wore to go hunting.

"Hi," I managed to say.

"Hey, Nova." He closed the door behind me as I stepped into the house. I let him lead me through the parlor toward the back room of the first floor. Which happened to be his grandfather's library. It was where he kept the old tomes about cryptids. The walls were lined with bookshelves, and all were completely full. Even on some of the shelves there were books stacked messily on top of each other.

In the center of the room there was an antique table and chair set. More books were strewn across it. Matt took a seat in one of the chairs and gestured for me to take a seat across from him. I strode to the chair and sat. He opened a book that was already on the table in front of him. It wasn't like any book I had ever seen. The pages were aged, but the cover was pristine. Ancient writing was engraved in the black leather on the front. There were also symbols etched into the pages. I had no idea what they meant but I didn't have a good feeling about it. He found the page he had searched for and leaned forward, sliding the book toward me.

My fingers grazed the edges of the pages. I glanced at Matt as I leaned forward and then peeked down at what he wanted to show me. An illustration. A male dressed in a knee length tunic with short sleeves. But that wasn't what drew my attention. There were horns sprouted from the man's skull and wings protruding from his back. Wings just like mine. White that gradually progressed into black tips.

The last hybrid.

"Turn the page," Matt said gruffly. And I did.

The hybrid from the previous page was on his knees and crowded by demons. One of which stood behind him. The demon held the hybrid's long hair between clawed fingers. A blade pressed into his throat. This was his execution. When Lucifer's soldiers were sent to murder him. My stomach twisted and I lifted my gaze to Matt.

"Where did you find this?" I whispered.

"Apparently, my grandfather has a secret hidden collection of his oldest books." I couldn't help but wonder how long Matt had this book. And why was he ignoring Tiffany's calls if he had information. He promised he'd give us any info he found. I cleared my throat before I asked.

"When did you find this book?" I tried to sound as nonchalant as possible. Matt's stare locked onto me and there was something indecipherable. In the years I had come to know him, I've never seen the expression he gave me now. My stomach curled with dread. He lunged across the table at me, but I anticipated it and threw my chair back. I jumped back to put distance between us.

"What the hell, Matt!"

"You think I want to be your little errand boy? Is that what you think? While you go around and whore yourself out." Jealousy. Plain and simple. He circled around the table, and I moved to keep distance between us. I didn't go for my weapons at my waist that I had hidden. I didn't want to hurt Matt, even if he didn't feel the same about me.

"Matt . . ."

"Shut up, Nova! I don't want to hear your bullshit excuses. I could've given you a somewhat normal life. Kids and marriage — a house. But you'd rather be with some random." My stomach soured. This was a side of him I had never fathomed. Hurtful and harsh words. This wasn't the person I knew for the last few years. The person in front of me was a stranger. I didn't want this to go to a place where either of us obtained injuries. Matt's face reddened more by the moment, and it was a sign of his brewing rage.

"Matt, calm down. We can talk about this like normal people." I held my hands up trying to show him that I wasn't the enemy here. I had no blades in my hands. But that didn't matter, Matt pulled out one of his own. We continued to circle the antique table.

My heart sank. He twirled it expertly in his hand.

"But you're not even a person, Nova. You're a hybrid whore." I jerked back. Too stunned to say anything. I felt like I'd been slapped in the face. "You know, I would've forgotten the deal I'd agreed to, if you'd chosen to be with me. But you didn't. I'm not good enough, right? I took that page from the book so you wouldn't find the writings from your uncle. So, you wouldn't know that I'd been the one to give him access to my grandfather's collection before I gave them to you. He needed the spell . . . to know how to take what he wants." Spittle came from his mouth.

"Please tell me you didn't make a deal with Azvameth." My blood drained from my face in realization. This whole time Matt had been collaborating with the enemy.

"He promised me power and wealth beyond my imagination." Matt had been siding with the on Azvameth's side the entire time. "I came by, expecting you to be home. But you were out with that guy." My gut clenched further.

"You killed Adalrik, didn't you?" I asked. The fresh wound in my heart from Rik's death burned. Now that I knew Matt was responsible for Rik's death, the shit was about to hit the fan. I reached under my shirt and pulled out my demon blades. The writing glowed brightly, fueled by my rage.

Matt pulled his arm back and threw his blade. I leaned to my right to avoid being hit. It managed to graze my upper arm. My skin burned. I hissed in pain, but I didn't hesitate to take my chance. I leapt onto the table and charged him. As I was about to land on top of Matt and take his sorry ass out, he disappeared. I landed in a crouch on the hardwood floor. I popped up and spun around searching for the traitor.

Matt appeared in front of me, and I staggered back in surprise. What the hell was going on?

He started laughing hysterically and twirled another blade in his hand. My shock washed away my thought process.

"The little troll didn't recognize me. I kept my face well hidden beneath my hood. Azvameth was so impressed with my ability to prove to him that I would go to such lengths — to kill one of your best friends — that he gave me this new ability. This new power inside of me — this is just the beginning, Nova. So why don't you surrender before you end up hurt?"

"Fuck. You." My wings filled the space around me and now it was Matt who was surprised. I lunged at him but he managed to take my legs out from under me. He pounced on me. The weight that pressed down on me smashed my wings beneath me. I cried out from the sensitivity and threw my arm up to stab him in his stupid face. I sliced his cheek. I could feel the wetness when it dripped down onto my lips. If I wasn't fighting for my life, I'd washed myself with bleach.

"You stupid bitch!" Matt back handed me across the face and pressed his blade to my throat. I saw stars from the force of his strike. I pried my already swelling eye open and glared up at him. This fight was *not* going to end in his favor.

"Matthew," a deep, velvety voice echoed throughout the library. "I told you to bring her to me, not kill her before I can take her soul." The fury in Matt's face didn't subside. His gazewas still locked on me. But Matt climbed off me and I scrambled to my feet. My wings thanked me. I managed to keep hold of my weapons.

My gaze landed on a tall man with dark hair and black eyes. Similar to Cyrus. He was in a form fitted suit and everything about him radiated power. He cocked his head to the side, and I realized he admired my wings that were splayed out behind me.

"I was wondering if your mishap with the wendigo had taken you to your mother. But obviously . . ." He stopped short and gestured a hand at my feathers. He took a few steps toward me, and my body shivered. I refused to show weakness by cowering from him. I held my head high and glared at the demon before me. His fingers brushed over my bruised face, and I growled in disgust.

"Don't touch me, you demon fuck!" I spat. The burning in my arm intensified. I couldn't understand why it was getting worse and not better. That wasn't normal for me. I should've started to heal. The pain was hard to ignore as it increased. My arms didn't budge as I swiped out with both of my demon blades. My fingers became weak, and I dropped my weapons to the floor. My last hope was to summon my fire. No amount of effort brought the blaze to my hands. Nothing.

I was so screwed.

CHAPTER TWENTY-FOUR

"Azvameth, do you need me to take care of her," Matt asked from behind the demon.

"No, Matthew. You've done enough by getting her here. And by using the Devil's breath."

My stomach sank as fatigue started to set in and I realized why my arm hadn't healed. Matt must've used the Devil's breath on his blade to incapacitate me. If he'd used enough of it from the flower, I may even start to hallucinate.

"Elias . . ." I tried to call for him and I was so tired and weak. I blinked slowly. My limbs grew even heavier. I fell to my knees. I tried to catch the edge of the table, but it was no use. With Elias's hearing, I didn't understand why he hadn't come.

Matt and Azvameth's voices started to sound far away. My vision started to turn to pin pricks, the edges faded gradually. I tried to pry my eyes open again. There was only blurriness.

I vaguely felt someone lift me into their arms and smell the scent of cedar and leather hit me. It was familiar so it must've been Matt. Once upon a time, I would've loved the sensation of his body as it held onto mine and his scent. But now I just wished I could kick him in the balls and take back my power. I needed Elias. He'd be able to get me out of here.

Azvameth stepped toward me and wrapped me in his darkness before I completely lost consciousness.

When I peeled my eyes open, my head pounded. Everything was blurry and I could only make out that I was laying down on a hard, cold surface. When I tried to put a hand to my forehead, I realized I wasn't able to move my arm. It wasn't from the Devil's breath either. I pulled harder but a metallic sound rang throughout the room. I felt the cool shackles around my wrists. My arms were extended above my head. I moved my legs, but they were also restrained. My feet were bare and cold. I turned my head from side to side and tried to figure out where I was. Azvameth must've faded us out. At some point my wings retracted because I didn't feel them under me any longer.

I hoped Elias knew I was in trouble. I knew he'd felt it before when the wendigo almost killed me. I hoped he felt it this time.

Candles were lit throughout the room that illuminated the dank walls. When I lifted my head, I saw a worn metal door that had once been blue. With how deteriorated it was, there were only a few sections of chipped paint left. No windows. I glanced to my left and saw a table with at least ten lit candles and dried herbs in glass jars. Great. An altar.

The door creaked open, and I jerked my head toward the noise. A woman with dark skin and a blood red cape covering most of her head came gliding in. I didn't recognize her, and I squinted. My gaze dropped to the large leather-bound book she had in her arms. She closed the door behind her and faced me.

"Oh good, you're awake," she said as she strolled to the table. She placed the book down on it. She lowered her hood, and I could see more of her features. A head full of tight curls framed her face and large earrings with pentagrams dangled from her ears.

"You're a witch," I rasped. My voice didn't even sound like my own. The Devil's breath left my mouth and throat raw. Her dark eyes locked onto me, and she gave me a grin but said nothing. "Please . . ."

"I am Azvameth's witch. I will not disobey him. He's

promised me too much."

"What are you going to do?" I feared the answer. My stomach burned with anxiety.

"We've been trying very hard to get the cryptids to bring you to him. But apparently you are quite the fighter. So, we changed our approach. Tonight, Azvameth will have what he's been waiting years for." I pulled on my restraints making the metal clang.

"My soul." It wasn't a question. This was what he had been after for a long time now. She gave me a slight nod and the back of my eyes burned.

"Yes. But it's more than that, my dear. Infinite power and control of the two highest realms. Once he has your soul, he'll be able to ramp up his power by staying in Hell for an extended period of time. Or at the very least, one of the realms in Hell."

Before I could respond, the door swung open again and Azvameth strolled in. Again, his power radiated. His dark eyes took me in as he came closer to the table I was chained to. His hands were clasped behind his back. He tilted his head to the side and examined me.

"Are we ready, Vita?"

"Wait!" I cried.

Azvameth smiled. "I've waited quite some time for you, Nova. And to think, the wendigo almost obtained your soul for himself. I would've had to wait another Satan knows how long for another hybrid. I don't think I can wait any longer." He curled a finger around a strand of my wild hair and pushed it out of my face. I shivered from disgust but tried to hide it.

"What are you going to do with the power? Take over the realms?" I asked, and he chuckled. If I could get him to talk, maybe it would prolong the process.

"That's none of your concern, really. But I guess since

you'll be dead shortly, I can tell you while Vita gets every-thing prepared." My eyes flicked over to the woman in ques-tion. Sure, enough she poured items and ingredients into a bowl. My gaze went back to the demon that glared down at me. "I intend to take over Heaven and Hell. Instead of there being two separate rulers for each realm, there will only be one. Me."

"Won't that cause a war?"

"Oh, I'm sure there will be a war. But in the end, I will win. And do you understand why I will win?"

"Because of me."

"Exactly. Your soul will allow me to overpower Lucifer and God. Perhaps even annihilate them both. I may even take over Earth when the other realms are mine." His black eyes gleamed with satisfaction in the candlelight.

"Azvameth, I need your blood," Vita called over. Azva-meth turned and went toward the table. He rolled up the sleeve on his crisp black dress shirt and presented his wrist to Vita. She took a dagger from her hip and sliced the demon's wrist.

Dark blood poured from his arm into the bowl she'd mixed everything else. Vita took a rag and pressed it to the demon's wound. While Azvameth staunched the flow, Vita placed her hands over the bowl and whispered words so low I couldn't hear. My heart pounded in my chest. I was in over my head.

I swallowed hard and pulled on my manacles. I tried as hard as I could to get my hands to slip through. But they were too tight, and my hands quickly grew raw from the metal. I tried again for my fire, but nothing even sparked. I wasn't sure there was any good it could do if I was able to summon it anyway.

I heard a deep chuckle and realized Azvameth was watch-ing me.

"Not only did the Devil's breath make your powers null,

but Vita charmed the chains. You are unable to use any of your abilities. Precautions and such."

"You can't do this!" I continued to pull my arms and kick my legs. But it was no use.

Vita came around the table and hovered over me. She dipped her fingers into the mixture she concocted and pressed her finger to my forehead. I thrashed my head so she couldn't write whatever it was she needed to. But Azvameth gripped my face roughly with one large hand and held me immobile. My cheeks ached from the bruising grip.

I closed my eyes tightly. Not wanting to stare at the demon who flipped my world upside-down the last few weeks. He was the reason why one of my best friends was gone and why another had turned his back on me. Betrayal. I silently promised myself if I managed to get out of this, Matthew was a dead man. But who was I kidding, I couldn't get out of this. If Elias hadn't been able to help me at Matt's house, how would he ever be able to help me here? In some abandoned room.

"Place your hand on her chest." Azvameth released his grip on my face and slid his hand down between my breasts. I knew he could feel the thrumming of my heart. I opened my eyes and my uncle stood above me with his large hand over my sternum. Eyes as black as night stared back at me.

Vita started to chant and at first nothing happened.

"You're a coward. You have the creatures and Matt come after me instead of yourself." I spat in Azvameth's face. He wiped the spit from his cheek and licked it off of his fingers. Disgusting.

"As much as I like a little fight from my victims, dear niece, now is not the time." His unfazed grin filled me with nausea.

After a few moments I felt the pain in my chest, similar to when the wendigo almost succeeded. One pulse and then a tug. I screamed in agony as pain ripped through me. My body tensed with each slow pull. A blue light flowed from my chest and wrapped around Azvameth's forearm. His black eyes turned the color of my soul, glowing intensely. With each drag of my soul leaving my body, the torment intensified and I screamed out again. My ears rang and I was quickly losing myself. I closed my eyes tightly against the pain.

My mind went to Elias and how I had never confessed that he was my mate. My soulmate. I would never free him from his punishment. My mother should've been able to help me but why hasn't she. *Mom, where are you?* I silently asked. I prayed that she could hear me and interfere in some way. *I'm dying.* I was close to losing consciousness and the tugging hadn't stopped. But I tried to hold on. My heartbeat slowed and my tense body started to give up.

A rush of energy and heat pulsed through the room. My eyes opened but my vision blurred. I blinked a few times, slightly clearing my sight.

"Azvameth!" a deep voice boomed. The walls shook with the force of it. I felt the demon's hand when it left my chest and I took a breath. The blue light that was wrapped around Azvameth's arm, released, and slammed back into my torso. My back arched off the table when I felt the sensation of, what I could only assume was my soul, settle back into my body. The voice was familiar. My head lolled to the side. The pain left my body, but I was incredibly weakened.

"Hello, brother," Azvameth said. I felt my brows pull into a frown. And then hands were on my face. Warm calloused hands.

Vita's chanting stopped. There was a gurgling sound.

"Dammit. Do you know how long it took me to find a loyal witch to help me?" Azvameth's voice rose in anger.

"You bastard! You try to take your own niece's soul? My *only* child." Cyrus's again.

I jerked at the sound of metal clanging and opened my eyes to slits. Blue ones stared into my own and I choked on a cry.

184

My heavy arms were released from their restraints.

"I got you, angel face," Elias whispered. He brought down his short sword on the chains that held my legs. The manacles were still intact, but I could move. With all my energy I threw my arms around Elias. His hands rubbed up and down my back. He lifted me from the table and placed me on my feet. I glanced down and Vita's still body was sprawled out on the stone floor. Her heart had been ripped from her chest and the blood was no longer flowing. I searched for Cyrus. His blood covered hands were on Azvameth and he kept him pinned against the wall. His face was in his demon form and a promise of death in his eyes.

Cyrus's clawed hand went to Azvameth's throat. The flesh of his neck, steaming from the heat of his hand. My uncle's face contorted in pain.

"Brother, please," he choked out. Even in my weakened state, rage overtook me. I could hardly move. But if I could, I would beat my uncle to a pulp. Cyrus's grasp loosened on his throat. Azvameth must have taken that as his opportunity because he snapped his fingers, and he was gone.

"Where did he go?' I yelled. Cyrus glanced at me; his demon features faded—aside from the black eyes.

"Most likely into hiding." I would've fallen back from fatigue if Elias hadn't been holding me upright. His arm tightened around me. If my father weren't here, I'd lean into him more, bask in the heat of his body to warm the deep chill that invaded me to my bones.

Cyrus's eye bore into Elias with anger. "This was your job. And you allowed her to go alone to that hunter's house."

"I'm the one that told Elias to stay outside, to let me go alone. Matt had information for me."

"I knew something was wrong. The moment I tried to get into Matthew's house a ward went up. I tried to break the windows, knock down the door. No matter what I did I couldn't get in. I knew I needed to get to you — that something was wrong." Elias choked. "I could hear you and then I couldn't, and I feared the worst."

"And what information could be more important than my daughter's safety? You should've been inside with her!" He glared at the arm Elias placed around me and snarled.

"You haven't been in my life for twenty-three years. And now suddenly you want to be part of it? Who said you get to choose what I do? Who am I allowed to be with?" I yelled and poked my finger into his chest.

"Allowed to be with?" he whispered and glanced at Elias. "Elias, I thought your punishment made it clear, to keep your low-ranking hands off of my daughter." He lunged for Elias and I stumbled putting myself between them. I threw my arms out to cover him with my own body.

"Keep your hands off of my mate," I growled as I stared him down. I felt my wings as they fought to come out. But I didn't allow it.

"Mate?" Elias whispered from behind me.

"You must've been talking with your mother when you had your little visit. Did she happen to mention you can have more than one mate?" Cyrus gave me cruel sneer.

"I don't believe you. But he's mine, so if you lay another finger on him, I swear, I'll flay your skin from your demonic body and feed it to the birds." I refused to believe my demon father over my angel mother. Afterall, demons were tricksters and liars.

"Now, daughter, you really do have a demonic side."

"I'm just getting started."

CHAPTER TWENTY-FIVE

Cyrus wanted us to come back to Hell so I could rest for a while and maybe acquire more powers. But that was the last place I wanted to be. I would rather be with Elias. Alone. Obviously, we had some things to talk about. He faded us into my bedroom, and I nearly fell onto my bed from exhaustion. Elias helped keep me upright and held my hand as I sat on the edge of the mattress.

He hadn't so much as glanced at me since the whole soulmate reveal. I felt hurt by his reaction. Even now he tried to turn from me, but I grabbed onto his arm.

"Elias." I stared at my dirty fingers as I gripped onto his forearm.

"How long have you known?" I swallowed. I wasn't sure if he'd be angry at me for keeping it from him. But this was what I was afraid of. That he wouldn't be able to accept it. I knew his heart still hurt from all those years ago when he lost his life and was punished for killing those men. I couldn't help but wonder if he thought he was betraying her. The wife who left this world hundreds of years ago.

"Since the healing tonic my mother gave me for you."

"Shit, Nova." My stomach sank. Elias ran his fingers through his hair.

"I didn't want to let it get in the way of what's already going on. And when you told me about your wife, I just figured it may never be a good time to tell you. But if it means that I can protect you from Cyrus's wrath, I'm willing to spill that detail."

I glanced up at Elias to see his eyes finally locked onto me. My chest ached. I was okay letting it be known if it meant he'd be protected. Even if he didn't want to be with me. He rubbed his scruffy jaw. Then, he planted both of his fists on either side of my thighs. His hands sank into the bed. He was close. I felt his breath on my lips, but I wasn't going to push this mate thing. So, I didn't move.

His eyes glowed and flicked to my mouth. I licked my dry lips. "I wish you would've told me. And I wish the first time I heard the truth wasn't in front of Cyrus."

I inhaled. "Why?"

"Because I can't get rid of you, Nova. No matter how hard I try. Every waking moment is filled with thoughts of you. Your violet eyes, your sassy fucking mouth, and the way you make me feel. You're a brat but I love every moment of it. Even feeling when things were wrong — like with the wendigo — it makes sense now."

"I am not a brat." I wrinkled my nose. "I didn't want to push things. Especially because of your loss."

"What if I want you to push things? What if *I* want to push things?" Elias leaned in and placed a tender kiss on my lips. My stomach clenched. "And my loss? Really? That was five hundred years ago. I've had plenty of time to work through the grief and accept it. I can move on."

"I think I might like that." I breathed a sigh of relief.

"When I couldn't get to you, I panicked. Cyrus was royally pissed. He promised me another whipping for not watching you closely enough. I knew better than to let you go to Matt's house without me, but I don't want to hold you back. I trusted that you could handle Matt. But I didn't expect your uncle to be there." For the first time, I saw pain in Elias's expression. Regret. "If Azvameth would've completed that ritual, I wouldn't be able to go on. I lost one love already. I can't lose another." My skin broke out in goosebumps at Elias's confession.

Could he really love me? I barely ever mumbled those words to Matt when we were together. I'm not sure I ever meant it either. Could I love Elias? I thought I could. But I didn't reply. My hands wrapped around the back his neck, and I pulled him to me. My lips molded to his. My tension from this hell of a night slowly dissipated. Elias's hands cupped my face as our kiss became more feverish.

I reached for his pants, but his hand stopped me. He broke our kiss. The fiery glow of his eyes told me he wanted me just as much as I wanted him.

"As much as I'd love to fuck you until you can't remember your own name, we should clean you up." I groaned. "And get these manacles off of you." His thumb brushed over the iron still wrapped around my wrist. Right.

Elias managed to break the manacles and helped me shower. He even went so far to help me wash my hair and combed out all the tangles afterwards. I never could've pictured this, but I wasn't complaining. By the time he helped me get into clothes, I was beyond exhausted.

Elias pulled the comforter and sheets down on my bed and I slid under the covers. He kicked off his pants, leaving him in only his boxer briefs that hugged him perfectly. He slid in behind me, wrapping me in his arms. I melted into him and the steady rhythm of his chest as it rose and fell against my back.

"Are we safe here tonight?" I asked.

"Cyrus put a temporary blockade around the house. Only you and I can come and go. It should last for at least two days."

"Does that mean my favorite uncle can't weasel his way in here."

"Azvameth can't break through the barrier. And if he did, I'd kill him on the spot."

"Not if I kill him first," I said.

"How about we kill him together?"

"Deal." My voice sounded groggy. I started to drift off to sleep but I felt Elias kiss my head.

"I'll protect you with my life," he said barely above a whisper. I smiled sleepily.

I snuggled in closer to him and enjoyed the heat from his body before the real war started.

The war between Azvameth and me.

CHAPTER TWENTY-SIX

I slept the hardest I ever had. I probably would've slept longer if Elias hadn't been peppering my jaw with soft kisses. His fingers dug into my flesh at my waist, and it caused me to rub my thighs together. My clit throbbed with need.

Elias's pushed his hand beneath the band of my shorts and brushed against my mound. I spread instantly. Elias pulled my panties to the side and he dipped his fingers into my wetness. The moment his fingers parted me, I let out a moan. He was so close to my clit but kept teasing me by bypassing it. He thrust two fingers into me, and I nearly shattered around him as soon as he entered me. Slowly and tortuously, he pumped his fingers into me. My back arched off the bed as I felt the tension build. I clenched and fluttered around his digits greedily. And when he brushed his thumb over my bud, it sent me into climax. Elias withdrew his hand from my shorts.

I pulled my shorts down my thighs and kicked them off completely. I reached over to Elias and gripped his hardness through his briefs. His groan rumbled through my body, and he pushed off his bottoms quickly. I gripped him again and stroked his silky flesh. My mouth hovered over his cock and licked the bead of moisture from his tip. He shuddered and I took him into my mouth completely. I moved my hand up and down as I bobbed on his length. A groan of satisfaction came from him, and his fingers tangled in my hair. He pushed me farther down, shoving his cock going deep into my throat. I gagged but continued to take him as deeply as I could manage.

"Your pretty mouth on me is perfect but I want to be inside of you, Nova." His hand released my tresses and I pulled away from him.

I turned to my side with my back against his chest, guiding him into me pushing myself back to completely sheath him. The pace was slow, and Elias moved his hips from behind me. He gripped my breast and nipped at my shoulder. His fingers created a series of goosebumps all over my body.

I peered over my shoulder at him, and the evidence of his pleasure was written all over his face. "You're so beautiful." I gave him a sultry smile and pushed my ass back harder wanting to have him fill me completely. My legs started to shake with my impending orgasm.

"Oh, Elias. I'm going to come." I squeezed my eyes shut tightly.

"No, angel face." He gripped my chin. "Look at me while I make you come on my cock."

I forced my eyes open and gazed at him as I spasmed around his hard length. My body quivered from the after-shocks of my ecstasy. Elias started pumping harder into me. His body stiffened, and he groaned as he released into me.

"That was not what I was expecting to wake up to," I said with a satisfied sigh.

"I feel like I let you down last night by not giving you what you wanted. But you needed your rest." I peeked back at Elias again and gave him a smile as I bit my lower lip. He pulled out of me and kissed my shoulder.

"Well, you definitely made up for it."

Elias stood and pulled on his briefs and pants.

"Where are you going?" He tossed my shorts to me.

"I want to show you something."

I pulled my shorts on. Elias grabbed my hand and pulled me up from the bed. He led me to my back door. I didn't know what he wanted to show me.

"Close your eyes." We stepped into the backyard, and he guided me a few steps before stopping me. He placed his hands on my shoulders.

"When I tell you to, open your eyes." He turned me around and stepped aside.

"Okay, open them."

When I opened my eyes, the sun was high in the sky. I viewed the area in my garden that was once dirt only a couple of days ago. The area where we had buried Adalrik. But instead of the dirt mound, there were flowers of varying colors in bloom. My whole garden was filled with the scent of them. From snapdragons to tulips to daisies—no dirt was visible with the vibrant flowers that took up the entire space. In the center of them was a ceramic garden gnome. It had a pointed red hat and blue shirt that were nothing like what real gnomes wore. But the beard was correct, and it made me miss Rik even more.

"You did this?" My voice cracked.

"I can't take all the credit. All I did was get a few plants and water the garden you admitted to neglecting. I bought a gnome to mark where Rik is. I tried to find one that resembles him the most, but this was the best I could do."

A warm breeze picked up my blonde strands and my eyes burned with the need to cry. Rik's body must have allowed the flowers to bloom in excess.

"Thank you." A tear slipped down my cheek.

"I hardly did anything. There's no need to thank me. Now I think I know why they call them garden gnomes."

"You've done more than you realize." Elias swiped his thumb across my cheek to wipe away the tear.

Just the garden gnome itself, as a memorial, was the sweetest thing anyone had ever done for me. Now I had a beautiful garden and memorial for my friend. I turned to Elias and wrapped my arms around his waist. My face burrowed into his hard chest and his hands came around me.

"Are you okay?"

"I'm perfect." I sniffled. We continued to stand in the grass for a while. I enjoyed the feel of the sun on my skin and the cloudless morning. The bumble bees buzzed around the flowers in the garden, and a butterfly floated by. I inhaled the sweet air and relaxed against my mate.

"I want to find Matt," I said into Elias's chest.

"We can go to his house. But I'm sure if he knows of your escape he won't be there."

"I still want to check."

"Okay, let's go get ready and I can fade us there." I nodded into his chest before we broke apart and headed back into the house to get ready.

Elias faded us to Matt's house right in front of the driveway. I untangled my arms from him and noticed the car in the driveway. So, Matt must not have heard of my escape. I glanced at Elias and gave him a grin. He must've understood my thoughts by my facial expressions because he just nodded. We both marched the path to the front door.

"Should we knock?" Elias asked.

"I have a better idea." I called my fire to my hands. It took a moment, but a few sparks came from my fingers. I furrowed my brow as I concentrated harder on what I wanted to accomplish. A few flames ignited in varying colors ranging from orange to blue. Small but there. Before they had the opportunity to resorb, I placed my hands against the cool wooden door, and it started to smoke and caught fire quickly. It was all luck because the moment the door erupted in flames, my hands extinguished. This was pure Hell fire. And I was ready to kick Matt's ass for what he had put me through. The door incinerated before us but didn't continue to burn after the door was destroyed. It snuffed out. Smoke curled and embers floated through the air. I stepped through the large hole that I'd had created and skipped over the ashes with my black boots.

Just as Elias stepped in behind me, Matt came around the corner. Probably to see what all the noise was about. His eyes widened and he turned to run. Elias faded in directly in front of him and grabbed him by the collar of his T-shirt. Matt was thrown to the floor in front of me with such force, I was surprised his shoulder wasn't busted from the jarring landing.

"Why didn't you just disappear instead of running? You know, your neat trick Azvameth allowed you to do?" I squatted in front of Matt, and he scurried back. He bumped into Elias's legs. I realized how tired and worn down he seemed. Dark circles beneath his eyes and a pale shade to his skin.

"I . . . He took the power when he took you." I clicked my tongue.

"I see. So, making bargains with demons isn't what you thought, now is it?" I stood to my full height again and threw my hair over my shoulder. "Now, I think you may have some information I need." Matt frowned and tried to get up from the ground, but Elias's large hand pushed him back down to the floor. He held him in place by his shoulders.

"I can't . . . he'll come back and kill me if I tell you anything."

"Well, here's the thing, Matt." I took my angel blade from my holster and used the sharp edge to pick at my fingernails. "You'll die either way. Because what you did to me is unforgivable. What you did to Rik, is unforgivable!" I shouted and threw my blade an inch away from his groin, imbedding into the wooden floor.

Matt visibly swallowed and opened his mouth to speak. I shushed him. "Can you believe I was actually going to try and be friends with you again? But then you stabbed me in the back in the worst way. I almost *died*, Matt. And you didn't care what Azvameth planned for me." I moved closer and crouched in front of him again, making us eye level. I pulled my knife from the wooden floor.

"I'm sorry, Nova. I really am. Please, please show me mercy. I'll do whatever you want."

"You're going to tell me everything I want to know either way." The rage burned of inside me and I knew I'd never be able to trust Matthew again. He needed to die. I would always be worried about him killing me instead. But there were some things I needed from him first.

"How do we find Azvameth?" Elias's head jerked up to stare at me. His eyes glowed lightly. I hadn't told him I intended to find my demon uncle and end him. I refused to be a victim again. And I didn't care if it was a demon, hunter, or human.

Matt shook his head and his lower lip trembled. "I can't . . ."

"You will! You screwed me over, Matt. You will tell me, or I'll cut your fingers off one by one until you have nothing but stumps left."

A tear rolled down his cheek. I wasn't sure if he cried because he was afraid or if he regretted his decisions. But I didn't care.

"Answer her!" Elias pushed down on Matt's shoulders, making him wince.

"The portal in the woods. If you go to the portal in the woods and think of where you want to go, it will take you there." Of course.

"Are you lying to me?" I cocked my head to the side.

"No, I swear! His witch opened the portal. She's the one that recruited me and told me how it works. She's had it open for a while now . . . even before the creatures started coming through. It was all in preparation to make sure she was able to keep it open for extended periods of time without having to go back and risk being caught."

"Vita . . ."

"Yes, Vita."

"Do witches' spells stay once they're dead?" I asked Elias.

"She's dead?" Matt interrupted. Elias ignored him.

"Depends. If she bound the spell to an object instead of herself, it's possible the portal is still there. If the portal has been open for so long, I would think it would drain her if she had it bound to herself. Or maybe she bound it to Azvameth."

"Let's go." I stepped toward Elias and Matt tried to stand again.

"Stay down, hunter." Elias growled as he pushed him back to the floor.

I grabbed onto Elias's bicep.

"Wait! What are you doing? I can't . . ." Matt's words were lost when Elias faded the three of us to the portal.

CHAPTER TWENTY-SEVEN

We ended up in front of the cave the portal was inside of. But this time fading in felt different. I glanced at Elias in question, and he shrugged. "It's harder to transport more people." I glanced down at Matt and his face was drawn. He looked like he was going to throw up.

"I thought you'd be used to teleporting," I said. His blood-shot eyes met mine.

"It never felt like that." Matt leaned forward to retch onto the dirt floor.

My lip curled in disgust. Not just from him vomiting but because of him in general. He disgusted me.

When he finished puking his brains out, Elias pulled him to his feet by his arm. We stepped toward the cave. I saw the light that emanated from the portal before we stepped inside. I followed the path through the cave with Elias and Matt trailing behind me.

I came to a stop in front of the portal and glanced over my shoulder at Elias. His eyes softly glowed in the dim lighting. I took a deep breath and reached out my hand. My fingers brushed through the mirrored gateway. Ripples expanded outward from my touch.

"Wait. Are you going to make me go through?" Matt asked from behind me. I pulled my hand back and turned to glare at Matthew.

"We aren't stupid enough to take your word for it. If we can go through the portal without being ripped apart or trapped, you wouldn't be so concerned with what's on the other side," Elias said and shoved Matt forward.

"If you're going to Azvameth, I don't want to go. I can't."

"Too bad. You should've thought of that before you betrayed me."

I reached out again, and the reflective surface started to reach for me in return. The aqueous substance wrapped itself around my fingers and glowed brightly. It was cool against my skin. I gave Elias another glance before taking a step forward. When I turned back toward the portal as it wound itself up my arm and started to pull me into it. It left my skin wet. I closed my eyes and thought about Azvameth before I stepped completely through. The sensation of being pulled through water hit me from every angle and I couldn't breathe. I held my breath, hoping there was enough air in my lungs that I wouldn't pass out before exiting the other side.

Pressure pushed in from everywhere—into every part of me. Just when I thought I wouldn't have much more air left, I was thrown forward, landing on my hands and knees onto a muddy terrain. Water shot out from my nose. My hair and clothes were completely drenched. The muddy earth coated my hands and squished between my fingers. When I inspected the world around me, I was somewhere I didn't recognize. The muddy field had no significant markers. The sky was a burnt orange and seemed like it was on fire. No clouds past overhead. I didn't get the feeling this was Hell but perhaps another realm I hadn't heard of.

A thud and coughing came from behind me. I turned and saw Matt and Elias exit the portal. Both choked on the fluid that entered their own nostrils and lungs. Their clothes were muddied and wet, clinging to them. I stood, and my boots nearly slipped in the sludge. But I caught myself and took a few steps to help Elias to his feet. His dark hair stuck to his forehead and his bright eyes were relieved when they landed on me. Once Elias was standing with me, I continued to hold onto his hand.

We surveyed the land together and Matthew slipped around until he finally managed to get to his feet.

"What is this place?" I asked.

"I'm not sure. Another realm, maybe. Azvameth either found a place outside of Hell to reside or the portal didn't work," Elias said.

I glanced at Matt and gave him a scowl. He threw his hands up in surrender.

"I have no idea. It worked before. I swear." Elias grabbed him by the front of his shirt and was inches from his face.

"If you tricked us, I'll kill you myself, hunter." Matthew looked like he might piss his pants.

He shook his head. "I swear on everything." Elias's nostrils flared with irritation, and he let his shirt go, stepping close to me once more.

"Which way do we go?" I asked.

"Normally, the portal drops you in the direction of where you intended to go. So probably straight ahead." Matt swallowed and pointed past me.

"You better be right." We started forward.

We trudged through the muddied ground which eventually turned to more solid land. We marched through it long enough for my hair to nearly dry into platinum waves and my shirt was no longer wet and stuck to my skin. Dried mud covered the majority of my clothes. I knew there had to be mud in my hair and on my face. On the horizon the top of a building came into view. I stopped and squinted, trying to make it out. Matthew and Elias both stopped beside me and stared into the distance with me.

"It looks like the top of a fortress." I said.

"There's only one way to find out," Elias replied, and we continued until we could see more of the stone building. It was a medieval tower constructed of gray stone. As more of the structure came into view, the tower was connected to a much larger building. The Gothic castle rose high into the sky and was surrounded by water. There was only one bridge which would ensure only one way in and one way out. If it was guarded, I couldn't see anyone, and no one seemed to be aware of our presence. At least not yet.

We stopped again and took in the scene. The feeling of darkness and power was overwhelming and pressed in on every inch of my body. I absently rubbed the center of my sternum.

"How many creatures do you think he has hiding behind these walls?" I didn't take my gaze off the building.

"Hard to tell. But there is a load of power behind those walls," Elias said.

"I just want to get to Azvameth. We need to go unnoticed."

"Nova." I tore my gaze from the building and peered at my mate. "We aren't prepared for this type of attack." I knew he was right, but we were here already. I didn't think there was any going back to gather troops and then coming back again.

"Don't you have any soldier friends?" Elias's lips kicked up into a grin.

"I do."

"And you've been summoned by Cyrus before. Does it go both ways?"

"It does." Elias's lips quirked up at the corner. "Having that sort of telepathy works well for us in battle."

"Good. Can you summon them?" I asked sweetly.

"We are all connected, but I am not their general. I can send out a mental message to them. Whether they come or not is up to them."

"Do it." Elias closed his eyes and sent off a mental calling to his battle mates. A ripple of power passed through the air as it was sent off. I hoped that Azvameth and whatever creatures inside of the castle were none the wiser. Hopefully there was enough power that moved throughout their own halls that Elias's wasn't noticed.

"Now what?" I asked as he opened his eyes.

"We wait and see. I can't promise they will come."

"Will your general get your call too?"

"He will be included in the message as well as Cyrus."

"If Cyrus knows, I'm sure he'll make them come." My gaze slid back to the fortress.

"He might, but they're loyal to Lucifer. What about your mother? Do you have any connection with her to send a message?" I frowned.

"I can try. I tried calling out to her when Azvameth had me shackled in that room. But she didn't answer. Maybe I wasn't doing it right? Tell me what to do." Elias stepped closer to me and gripped my dirtied hand in his.

"I often close my eyes to focus on who I'm sending the message to. But my brothers are connected to me. I assume she is connected to you since she can tell when something is wrong."

"She didn't come last time," I mumbled.

"Who do you think told us where you were?"

"She . . . she told you and Cyrus?" My brows dipped into a frown.

"Yes, in my frenzy she came to me and told us exactly where to find you. She wasn't physically there but she seemed like a hologram." Why didn't they tell me this before? Seraphina really was watching out over me.

"Cyrus was able to find me before and so have you. Why not then?"

"For some reason we were blocked. He probably had his witch do a spell of shielding. He obviously didn't take into account that your mother is watchful over you." I gave him a nod of understanding.

I tried to focus on my mother and blew out a breath before I closed my eyes. I thought of her eyes, so much like mine. Of how I needed her assistance. I felt a wave of power push from me and ripple through the air. Not as strong as Elias's but it was there. I opened my eyes and we waited.

We waited for about five minutes and then I had the sinking feeling that maybe no one was going to come. It was quiet and the only sound I heard was the slight breeze as kicked up some of the dirt in this hell hole.

Intense heat surrounded me, kind of like when Elias faded in but way stronger. Several men appeared before us dressed all in black with various weapons strapped to them. A dark-skinned man stepped forward.

"Brother, we got your message," he said.

"Our enemy is behind those walls." Elias nodded toward the fortress. "Did you get permission from Lucifer?"

"Perhaps not *permission*. But what he doesn't know immediately may only lead to lashings." He gave us a wicked smile, showing his straight white teeth. Only? This guy was legit crazy.

"And the general?"

"You know General Arlas never backs down from a fight. He loves this shit."

I couldn't help my grin that spread from ear to ear. Heat rippled again at my back. More soldiers appeared in the dreary dirt field around us. Matthew's brown eyes were wide. He had been quiet and watched the interactions between Elias and me.

I pulled Elias closer to me and whispered into his ear, "I lost my demon blades when Azvameth took me. I only have my angel blade." His short sword appeared in his hand, and he passed it off to me.

"I can't take this." I pushed the hilt back into his hand.

"Angel face, I have plenty of other weapons at my disposal. I can lend you my demon blade for this fight."

"This is your favorite weapon, give me another one you

don't use."

He grabbed my hand and put the hilt back into it my palm. "I would much rather you have the reach with this sword. Besides, my favorite sword for my favorite hybrid." He smirked. My heart melted in my chest, and he leaned down and gave me a quick kiss on the lips.

"Does Cyrus know you're wooing his only child?" Another of the soldiers teased. He had sandy blond hair and brown eyes. A scar across his cheek stood out from the rest of his tanned skin. Even with the disfiguring scar, he was a handsome man. His armor was a matte black chest plate and leather pants. A variety of daggers in different shapes and sizes were on a strap across his chest. There was even a battle axe attached at his hip and on the other a side, a longsword.

My eyes met his. "Cyrus doesn't get to tell me who I can be with. Even if he is my demon daddy."

"I like a woman with her own mind," the soldier said with a deep chuckle.

"Get your own hybrid, Andras." There was still an edge of possessiveness beneath Elias's words.

"Sure thing, brother. Just tell me where to find one." Blondie's grin split wider. I let out a soft laugh.

"I'm Andras. It's nice to finally meet the hybrid warrior we've all heard so much about."

"Nova." I reached out to shake his hand. "And I'm not sure I'm much of a warrior."

"We can let today speak for itself. But Elias would never choose a weak woman to stand at his side."

I peered up at Elias and if I didn't know better, I'd say his cheeks had gone a little red.

A rumble under our feet caused me to sway.

"They must know we're here now," I said. The ground trembled and shook, making it hard for me to keep my footing. The dirt cracked into small fractures, and it spread quickly.

The soldiers turned toward the fortress, and someone strode past me with dark brown hair and a long beard. He was taller and bulkier than the others and wore metal armor. His bare biceps were completely covered in unholy writing and symbols.

"That's General Arlas."

"I wouldn't have guessed," I responded sarcastically. This guy screamed superiority. He weaved his way through the men and pushed to the front.

"Get ready, soldiers!" his voice boomed and echoed all the way through the sea of people that surrounded me.

A shriek ripped through the air right after he gave his command. The front line jumped back, as a worm-like creature burst through the dirt, sending clods of dirt flying into the air. There was only a massive mouth filled with razor sharp teeth.

"Holy shit. It's a Mongolian death worm." Just like the one I'd seen in the book. The hideous creature spat its acidic venom at the crowd of soldiers. Some of them screamed in agony. Nope. Worms were a big nope for me. I stumbled back a step and Elias caught me by the arm.

"What's wrong?"

I shivered as I couldn't take my gaze away from the disgusting cryptid. "I hate . . . I hate worms."

In the distance, a black sea of something moved toward us. I couldn't tell quite what it was, but it was coming quickly.

The men ahead of us charged the worm and within moments a sword was lodged into its side. The cryptid let out an ear-piercing scream as it went down and the ground shook from the weight of the massive beast as it collapsed. The uneasiness that had spiked inside of me eased at the death of the creature.

The sea of darkness was getting closer. It wasn't a solid mass or fog. It was an army of cryptids.

CHAPTER TWENTY-EIGHT

The number of cryptids that charged toward us left us severely outnumbered. I had no idea how we would be able to hold them back. Azvameth held out on the amount of them he had sent after me. When they hit the front lines, Elias and I ran toward the mayhem side by side. My legs pumped hard. I tried to get there as soon as I could to help the soldiers.

When we reached the front, the only remnants of the slaughtered cryptids were black gore. The soldiers that had been injured were still going at it. I was certain the ones that took more blows probably disappeared back to Hell to recover.

A werewolf charged toward me, full force. Its front two paws came up onto my chest and knocked me onto my back. It whined as my blade pierced through its fur coat and flesh. The warmth of blood coated my fingers. I rolled the beast off me before I pulled my sword free.

Elias battled two upir. They blurred around him as he tried to strike at them. My brows slammed down. I knew they were playing with my soulmate. I ran toward him and jumped into the air as I threw out my arm. My angel blade caught the male upir in the neck. He grabbed the hilt and pulled it free, dropping it to the floor. Blood squirted from the severed artery. His hands clamped onto the wound, trying to staunch the flow. His hands were painted black, and he fell to his knees.

The female upir stopped circling Elias. She screamed, her mouth opened unnaturally wide, showing her razor-sharp canines. Elias took the opportunity and cut the woman's head from her body. It rolled across the dirt, leaving a trail of blood as her body dropped to the floor. Her expression was frozen in rage.

I was knocked into by General Arlas and nearly lost my footing. He killed the creatures without even breaking a sweat. His powerful arms cut and sliced through the cryptids repeatedly without strain. Blood splattered his face, beard, and arms.

When I turned back to Elias, we were surrounded by five rakes. They started closing in around us until Elias and myself were back-to-back. Two launched themselves at us. I jumped forward and blocked the blow. Its nails sliced into my thigh as it landed. I gritted my teeth against the hot pain that blossomed in my leg. The other came forward and I twisted out of the way as it dove. I slashed down with my sword, knocking it to the ground and sliced into its back.

The next rake was on me in an instant. It jumped onto my back, it's teeth too close to my neck. Its rancid breath as it huffed in my face and he gripped my hair, making my eyes water and my scalp burn. He needed to get off *now*. I jumped into the air like I was going to do a backflip. Only I landed on my back. The rake took the blow and shrieked in pain. I scrambled to my feet and pushed my angel blade into the creature's eye socket. There was no resistance as it pushed in. When I pulled my blade back out, the eyeball was still on my weapon. The black eye was stuck. So I touched the disgusting thing, pulling it off and dropping it to the ground. I wiped my blade and my hand on my already filthy pants. Elias came to my side having fought off the rest of the rakes.

The fight seemed to be dying down. Even though we were outnumbered, the soldiers had taken care of the mass majority of Azvameth's soldiers.

General Arlas's voice boomed as he yelled, "He's sending more! Get ready!"

More? We glanced toward the fortress. Sure enough there was another wave of cryptids headed right for us. I never even knew this many existed. How had Azvameth convinced this many creatures to work against us? He must have a lot of power and persuasion to get everyone on his side.

"What if he has even more after this?" I asked.

"Hopefully this is the last wave."

"And let you guys have all the fun?" I spun around at the sound of my sister's voice.

"Oh my god, Tiffany. What are you doing here?" Before she could answer, my adoptive father stepped forward. He was in full battle gear with over twenty men I didn't recognize behind him. His dark hair was pulled back in a low ponytail, and he wielded some serious weaponry.

"Well, funny thing—when you don't tell us where you're going and then a woman that looks a lot like you came and told me you went through the portal. I knew I needed to come after you and I happened to come up on Dad as he and his friends were going through too."

I threw my arms around my sister and felt the tears well in my eyes. I shook my head and tried to shake away the feeling. I knew our reprieve was short—until the new mass of creatures finally reached us. I pulled back and stepped toward my dad.

"You disappeared! Why the hell would you scare us like that? I even thought maybe you found a new woman." I punched him in the shoulder.

"I would never hurt your mother like that. I was gathering my own army. I had a feeling that I should gather as many hunters as I could find. I had a dream of your real mother. She told me we'd all be needed soon to assist you. So, I'm calling in a few favors. There were others who were more than happy to come out of retirement to help." My mother knew how to get around to everyone. She's had my back my whole life and

I hadn't even realized it. I just wished that she had shown up, too. I owed her my life and then some.

I stepped into my father's space and wrapped my arms around him.

"You didn't tell anyone," I murmured into his chest. His hands came to my matted hair, and he kissed the top of my head.

"I didn't want your mother to insist on going with me. You know how she is."

"About that . . ." Tiffany chimed in. "Mom's here."

I stepped back and my father's eyes were like saucers.

"Vincent Alexander. You and I are going to have quite the conversation when we get back to the house." My mother stood beautifully with her hands on her hips. Her long dark hair braided back away from her face and in black leathers tight against her body. Weapons were strapped along her hip and at her ankles. She was a badass warrior.

"I'm sorry, I didn't want you to worry but it was something I needed to do alone." He reached out to grip my mother's hand in his. The other hunters with him chuckled softly and his brows slammed down. My mother opened her mouth to respond but before she could get anything past her lips, Elias interrupted.

"I know you all have a lot to discuss, but the cryptids are almost here." He glanced back over his shoulder at our approaching enemies. The snarling and keening was getting louder with every moment that we stood around.

Everyone spread out and prepared for the second wave to reach us. I squinted and saw a horse in front of the others. My stomach sank when I realized that Azvameth was atop the black behemoth of a horse. If that was what you could even call it. It was larger than any horse I'd ever seen. They slowed and eventually came to a stop before they reached our front line of defenders. I pushed my way through the crowd of soldiers. There was only one reason Azvameth came out of his high castle—to try to take me without more deaths. Not that he cared about anyone else's life but his own.

I stepped out from behind General Arlas's enormous body at the front line, and he gripped my shoulder to stop me. I glanced up at him and he must've seen something in my expression because he let go and gave me a slight nod. "If you need us, holler," the general said. I didn't respond and Elias came to stand beside me. I took a few more steps toward my enemy. Azvameth was in head-to-toe black leather and his dark hair perfectly coiffed.

I stopped and gripped my weapons, twirling my angel blade in my one hand.

"Nova, this can all be over, and we both will have no more blood on our hands, if you just surrender." I wanted to throw my blade at his face. But I would have to be one hundred percent sure that I'd hit my mark. I scoffed.

"No more death? You say that as if my death means nothing," I said loudly enough for him to hear me. His horse's hooves beat against the dirt and seemed to grow agitated with being at a standstill.

"One life for many. Do you know nothing of sacrifice?" He grinned and there was a gleam in his black eyes.

"And we are to believe you wouldn't kill more? That you wouldn't slaughter all who stood in your way of taking over the realms? You're a lying son of a bitch."

Azvameth clicked his tongue. "Now if I had a mother, that may have hurt my feelings," he said with mock shock. "But Lucifer created me, and your insults mean nothing to me. I've grown tired of playing nice, niece." This time his grin turned feral. He bared his too bright teeth at me. "Now surrender, you little bitch, before I massacre your entire army and make you watch while I slice your mate's head from his shoulders and let my creatures fuck his corpse." Elias tensed next to me and the rage that boiled beneath his skin was palpable. He stepped forward but I threw my arm out to keep Elias from attacking. My eyes didn't leave Azvameth even for a moment.

"Screw you, *uncle*." I gave him my best smile.

"So be it." Azvameth threw up a leather gloved hand and then they charged forward.

CHAPTER TWENTY-NINE

My allies started forward and I was swept up in the crowd of soldiers and hunters. I lost sight of Elias, but I wasn't going to stop. He may have been sent as my protector, but I would be the one to finish this. I wouldn't allow Azvameth and his creatures to take me without a fight. I ran as fast as I could to meet at where the battle ensued. The sound of cryptids shrieking was lost to my own breathing and the pounding of my own heart now.

The moment our troops met Azvameth's, our weapons swiped through the air. The shouts of injured men and creatures echoed throughout the demon's realm. With the amount of varying beasts all together I almost tripped over my own feet. There were werewolves, shapeshifters, ghouls, rakes—the list could go on and on. Some of them were humanoid and others were completely beast-like. Cryptids from all over the globe. I knew that if Azvameth succeeded in taking my soul, it wouldn't matter whether or not he kept his promises to the cryptids. He would be able to kill them at the drop of a hat. There would be nothing they could do about it.

I came face to face with a deer woman. Her upper half was human, and her lower extremities were that of a deer. She was shirtless and her pert breasts were out for all to see. Sounds innocent enough. But the large ax in her hand said otherwise. She had long dark hair with a small set of antlers that protruded from her skull. The ax was large with her slender arms and delicate hands. I ducked when she swung at me.

"Your tits are distracting," I said as I shot my arm out to

stab her. I missed. She cocked her head to the side and gave me a hateful grin. I grimaced in disgust at the row of blackened teeth.

"Gross, and so are your teeth." Her sneer dropped from her face and her brows slammed down. She jumped forward and lunged at me. I used her own move against her and leaned into her attack. Elias's short sword plunged through her belly. Blood dribbled from her mouth and her delicate hands dropped the ax. I pulled my weapon free and moved onto the next creature.

I cut them down one by one. When I had a moment in between, I searched for Azvameth. His big ass horse wouldn't be hard to miss. But I didn't catch sight of him. I was covered in creature gore. We may not have the upper hand at the beginning of the battle, but we definitely seemed to be holding our own. To have this amount of people — if that was what you'd call them — fight with me, had me grateful. If it weren't for Elias and my adoptive father, I would've been on my own.

Just as I finished slaying a ghoul who stopped to feast on a severed appendage, a large hand grabbed me by the upper arm. I spun to jab my blade into whoever or whatever it was. I stopped short when I saw a handsome, bloodied face and cerulean eyes.

"Elias!" A couple of werewolves decided now was a good time to get ready to pounce. Elias and I pushed away from each other. Elias's arm went up and gave his opponent a killing blow as I sliced the short sword entirely through the torso of the beast.

"If we weren't in the middle of a field of slaughtered creatures, I'd take you right now." Elias grinned wickedly. My stomach clenched.

Hooves pounded against the ground as Azvameth galloped toward us. My rage sent my hands enveloped in flames, quickly sputtering out. He stopped his horse a good distance away from us and chuckled.

"Stupid girl, you think you can control your powers without some sort of training? This is how I know you don't deserve such gifts. And even if you were successful in throwing your sorry excuse of Hell fire at me, it would do nothing." I remembered then how my hands were engulfed in flames when Elias and I kissed. He had said it didn't hurt. Made sense. But that left me with less power to fight Azvameth

I felt my family as they came up behind us and the hunters came to stand at their sides. Then, the remaining soldiers that were not injured crowded in to stand with us too. I hadn't realized it, but the creatures ceased their fighting. Our enemies crowded around Azvameth. They waited for his command to slaughter us and finish the battle.

I felt heat lick at my side. Cyrus appeared next to me, his black eyes trained on my uncle. Azvameth's brows rose. "I didn't expect to see you here, brother. Suddenly caring whether your only child lives or dies?"

"Shut up, Azvameth. You're only trying to acquire power to go up against Lucifer since he no longer wants you in Hell. Poor Azvameth, no longer Lucifer's favored."

"Fuck Lucifer. I'd make a better ruler than him," my uncle spat.

"Well, I'm here to retrieve you. He wants your punishment to be by his hand." The sneer that crossed Cyrus's face gave me the chills. Creepy. I wouldn't doubt that Lucifer's punishment would be worse than death for him. But Azvameth didn't seem afraid. He was pissed off. His nostrils flared and I would have bet money that he hadn't expected Cyrus to come help me once again.

"I'm not going to allow that, and you know that, Cyrus. So, let's end this already. I'm eager to be the new leader of Heaven and Hell," Azvameth said.

Azvameth jumped down from his stallion and the beast

took off. He stood at the front of the creatures, withdrawing his sword. They snarled and their inhuman noises rose again.

Cyrus stepped in front of me to shield me. Matt stepped to my side. I glanced at him unsure of what to expect from him. But his once empty hands wielded weapons and a frown marred his face.

"What do you think you're doing?" Elias asked from the opposite side of me.

"I'm going to help return Azvameth to Hell." Matt glimpsed at me, sadly. "I'm sorry, Nova. I should've never betrayed you. Let me prove to you that I'm on your side." I gave him a slight nod. Not that I forgave him. But I wasn't going to say no to another person in our army of hunters and soldiers. I would handle him later, after the war was finished.

Cyrus's voice came back in. I tore my gaze away from Matt to take in the scene of my demon dad and demon uncle as they argued.

"I'm tired of exchanging words, little brother. Your daughter will not live through this. Her soul belongs to me!" His face turned a bright red as he yelled.

As soon as the words left Azvameth's mouth, Cyrus and Elias charged forward. Creatures unleashed. They blocked Elias and me reaching him. We cut through them as quickly as we could. When I caught a glimpse of Cyrus and Azvameth, I saw them heavily battling against each other. I didn't want Cyrus to have this one. Azvameth was mine to deal with. I just needed to get to them—I wouldn't promise I wasn't going to kill him. It may end in one of our deaths. Even if it was too merciful to end my uncle, Lucifer's punishment would definitely be more fitting.

The sound of my short sword clanged against the horned head of a minotaur. The muscled beast tried to spear me with his big horns. I jumped out of the way and dove toward the creature, slicing his arm. Muscles and tendons shredded. He let out a deep guttural bellow. He used his other hand to grab the wound. I shoved the short sword through the side of his thick neck. He tried to roar in outrage and pain. But the only sound that came from him was a gurgle as he fell to his knees and then to the ground. I moved on before he disappeared. I had lost sight of Cyrus and Azvameth.

I searched over the crowd of the battle trying to spot Azvameth. Cyrus's dark head caught my eye. He faced me and his face was covered in blood. But it wasn't Azvameth's. It was his own. He moved away from the crowd of cryptids and clutched his side as he limped.

I moved to go to him. To help get him to safety if he was severely injured and could no longer fight. But as soon as I moved an inch, something slammed into me. I was thrown to the side with the force of a body colliding into mine. I tumbled ass-over-head multiple times and was unable to regain my balance. I crashed into the dirt, stomach first and slid. The dirt burn was unreal. If dirt burn was even a thing.

I groaned as I tried to get up off the ground. My weapons ended up a few feet away from me. I pushed to my hands and knees. I crawled about a foot before I felt a booted foot slam into my back. I fell back onto my stomach and lost my breath.

A dark chuckle caused my mouth to go dry. I tried to push up again but was stomped on again. My torso crushed by the weight of my enemy.

"Your father must be as stupid as you are."

It was Azvameth. He somehow managed to lose my father in the crowd and find me.

CHAPTER THIRTY

M y spine felt like it was crushed by a mountain. My face was smashed into the ground. The dirt stuck to my sweaty skin along with the dried blood and mud that already covered me.

"Screw you." His boot pressed harder on my back and a yelp tore from me. Tears crowded my vision as my face was pressed into the ground.

"Oh, I wouldn't be so crass if I were in your position. But who am I kidding, I'd never be in your position. This is why I deserve to have the power you hold. You have no idea how much more you're capable of. If only you spent a little more time in Heaven or Hell. You might actually have a chance against me." He clicked his tongue.

Azvameth's large, gloved hand went to my arm in a bruising grip. He flipped me onto my back like I weighed nothing. My breath was knocked out of me as I hit the ground again. I stared up into his black, soulless eyes. "Just think of all of the terrible things I can do once I have the power. I just have hide away in Hell for a while to gain the power you lack." His smirk was wicked. I suddenly felt that pull from deep within me. It left me breathless as Azvameth's outstretched hand took from me. Just like when Vita was assisting him.

"How?" I choked and my eyes widened.

He chuckled deeply. "You think I wasn't able to grab onto my witch's power when she died. One mistake your father made was killing her in my presence. Besides, the spell was never finished." Tears tracked down into my hair. I grabbed onto his ankle and tried to break the hold he had on me. I was no match for him. Not in the position I was in.

A shadow soared overhead. Before Azvameth could glance up, he was tossed through the air. He landed hard a few feet from me. The dirt kicked up where he landed, and I scrambled to my feet. The pain still radiated in my stomach and back. Elias appeared in front of me, and I nearly screamed in surprise. His large hands gripped my dirty cheeks, and he searched my face, assessing my injuries.

"I'm okay," I croaked. I covered his hands with mine. I peered over my shoulder to see Azvameth already on his feet. He stalked toward us. Elias disappeared and faded in front of him. His fist connected with Azvameth's face so hard, it sent the demon back to the ground.

Elias caught him by surprise. But Azvameth was on his feet in no time. I rushed to pick up my fallen weapons and ran over to where the altercation took place. My uncle and my boyfriend punched the hell out of each other. Although Elias did have the upper hand. When he threw his packed punches, his muscles bunched and rippled. Azvameth smiled and let out a deranged laugh. Dark blood painted his teeth.

"I do have a fondness for pain." He beckoned him forward, inviting more violence.

I threw myself in front of Elias and slashed downward with my sword. I grazed Azvameth's chest and cut open his uniform. He jumped back and pulled out his own sword. He'd swung at me. I parried and pushed forward making him stumble back a step. I propelled forward and lunged, aiming for Azvameth's gut but he blocked my move. I came at him again and again, but he was too fast.

He quickened his moves and swiped out low, aiming for my legs—after all he couldn't kill me before he took my soul. I narrowly escaped his assault and jumped over his blade. My boots hit the ground and I caught Azvameth off guard when

I backhanded him across the face. His head snapped to the side. I pierced his shoulder with my short sword. He let out a ferocious roar of pain. Blood spilled from his fresh wound, but it was hardly visible on his dark clothing.

"I thought you like pain," I bared my teeth as I twisted the sword in his wound.

I planted my boot on his abdomen and kicked out. I successfully withdrew my sword from his flesh. Azvameth fell back onto his ass. The anger in his black eyes told me there will be more than hell to pay. Not if I could help it. I stalked toward him and kicked his discarded weapon. His gloved hand gripped his shoulder, likely trying to heal himself. But my blade was a weapon created for unnatural creatures such as himself. And if I'd lodged it anywhere more vital, he wouldn't have been sitting there as he hissed in pain. I stopped in front of him.

"You stupid bitch," he spat. "You think this is over? That you can end me and there won't be someone else taking my place to consume your soul?" I shrugged nonchalantly.

"It's not a problem today. I'll worry about that when or if it happens again," I replied. I hit him upside the head with the hilt of my sword, knocking him unconscious.

I raised my sword to take Azvameth's head from his body while he was down. Just as I was about to bring my sword down, Seraphena stepped into my view. I froze.

"Daughter, you must let Lucifer handle his punishment," she said.

"This is my kill." I lowered my sword. "And where were you when I called for you? You sent others but couldn't come yourself?"

"I got here as soon as I could. I've been fighting for you." I glanced down at my mother's gold-plated chest with splattered blood across it. I noticed how wild her hair was compared to the last time I had seen her. Stray hairs came loose from the long braid she had it pulled into. No longer was she so clean and pristine.

"Let Lucifer handle his punishment, Nova. If you don't, he will be angry and come after you himself." Her eyes pleaded with me to listen. The rage inside of me wanted to be the one to dole out Azvameth's death blow—the ultimate punishment. He had put me through enough. If it wasn't for him, I would still have Rik. I'd would never have been duped by Matt. My life would be normal still. My adoptive father wouldn't have left his wife and everyone else worrying about him while he recruited backup. *But you wouldn't have met your mate.* A voice in the back of my mind said. Some of the anger receded at the thought.

At the time I had met him, I didn't know that the strange pull in my chest that I felt was anything more than lust. I felt the connection and wanted to deny it so much. I never would have thought that he felt the same. To become my partner in everything. My gaze found Elias. He battled a creature. I knew he would stand by my side either way. I knew that he would go up against Lucifer with me. I would never put my mate in that kind of harm. Especially for selfish reasons like vengeance.

My shoulders slumped and I dropped my arms to my sides. My mother held out her hand to me and I reached to take it. Her head jerked back and Azvameth's blade was at her throat. Her eyes widened. No. He glided the steel across my mother's delicate neck. Blood welled instantly. Her gold chest plate was quickly covered in her blood.

I realized my mistake; I had taken my attention off Azvameth to listen to my mother's pleas. The pleas to let go of my rage to allow for a more fitting damnation. My mother's body fell to the side and landed hard to the dirt ground. Rage burned in my gut. I screamed, taking two steps toward Azvameth and his wicked grin. I was ready to decapitate him when two strong arms came around my waist and pulled me back. A shriek of fury escaped my throat and I kicked as my feet came off the ground. I knew it was Elias that I was pinned against. His scent with a trace of sweat and blood wrapped around me. I sobbed as I glared at my mother's murderer. "I'll kill you!" I screamed. "I'll kill you!" My voice broke as I yelled at my enemy.

Cyrus appeared behind Azvameth and wrapped an arm around his neck and squeezed. He'd dropped his blade from the surprise of his brother behind him. Azvameth's hands tried to loosen Cyrus's hold but he squeezed his neck until Azvameth was almost purple. Azvameth lost consciousness again and slumped. Cyrus pulled rope from a small satchel at his hip and quickly bound his brother's wrists and feet together in a hogtie with the help of General Arlas. Once Azvameth was detained and I took a few deep breaths to calm myself, Elias loosened his hold on me. I turned around in his arms and sagged against him.

"I wanted to know her," I cried. Elias's hand rubbed up and down my back in soothing sweeps. I peered back over my shoulder at Seraphena's body.

Cyrus kneeled next to my mother's limp form. There was sadness in his black gaze. Pain. Love. Something I had never expected a demon to feel. Tears flowed down my cheeks. Cyrus pulled my mother's lifeless body into his lap, and I didn't fight him. He kissed her parted lips gently and ran his thumb over her alabaster cheek. The way he studied her face . . . Like he needed to memorize it for the last time. It broke my heart even more.

"I couldn't forgive her for taking you away," he said gruffly without taking his gaze off her. "I wanted to have you and her. She took that decision away from me. I couldn't forgive her. I couldn't see past it. I couldn't see that she was protecting you while breaking us apart. But then when I found you and was made aware of plans to take you away for good, I had to protect you." Cyrus's attention shifted to me. "If I would've known that Elias was your mate, I wouldn't have punished him so harshly."

I scoffed. "So harshly? So, you still would've punished him?"

"I cannot be seen as weak in my position. I wouldn't have been so . . . cruel. But what's done is done. And believe it or not, your mother was my only love. I still love her. I will *always* love her." My heart broke a little more with his words.

"Why hasn't she disappeared?" I asked and stepped out of Elias's arms.

"I'm willing her body to remain here until you can say goodbye," Cyrus said. I swallowed the lump in my throat. I kneeled on the opposite side of Cyrus. I stared into the frozen face of the mother I wanted to know more. Her lifeless violet gaze was fixed on the sky above her. I tried to keep my stare from roaming to the rest of her and her blood drenched armor. Her wounded throat. I ran my hand over the top of her head and leaned down to kiss her forehead softly.

"I wish we had more time." I sat back on my heels, and I glanced toward Cyrus. His black eyes were sad and hopeless. I gave him a slight nod and my gaze slid to my mother again. She slowly started to disappear and unlike when the cryptids evaporated, a light glowed from her. After she was gone Cyrus and I stood. I wiped the remaining tears from my face.

"Nova!" I heard my name being called from behind. I turned to see Tiffany who ran toward me. "Oh, Nova." Her arms wrapped around my shoulders, and I leaned into her.

Elias dragged Azvameth's limp and bound body toward us.

"He isn't dead," he said. "But he should be."

Several soldiers came to take his battered body. Elias gladly gave him over. Tiff's hold loosened and when Elias held out his hand for me to take. I placed my hand into his and he pulled me toward him with such force I crashed into him. His fingers tangled in my hair, and he bent to put his lips to my ear. "I'm so sorry, Nova. I should've gotten to him before he hurt your mother. I'm so sorry." He squeezed me tightly. I wrapped my arms around his waist.

"It isn't your fault. I should've . . . I should've . . ." I gasped as I tried to push the words past my lips but couldn't. "I saw you fighting. I don't blame you." My face crumbled and my body shook as I pressed my forehead into Elias's chest. I noticed that all the fighting stopped. It was quiet. I turned my head and scanned the land where we had just held the hardest battle of my life. More hot tears cascaded down my face.

The creatures that weren't slaughtered retreated after Azvameth had been captured. They no longer had him to stand behind.

"I need to get him to Lucifer before he wakes up," Cyrus said. I let go of Elias and wiped my face with the back of my arm.

"I'm going with you," I said.

CHAPTER THIRTY-ONE

"It's not wise, Nova," Cyrus replied. "What do you think Lucifer will do if the hybrid comes to his palace? You will gain more power and abilities the longer you stay there."

"I don't really care. I want to be the one to take Azvameth to him."

Cyrus focused on Elias as if he could talk some sense into me. I gazed up at him and his attention was locked onto me.

"I'll follow Nova wherever she wants to go. And if she wants to take Azvameth personally to Lucifer, then I'll stand by her side." I slid my hand into his much larger one.

"You are jaded by love." Cyrus sighed but didn't fight me anymore on the subject.

General Arlas and another soldier held onto Azvameth's limp body and faded out.

I felt the ripples of Elias's heat and he faded us to Hell. I gripped his hand a little tighter. I took a deep breath, closed my eyes and let Elias take over.

I felt the shift in energy when we reached Hell. It was a heavy feeling that grated against my skin and a shiver ran down my spine. When I opened my eyes, a very large, very black castle stood before me. Think *Sleeping Beauty's* castle from the movie. But much, much darker. The skies still appeared as if they were on fire, but it was surprisingly a decent temperature. My dirt and blood caked shirt clung to my chest and stomach. I couldn't imagine how I'd appear to the Devil when we strolled inside.

The others started forward, but Elias gripped my hand tighter and pulled me back for a moment. "Don't let him see any weaknesses, he'll use them against you." I gave him a nod. He brought my hand to his lips and placed a kiss on my knuckles. "That includes me," he said. My eyebrows rose. I hadn't thought of that, but Elias was right. If he was as wicked and cruel as his reputation stated, then he may punish me by hurting Elias. I couldn't stomach that. Not again.

He let go of my hand and we trudged the path to the entrance of the castle. General Arlas, Cyrus, and the other soldier waited for us until we reached the gatehouse. There were guards stationed at the entrance and my stomach dipped with nervousness. They recognized Cyrus and General Arlas, waving them through the front gates. Maybe I should have just let the General and Cyrus take Azvameth to Lucifer. It was too late now. When we entered the hallway to the castle there were two men that waited to take us to their master. They were identical twins and seemed surprisingly human. Except when they smiled, their teeth were sharp points. I realized their eyes were as black as Cyrus's.

"Master has been waiting for you. What took you so long?" one of the demon twins asked.

"Apprehending Azvameth was a little more difficult than anticipated. He had help from the cryptids," Arlas replied. The other twin grunted in understanding, and we continued down the hall. I noticed as I surveyed the castle it probably hadn't been remodeled since Elias was brought here. There were tapestries hung on the walls as well as grotesque paintings of demons in sexual acts with humans. One of them was of a woman being mounted by a demon with scaly skin and clawed hands. Even though the creature was disgusting in the painting, the woman appeared to enjoy it. A shiver ran down my spine and it took a second to realize I had stopped in front of the image. Cyrus placed a hand on my shoulder. I peered up at him.

"We can't keep him waiting any longer. Perhaps after this I can take you on a tour if you wish to see more of the artwork Master has acquired over the centuries."

"Let's just see how this meeting goes first," I said. Cyrus nodded before he guided me back toward the way we had been headed.

We continued down the corridor and followed behind the twins. I stayed at the back of the group. I kept my attention on Elias's muscular form and prayed that this didn't go down horribly. We reached a tall set of ancient doors, and the twins pulled them open. The hinges must've never have been greased because they creaked loudly. Arlas and the soldier headed in first. Elias gave me a glance over his shoulder before he stalked through the doors. Cyrus and myself stepped into the room a few feet behind them, the doors closing with a bang. When I glanced back, I noticed the twins decided to stay on the safer side of the door.

The large room had the same theme as the corridor we came through. Not a thing updated in centuries. The stone walls didn't have tapestries, however. There were carved scenes that depicted a war between angels and demons. Both sides had sets of wings and swords. Gory depictions of death were created within the stone. It was beautifully disturbing.

I hadn't paid enough attention because I ran into the hard back of Cyrus and stumbled back a step. Luckily, I caught myself before I fell. Arlas and the soldier dropped Azvameth's hogtied body with a thud onto the ground. Then they both kneeled. Elias and Cyrus followed suit. Their big bodies no longer blocked my view. My eyes widened when I saw a beast of a man that sat on a throne. A throne constructed of animal bones or maybe they were the bones of his enemies. Smooth black leather tightly formed around the seat and armrests. A wall of flames licked up the stone wall behind his large chair.

He was surprisingly the opposite of what I would have thought. Blond hair combed neatly back, eyes black as coal, and bare chested. And, I hated to say it, but the dude was ripped. Black leather pants hugged his thick legs, and the muscles were prominent underneath, his feet were bare. I swallowed.

Cyrus pulled me by the hand, so I kneeled next to him. Lucifer cocked his head to the side in a creepy way and his eyes locked onto the movement. I noticed then that he had two chained people who sat at his feet. A male and a female. Both were practically nude. The woman had long dark hair, her eyes were downcast on the stone floor. Her complexion, sallow. The woman's small breasts were only covered by a sheer black cloth draped across her chest and a skirt with slits all the way up both thighs. It revealed that she had nothing on underneath.

The male was shirtless and dressed in nothing but linen shorts that covered his bottom half. The sheerness of them revealed a little more than I would've liked to see. Both had collars on with a chain connected to the throne Lucifer was seated on.

"You have brought me Azvameth," his booming voice said. I snapped my attention back to Lucifer.

"Yes, Master. We owe it to Nova," Arlas said as he rose. The rest of us rose from the floor.

Lucifer's eyes slid to Cyrus. "Your daughter." Cyrus only nodded and he pulled me forward. My skin felt hot all over from the nerves that took over my body.

Lucifer's black glare met mine and the hair on the back of my neck stood on end. Being in the presence of someone as evil as Satan himself put my body on high alert.

His eyes took in my filthy body greedily. He gave me a wicked grin and pulled his lower lip in between his teeth.

"I do enjoy warrior women. They make my cock hard."

Elias stiffened next to me. But he said nothing and didn't move closer to me.

"I'm only here to escort Azvameth and to make sure he is punished for the shit he put us through." My voice didn't waiver. I refused to acknowledge his cock comment. I curled my fingers into my palms and my fingernails dug into my skin. I tried to remain calm.

"Maybe I can change your mind about that being the only thing you are here for." His wicked grin caused my stomach to ache.

"Not interested. But thanks for the offer." I forced a smile.

"Too bad." He sighed and flicked a hand toward Azvameth just as he started to stir. Out of nowhere several soldiers in full gear came and lifted him to carry him away. "Make sure he is put on the rack and ready for me within the hour," Lucifer commanded. Even his torture devices were medieval.

I swallowed before I stepped closer to the throne. "We brought you Azvameth, now I'd like to request a favor in return."

CHAPTER THIRTY-TWO

"**N**o!" Elias and Cyrus both shouted at the same time. Lucifer's eyes narrowed on the two men.

"You can't ask him for anything," Elias whispered.

"Why not? He got what he wanted from us. I think it's only fair if I get something in return," I replied. A deep laugh echoed from Lucifer. It sounded unnatural and my spine stiffened as I tried to control my trembling limbs.

"There is no such thing as fair. But ask what you want of me. Do not allow these two to tell you what to do." He waved his hand between Cyrus and Elias. I gathered all my courage, and I crossed the remainder of the space between Lucifer and myself. The protests of Cyrus and Elias were ignored. I stopped in front of slaves at his feet.

"Come closer. Do not mind Sarah and Kade, they are my pleasure slaves and know better than to bother my guests." My brow furrowed as I glanced at the both of them and my stomach clenched. Lucifer tsked and said, "No, do not feel sorry for them." His voice came out hard and I tensed further. "They lived a life of murder and revenge. They did not think before they slaughtered the people they did. Sarah is a whore who pleases whomever I demand and Kade likes to take it in the ass as punishment for their sins." I didn't respond and swallowed, taking a few steps closer to Lucifer until I stood directly in front of him.

"On your knees." I didn't want to obey the command but I listened. I dropped to my knees slowly and never took my gaze off the Devil. The darkness in them could have swallowed me whole. I realized that this creature had seen more than I could have ever imagined. Wars, bloodshed, demons against angels, God against Lucifer. With the abilities I had at the moment, I wouldn't be able to take him on. I hadn't spent enough time in either realm for my full power to come out.

Lucifer's blond brow arched as he waited for my request. His handsome face was clean shaven and if I didn't know what or who he was, I may have even been attracted to him on some level. But the evil inside of him let off an energy that sent my nerves spiraling and my gut twisting. I was surprised I hadn't vomited on his feet by the close proximity.

"Well?" His lush mouth tipped up in a smirk. I gathered my nerves and leaned forward. Lucifer put his forearms on his knees. His face was so close to mine I could smell him. He smelled like a fire in winter.

I opened my parched mouth and I spoke quietly so the others couldn't hear. The men at my back shifted as they tried to listen in on my conversation with the King of Hell. I figured that Elias would pick up on the words I spoke softly to Lucifer. When I was done. I sat back and waited. Lucifer's stare darted to Elias behind me and then back.

His hand wrapped around my throat so quickly I didn't even get a chance to defend myself. His grip was firm. I gasped for air, as I tried to pull his hand from my neck. My hands erupted into flames and my wings tore from my back, but he just laughed. A cruel laugh that chilled my very soul. Elias and Cyrus tried to rush toward the throne to help me, but I could only assume Arlas and the soldier held them back.

"Master, please," Elias begged. Lucifer paid no attention to my mate and his stare continued to burn into mine.

"I will give you what you wish, hybrid. However, you are never to return to Heaven nor Hell. You are too much of a threat to me and my kingdom. If you ever step foot inside my realm again, the deal is void. Understood?" I nodded as much as I could while I tried to pull air into my lungs.

He released his hold and shoved me back. I fell to the floor on my side. I coughed and greedily gulped in the air. My wings disappeared into my back and my flames died out. Lucifer was on his feet and brushed his hands together as he towered over me. I scrambled to my feet and backed up, nearly tripping over Sarah and Kade.

He turned and started to stalk out of the room. He went the same way as the men who had taken Azvameth. I assumed he was going to start his torture session.

"Wait!" I called after him. Lucifer stopped and peered back at me. "What about the deal?"

"You have what you want, hybrid." His gaze flicked to Elias again as he smirked. I turned and glanced back at my mate.

Elias was restrained by Arlas and his face grimaced in pain. And then his screams echoed through the room.

Elias fell to his knees, and I rushed to him. I slid on my knees in front of him. The biting pain of my knees knocking off the stone floor went ignored as my hands cupped Elias's face. "Tell me what hurts?" The panic was evident in my voice.

He grunted and fisted his shirt, tearing the fabric over his chest. The *S* on his chest appeared as a fresh burn as it bubbled across his skin.

"What did you do," I screamed at Lucifer but when I whipped my head back toward where he last stood, he was gone.

I gaped at Cyrus, Arlas, and the soldier. The concern was evident on their faces, but they didn't know what to do. I stared back to my mate's face and rubbed my thumbs over his scruff on his jawline.

"What do you need me to do?" I asked. "Please, tell me what I can do to stop the pain."

Elias's hands covered mine and I leaned my forehead against his. He clenched his jaw and continued to groan in agony.

"I feel like I'm being branded all over again," he said through clenched teeth.

"I'm sorry. I didn't know this would cause you pain. I didn't know." A tear snuck out from beneath my lashes. Elias's pain shredded my heart.

I stayed with him as the searing pain burned his chest. Minutes passed before I felt Elias's body relax against mine. I blinked open my eyes and his breathing evened out.

"It's gone." I heard the general's voice say from behind me.

"What's gone?" I pulled myself away from my mate.

"His sinner's brand," Cyrus said.

I peered down at Elias's chest the same moment he did and there was nothing but smooth skin across the area where the brand once was. My mouth hung open. I trailed my fingertips over the section that, just moments before, caused him so much pain. Elias's hand enveloped mine.

When I peered into his eyes there were no glowing embers like there normally were. Just the prettiest humanly blue eyes I'd ever seen.

"What did you ask Lucifer for?" Elias asked. His voice rumbled and vibrated against me.

I only stared at him for a moment before I answered.

"I thought you had super hearing," I teased.

"Nova, please. What did you ask for?"

"Your freedom."

CHAPTER THIRTY-THREE

"Nova, you owe me nothing," Elias said in a strained voice as he squeezed my hand.

"I owe you everything. You are everything to me. I never thought I'd find this—what you and I have. I'll be damned if you stay here, and I have to go back to living a cryptid hunting life without you." His fingers entwined with mine just as a scream split through the room. We all jerked our heads toward the sound.

"As much as I love a happy ending, I think that it's your time to go," Arlas said.

I nodded and Elias stood, helping me to my feet. Cyrus gripped Elias's shoulder.

"Take care of my daughter." I rolled my eyes, but Elias nodded and gripped his shoulder in return. Cyrus turned my way, and his black gaze took me in.

"I know I haven't been around, but if it's all right with you, I'd like to visit when I can."

As much as I was angry at Cyrus for not having been in my life and hurting my mate, I thought I could start to slowly build our relationship. I had to remember; my mother found something to love about him. So maybe I could too.

"Okay. But call first." I pointed a finger at him. "No popping in unexpectedly. We're going to need our privacy." Cyrus grimaced and turned a wicked stare over to Elias. Elias just smirked. Another scream echoed. I could only imagine what Lucifer's punishment felt like for Azvameth. I shuddered at the thought.

I grabbed Elias's hand and started to pull him behind me. "Let's go home."

"I'm not quite sure he'll be able to get you back to the human realm," Arlas said from behind us. I stopped in my tracks.

"What do you mean?" I asked. I peered at the Viking-like general.

"When he loses his station as Lucifer's soldier, the powers tend to be taken away with it." I hadn't thought of that. Did it mean he was human? Will he live a long life like me? Or will he end up living a human's lifetime? I wanted to throw up. Arlas moved toward us and placed a hand on each of our shoulders.

"I can help you though." I opened my mouth to respond but before I could, heat wrapped around us and we stumbled into my small living room. With both of the hulking men, I had barely any room to move.

"Thank you, Arlas," Elias said.

"I will miss having a fine soldier like yourself." The general nodded his head toward me. "Nova, you are quite the warrior. I may have to call upon you sometime when we are in need." I laughed off his compliment and he faded out of the room without a goodbye.

The silence in my small home caused the realization of my actions to crash down on me. Lucifer tricked me.

"Do you think it's true? Lucifer turned you into a human again? Do you think you'll have a human's lifespan?" My heart beat double time in my chest. I placed my hand over my sternum.

"Let's not think about that. We have here and now. You freed me from the prison I was in. I'll never be able to repay you." Elias gripped my hand in his and pulled me toward him. His mouth crashed down onto mine. I pulled away.

"But . . ." His mouth slammed into mine again.

"Not now, Nova," he murmured against my mouth. Elias wanted to live in the moment, and I couldn't blame him. He'd lived as a prisoner for the last five-hundred years. This was the first time he could actually think and feel freely without any restraints. He kissed me senselessly. I placed my hands on Elias's chest as I gently pushed him away and broke our kiss. I rested my head against his chest and listened to his rapid heartbeat. "As much as I'd like to bump uglies, I'd really like to shower all this gore off of me before we get naked."

His arms wrapped around me and hoisted me up making me squeal. "What are you doing?" I shrieked as my legs wrapped around his waist.

"We're going to shower," he growled and started toward my bathroom. I reached down and peeled my shirt over my head and he kissed me again. He kicked the door closed behind us. Elias set me down on the counter. He turned on the shower to allow it to warm up, then pulled his shirt over his head. Elias came back to me and settled between my thighs, kissing me gently at first and slowly started to pull off my bottoms. They were stiff from blood and mud. I lifted my butt so he could take them off along with my panties. I reached behind my back and unhooked my bra, letting it fall to the floor.

Elias started to work on his own pants and only broke our kiss so he could remove his remaining clothing. His large cock sprang free. My hand immediately went to it to stroke the soft head. Elias groaned into my mouth and his hand went beneath my thighs and lifted me from the counter. I slid down his body until my feet gently touched the floor. I released his cock and strode the couple of steps to the shower, pulling back the curtain. I stepped into the tub and peeked back at Elias. At his rock-hard body and rock-hard length. I bit my lip, and he followed me. He stepped into the small shower. There was hardly any room in the shower with the both of us.

But we managed to wash the grit and mud and blood off each other.

I wrapped my arms around his neck and pulled him down to my level and nipped at his lips.

"There isn't enough room in this shower for me to fuck you properly," he said huskily.

"No one said we have to stay in here," I teased. I closed my eyes and I thought of how we'd had sex in my bed the last time. I kissed his jaw and neck. When my eyes fluttered open again, we no longer stood in my shower. We were in my room. I stumbled back a step.

"You just faded us to your bedroom." Elias chuckled. It had to be me since Elias was no longer immortal and was without any of his abilities. His body was dripping wet, and he snagged me by the hips, tossing me onto my bed like I weighed nothing. I was flipped onto my stomach and my hips pulled toward him. I pushed up onto my hands and knees. Elias nudged my thighs open with a knee and his cock pushed at my wet entrance. I gasped as he slammed himself into me and thrusted roughly a few times. Elias pulled out of me all the way and he slapped my clit with his wet erection. I cried out and sent my hips back toward him greedily. His tip rested at my entrance again. A slap landed on my ass with an open hand, making me shriek in surprise. The stinging pain turned me on even more and he thrust into me again. He propelled at a steady pace and I balanced on the edge of utter ecstasy.

"Don't you ever. Make. A. Deal. With. Lucifer. Again," he said as he thrusted in and out of me. Elias slipped his hand between my legs from my front and rubbed my clit in firm circles. Just as I was about to spiral out of control, he stopped. I pouted and whimpered at the loss of the friction. I tried to move my hips to take my orgasm.

"Do you understand, Nova?" He stilled his movements completely.

"Yes," I said. "Please . . ."

"Please what?"

"Please make me come," I begged.

Elias rocked into me feverishly and his hand continued again on my clit. He slapped my clit lightly a few times and I fell over the edge. My arms lost their strength and I fell onto my bed. My face landed on the mattress and my ass was still up in the air. Elias pumped into me at a quick speed. I felt his cock spasm inside of me as he growled his release. His pace slowed. He leaned forward and placed gentle kisses to my shoulder as I caught my breath.

He pulled out of me and sat on the bed next to me. Elias hauled me into his lap and stroked a hand down my arm.

"Promise me," he whispered against my ear.

CHAPTER THIRTY-FOUR

"Just try it," I told Elias as I shoved a milkshake drenched French fry in his face. The scowl he gave me did nothing to deter me from putting it even closer to his mouth. Ever since he'd been back in the human realm and without his powers, he had an insatiable hunger. He practically ate me out of house and home. Our training sessions burned a ton of calories, but I doubt that was the only reason. He hadn't eaten in centuries. And he was a human again.

"If I try this and hate it, will you finally leave me alone about it?"

I gave him a smirk. "Maybe." I giggled. His upper lip arched in disgust. But he finally opened for me to pop it into his mouth. He chewed for a few moments and his gaze snapped to mine. Elias finally figured out it wasn't as gross as he'd thought.

"Okay, now I see why you are so into this."

"I told you." I grinned in triumph.

My phone rang and I pulled it out of my pocket. Tiffany's name lit up my screen.

I answered. Only because I was trying to be a better sister and daughter.

"Hey, Tiff. What's up?"

"Hey, Nova. Mom told me to call and tell you that we're having dinner tomorrow night. She wants you and Elias to be there." I covered the mouthpiece and asked Elias if he was okay going. We'd been to my family's house for dinner about the hundred times since we'd returned Azvameth to Lucifer.

Elias nodded. He took my milkshake and fries, setting them in front of him to eat.

"Hey! You better not steal all my fries. It's called sharing."

"Never heard of it." Elias dipped a fistful of fries into the shake and shoved it into his mouth. Melted ice cream dribbled down his lush bottom lip and into his scruff. I bit my bottom lip, wanting to lick it from his sexy face. I uncovered the mouthpiece.

"Sure, we're down. I'll see you guys tomorrow," I told Tiffany and hung up.

We still hadn't gotten information about whether or not Elias would live a long life. Or if my time with him was limited. I researched in secret when I was alone. Every time I tried to bring it up, Elias didn't want to talk about it. He just wanted us to live in the moment. What a nerd. I would do just about anything to make sure he was by my side for the rest of eternity. Even if it meant making a deal with Lucifer again. Every time Elias mentioned the promise of never doing something so reckless again, I avoided it. Because I knew that if I were to have the opportunity, I would make a deal. I wanted to give Elias his immortality back. While keeping him free.

Matt disappeared after the battle. We hadn't heard anything about what happened to him. His grandfather reached out to me to see if I'd heard anything. But I wasn't able to give him any information. He'd let me know his library was open to me anytime. I couldn't bring myself to tell him about being backstabbed by his grandson. Honestly, I wouldn't be surprised if Matt was in hiding. But whether he came back from the realm we were in, was unknown to me and my family.

Elias and I finished our meal and headed back to my house. It was good for me to not be alone since Rik's death. In the mornings, I sat by his burial spot in my yard. I drank my coffee and talked to him. I talked about everything and nothing. About how I met Lucifer and about how I might love Elias.

Even though there was never a response, I felt like he listened. The flowers continued to grow without hardly being tended to. For me, that was enough confirmation that he was there.

I strolled through the front door, and I flipped on the lights. Startled to see Cyrus and Arlas in my living room. "Didn't I tell you to call before you just popped in?" I asked Cyrus.

"Sorry, I left my phone in Hell," he replied dryly. I was surprised to see Arlas was with him. This was the only time he'd come top side to see me since he dropped us off.

"Heya, Arlas. What brings you along with my demon daddy?" I joked.

He didn't smile like I'd expected him to. "Serious business, I'm afraid." The smile dropped from my face. I should've known the general of Lucifer's army didn't bring any good news. He hadn't come any other time.

"What's going on?" Elias stepped next to me and wrapped an arm around my waist. His hand squeezed my hip gently.

"Apparently, Azvameth seems to have more followers than we expected. He was freed and has disappeared," Arlas said. My stomach twisted.

"Why didn't Lucifer just kill him?" I asked.

"I cannot answer that. It would have kept others in line, and he would not have been a problem anymore. My brother is a strong demon. For Lucifer to let him live was a mistake," Cyrus said.

I should've killed him when I had the chance. Consequences be damned. My mother could have figured something out and I was almost positive Cyrus would've assisted.

"So, what do we need to do?" Elias asked.

Cyrus and Arlas focused on me. I glanced between the two of them.

"What?"

"Lucifer has requested your presence," Arlas said.

I choked and nearly had a coughing fit.

"Lucifer said I can't come back. He'll make Elias his soldier again."

"He won't, he gave his word." Arlas was monotone. Lucifer's word wasn't worth much to me. I glanced up at Elias and he seemed concerned. He waited for my answer. I didn't really have a choice in this. If I didn't go, Lucifer would come and get me. Or worse, take Elias. Or Azvameth may send his minions to destroy my home again and try to take my life. It was a lose-lose situation.

I locked eyes with General Arlas. This may be the way I could ensure Elias's immortality was returned. Then we could spend the rest of our long lives together. If we managed to survive a second time. A grin spread across my face, and I peered up at Elias again.

"Feel like making a deal with the Devil?"

ABOUT THE AUTHOR

Christina Abu-Khalaf is a California native that moved to Colorado with her husband and two children in 2021. Working in administrative settings her whole life, she took up writing as a way to put her ideas onto paper. She writes about love, fantasy, and enjoys dipping into the world of the paranormal.

www.ingramcontent.com/pod-product-compliance
Lightning Source LLC
Chambersburg PA
CBHW051452170626
46811CB00002B/453